MW01595202

ABOUT
GOING OVERBOARD

Second-class petty officers Dalton Taylor and Chris Ingram have been best friends since coxswain's school. Now they're stationed together in the harbor patrol unit of NAS Adams. They're content as friends, but secretly, they both ache for more. Neither makes a move, though; while Dalton is out and proud, Chris is closeted—even from his best friend.

Then another coxswain's negligence nearly drowns Dalton. After a taste of how easily they could lose each other, neither man can keep his feelings hidden anymore, and it turns out love and sex come easy when you're falling for your best friend.

Things aren't just heating up between the friends-turned-lovers, though. The Navy is investigating the accident, and the harbor patrol chief isn't going to let his star coxswain go down for dereliction of duty, even if saving him means throwing Dalton under the bus.

As the threats and gaslighting pile up, Chris and Dalton need each other more than ever—as shipmates, friends, and lovers. But if their chief prevails, the only way they can save their careers is to let each other go.

Riptide Publishing
PO Box 1537
Burnsville, NC 28714
www.riptidepublishing.com

Going Overboard

Cover art: L.C. Chase, lcchase.com/design.htm
Editor: Chris Muldoon
Layout: L.C. Chase, lcchase.com/design.htm

ISBN: 978-1-62649-701-6

First edition
February, 2018

Also available in ebook:
ISBN: 978-1-62649-700-9

GOING OVERBOARD

ANCHOR POINT

L.A. WITT

RIPTIDE
PUBLISHING

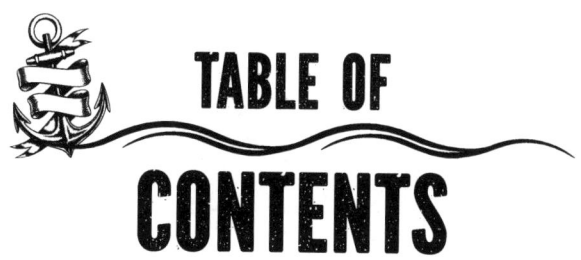

TABLE OF CONTENTS

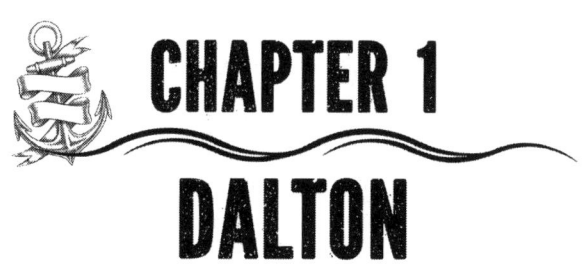

CHAPTER 1

DALTON

"You know, with as much money as the Navy spent to send your ass to coxswain's school," MA3 Rhodes said as she put on her police belt, "you'd think someone would actually let you drive the boat once in a while."

"No shit." I scowled and slung the M4 rifle over my shoulder. "As long as Chief Lasby's golden boy is running our section, though . . ."

She frowned but said nothing. What was there to say? Chief Lasby played favorites, Chief Lasby ran Harbor Patrol, and Chief Lasby thought MA1 Anderson was the Second Coming. The fact that Anderson was only a basic coxswain and I'd graduated Level II coxswain's school at the top of my class and could drive that fucking boat in my sleep didn't mean a goddamned thing, because the dirt bag was our Lead Petty Officer. And the only reason he was our LPO was because he outranked us all, which was because Chief Lasby had given him a glowing eval he *totally* hadn't deserved. Not that I was bitter.

Between the extra chevron on Anderson's uniform and how deeply his nose was planted between Lasby's ass cheeks, he got to call the shots when we went out on patrol. And his call was . . . he drove while I carried the gun.

I adjusted the sidearm strap around my thigh. "Think we'll at least get the Metal Shark up and running soon so we don't have to bring the rifle anymore?"

Rhodes snorted with laughter. "Senior Chief Curtis has been after Port Ops for months to fix that stupid boat. At this rate, we're going to break the little boat too, and then we'll have to . . . I don't know. Patrol the harbor in a kayak or something."

"Don't even *joke* about that," I groaned. These days, there wasn't much I'd put past our command.

I gazed out the Harbor Patrol Unit building's second story window at the boats below. The wind was brutal today, rattling the windows and even the walls of the mostly concrete building. The usually calm water of the harbor was rough as hell, waves slamming into the seawall and tossing our boats hard against the pier.

In the slip closest to shore was the Metal Shark—the biggest, most capable vessel we had. I loved those boats. They could turn on a dime, they hauled ass, and they were pretty stable even in rough waters. Unfortunately, ours had been out of commission for . . . hell, no one even knew anymore. I'd been here almost a year, and I was pretty sure I'd only seen that bad boy leave the pier twice.

With that boat still waiting for repairs, and the larger fast boat on reserve in case of emergency—and because it was too expensive to operate on a daily basis—we were stuck with the piece-of-shit smaller craft, which was currently out on patrol. It was tiny, rickety, and didn't steer for shit. It could haul ass, which was good, but it didn't maneuver nearly as cleanly as the Metal Shark. And that was in calm waters.

The best part? It was a small craft that couldn't support a mounted machine gun like the Metal Shark. Since we had to have at least one large weapon when we patrolled, we had to go with the next best thing—the hand-carried M4 currently hanging off my shoulders. All eight-plus pounds of it. On top of the heavy vest. And the trauma plates. And my loaded sidearm. And my boots. And my police belt. I didn't even know why they bothered having inflators in our vests. Didn't seem like they'd really help when we were weighed down like fucking anchors.

I shifted my attention out to the mouth of the harbor and beyond. The green water was churning violently, the swells making me a little queasy even from here. I wasn't prone to seasickness, but I knew what seas like that could do to a boat. My nausea was nerves and nothing else.

We shouldn't be out on the boat. Not tonight.

I shifted my attention to the sky. We had about an hour and a half of daylight left. Going out in this weather was dangerous enough. As our visibility faded with the sun, it would only get worse. Going out for night ops in these conditions, on that boat, was suicide. Plain and simple.

But the powers that be insisted. After all, what better time for terrorists or something to infiltrate our harbor than while we were hiding from the elements?

Rhodes appeared beside me, gazing out the window as she fussed with something on her belt. "You know, it's actually a good thing you're the gunner today."

I glared at her. "Why's that?"

"Because if I had the rifle, I'd probably club Anderson to death with it." She nodded at the parking lot below us, where Anderson was having a cigarette with Chief Lasby.

I turned away in disgust and pressed my back against the window. "One more year, and he's not our problem anymore."

"Yeah." She sniffed bitterly. "Assuming he doesn't get an extension and stay here. And even when he transfers, we're still stuck with Lasby."

I shot her another glare. "You are one gigantic ray of sunshine today, you know that?"

She smiled brightly and patted my shoulder. "That's me."

I couldn't help chuckling even as I rolled my eyes. "Come on. The boat's on its way back in."

We didn't speak as we clomped down the stairs and went outside into the vicious wind. Being February, it was cold as balls even without the wind and sea spray, and it was just getting colder.

"Holy shit." I almost choked on the words as I walked. I'd been out here an hour ago, and damn but the wind hadn't been *this* strong. We both had to shield our mouths and noses just to breathe. At the edge of the parking lot, the American and Navy flags were snapping and whipping in the wind, the chains pinging loudly against the poles. In this kind of weather, the flags shouldn't have even gone up, but as with everything, it wasn't my call to make. I just hoped neither of them broke off and wound up in the water. The seas were way too rough to try to rescue anything, and it didn't take a genius to figure out who'd be the one leaning over the side to fish out the ruined flag while Tweedle Dipshit was at the helm.

I shook myself and continued down to the pier. Up ahead, the boat was on its way back in, and I couldn't help feeling a little better. My best friend was aboard right now, so we'd get a minute to cross paths while his crew turned over the boat to mine.

I stopped near the slip and watched them battle the waves to park the boat. As the ass end swung around, I caught sight of him, and my heart did a little flip.

There you are.

MA2 Chris Ingram and I had been close since coxswain's school, and I'd secretly had the worst crush on him. Not just because he was the sweetest guy I'd ever met, but because dear *God*, he was gorgeous. Our base hadn't yet switched over to the new green camouflage, so we were still wearing blue, and I loved how it looked on him. Something about the color made his black skin look even darker and brought out the warm brown of his eyes. The cut of the uniform made his shoulders seem broader and his arms seem bigger. The rest of us looked like shit in these things, but trust him to look good even when his police belt masked his narrow hips, which I'd memorized a long time ago anyway.

It didn't hurt that he was built like a brick shithouse. He and I were about the same height—six-one, give or take—but he was definitely bigger. And so, *so* hot. Especially with that black vest over the top of his camouflage and the laced-up black boots and—

I tore my gaze away before someone busted me. Last thing I needed was Lasby catching wind that I was checking out another MA. I was out and everyone knew it, but it didn't hurt to fly under Lasby's radar as much as possible. He was one of those homophobes who wasn't obvious about it, but wasn't all that subtle either. A few comments here and there about marriage equality, DADT, and our senior chief's recent wedding had been enough for me to read between the lines. Besides, Chris was straight. I didn't need him to bust me ogling him and get uncomfortable.

The boat was finally close enough to the pier, and Chris tossed me a line. Rhodes and I helped him and his crew tie the lines, and in a matter of minutes, it was secured. The crew disembarked, and they were all a little unsteady on their feet. None of them were new to being out on the water, either—Chris and MA3 Powers had better sea legs than I did. If they were that wobbly, I was fucked.

Well, this is going to be a fun watch, isn't it?

I smirked despite my nerves. "You boys doin' a little drinking out there?"

"I wish." Chris's dark skin actually looked a tad green, and he eyed the pier like he was trying to find a spot to heave over the edge. "Man, those waves are no joke today."

"Great. And Mario Andretti over there is driving." I motioned toward MA1 Anderson, who was sauntering down the pier.

Chris's eyes widened. "You're shitting me. Again?"

Sighing, I nodded. "Yeah. God help us all when he gets back from Level II school."

Chris snorted. "They'll boot him out of there the minute he gets out on the water."

I held up my hand, my gloved fingers crossed.

He didn't laugh. Stepping closer, he lowered his voice. "I'm not kidding about those waves out there. And with as fast as he drives?" His lips pulled tight. "Don't let him go out of the harbor."

"In this weather, only a complete idiot would try open seas."

"But you know how Anderson likes to do his outer harbor sweeps."

I rolled my eyes. "Fuck. Well, hopefully even he's not that dumb."

The quirk of Chris's lips told me he was pretty sure Anderson really was that dumb. "Be careful out there."

"I will."

Our eyes locked just long enough to fuck with my pulse.

Then he smiled, gave my arm a light squeeze, and headed up to the Harbor Patrol building.

I watched him go, but only for a couple of seconds. I definitely didn't need anyone in our unit—least of all Chris—catching on. What I wouldn't have given, though, for a chance to put my hands on those shoulders, especially without the uniform in the way, but he didn't need to know that. No one in our command did.

I focused my attention on carefully boarding the wind-tossed boat, but part of my mind was still on Chris. I wished like hell I could go out on patrol with him more often, and not just so I could ogle him. He was a solid Sailor and a more than competent coxswain. We worked well together, maybe because we were both on the older end for our rank. Most people in our rate advanced to MA1—E-6— around the ten-year mark. We'd both been in fifteen years, and we were still MA2s. The last few advancement cycles had seen a lot of younger MA2s advancing while those of us who'd been in longer stagnated. Hence why we were both answering to MA1 Anderson—a cocky, ambitious kid who was great at kissing ass but not so great at doing his job.

As younger guys advanced past us, Chris and I commiserated about being ordered around by kids who couldn't find their own asses with a flashlight and an anatomy chart. At least he got to be at the helm once in a while.

Joking and grumbling aside, we really did need to advance soon. Both of us. We had until our sixteen-year marks to make MA1, and if we didn't, we could kiss our careers and retirements goodbye. Chris had been held back at his last few commands thanks to political and quite possibly racial bullshit. I didn't have anyone to blame but myself. It had been ten years since my dumb ass had gone to Captain's Mast and been summarily demoted a rank, and that incident was *still* following me around. At the end of the day, we each had two advancement cycles left to get promoted, or the Navy was done with us. No pressure.

So, as I settled in on the boat, I reminded myself to spend a couple of hours studying tonight after I came off watch. The advancement exam was coming up fast, after all, and I was going to *own* that fucker if it killed me.

Anderson and Rhodes came aboard, and after we'd pulled in the lines, Anderson steered the boat away from the pier.

The second we were clear of the slip, the boat rocked hard. Shit. The guys hadn't been kidding—even inside the harbor, the water was rough. Bearable, though. It didn't take me or Rhodes long to get our legs under us.

Half an hour into our watch, Anderson called me into the cabin.

Bracing myself against the metal frame and planting my feet wide on the deck for balance, I leaned in. "Yeah, boss?"

He shifted in the coxswain's chair, gripping the helm tightly in one hand while he gestured with the other toward the mouth of the harbor. "There's a disabled vessel about a hundred yards past the gate."

I looked out, and there was definitely something out there. An indistinct shape that seemed to disappear between swells. Probably a boat, though I couldn't fix my eyes on it enough to decide if it had lights or if those were just reflections from the half-moon or the base lights.

"Call in the Coast Guard," I shouted over the wind and the engines. "There's no way this boat can handle those waves."

Anderson shook his head and throttled toward the open ocean. "We'll be fine."

"Uh, no. MA1, I'm serious." I gestured at the violently rolling seas. "Even if we can get to that vessel, there's no way we can help them without—"

"We're going to help them, MA2." He shot me a glare.

I stared at him, jaw hanging open. "It's too dangerous!"

"And it's too dangerous to just leave another vessel out there!" His glare hardened, and I could almost hear the accusation of insubordination.

Gritting my teeth, I stepped out onto the deck and made my way to Rhodes, who was trying to keep her balance near the stern.

"Hold onto something," I grumbled. "We're heading out into open water."

Her eyes were instantly huge. "Is he *insane?*"

"Probably. He thinks we can do something about that." I gestured at the possibly disabled boat.

She looked past me and scowled. "Shit. What do we do?"

I swallowed. So did she.

She said something I couldn't hear, then grabbed her radio to call for a fast-boat response to be on standby and to get the Coast Guard mobilized. While she did that, I went out to the bow to watch for debris or other vessels; with swells that big, we were liable to crash into something without even knowing what we'd hit. Hopefully if I saw something, Anderson would be smart enough—and fast enough—to avoid it.

As soon as we crossed from the harbor into the open ocean, the ride went from rough to terrifying. The deck pitched hard under my feet. We crested a swell, and my heart lurched when I realized we'd almost completely cleared the water. We came down hard, the impact driving me onto the deck with a painful crack of kneecap to metal.

My eyes watered. It took a second for me to catch my breath, and by the time I did, we were going up over another wave. The second impact made my teeth snap together. Then we were going up again. A wall of ice cold saltwater reared up over the side and slapped down hard on top of me, stunning me for a second and soaking me to the skin. Before I'd finished sputtering and regained my footing, the boat slammed downward again. More spray. More water. More violent pitching and listing.

Shit. We were going way too fast, and the waves were even bigger than they'd looked from the harbor. Maybe the Metal Shark in the hands of a competent coxswain could've handled these seas. The *USS Minnow* with Gilligan and his ego at the helm? Not a chance.

I motioned to Anderson to go back.

Through the windshield, he shook his head. The boat stayed the course.

For fuck's sake.

"MA1," I shouted. "Go back!"

"We're fine, MA2! We're almost there!"

"Go *back*, you fucking idiot!"

He glared at me with *you're going to hear about this later* in his eyes. I didn't give two shits about insubordination. Not when he was going to get us killed.

A wave tossed me hard enough I nearly lost my footing. At the stern, Rhodes stumbled hard and hit the railing. She nearly went over, but caught herself.

Our eyes met. The fear in hers echoed what was surging through my veins. This was insanity.

Fuck insubordination. Anderson was out of his mind, and he needed to be out of the coxswain's seat. Fortunately, I was big enough by comparison that overpowering him wouldn't be too difficult. I might not even have to cuff him, which I didn't want to do in case the boat went down or he went overboard.

If it came down to it, though . . .

I took a step toward him, struggling to stay upright as the boat pitched and rolled.

But then the deck wasn't under my feet anymore.

Nothing was.

I was weightless for a split second.

Speeding away from the boat. Over the railing. Then down.

And as soon as I hit the water, I was the opposite of weightless. I sank. Fast.

I swam hard and managed to break the surface. As I gulped in air, I tried to inflate my vest, but I was getting tossed around too much. I'd get my fingers on the pulls just in time for the violent seas to toss me like a ragdoll, and I'd lose my grip. The rifle was simultaneously dragging me down and narrowly missing my face as the waves threw me around. I couldn't get the strap over my head. Even when I surfaced, it was only for seconds at a time. Never long enough to breathe. Couldn't pull the tabs on the vest. Couldn't gain any purchase, any control, and each time I went under, it was harder to come back to the surface. Too much gear. Too much heavy, constricting gear, and I couldn't get my hands on any of it long enough to—

"MA2!" Rhodes's voice cut through the chaos. "Look out!"

I turned my head just in time to see a wall of gunmetal gray coming at me, and coming in hot. I put up my arm, but it caught on the rifle strap.

The hull slammed into me.

And everything went black.

Cold saltwater in my throat made me cough, but there was no air. Just more water. My lungs screamed. Pain exploded along the side of my head. Still no air.

Up? Where is up?

I opened my eyes. Bubbles were going . . .

That way.

I swam as hard as my numb, heavy limbs would swim, and followed the bubbles, but they were faster than me.

Heavy. Too heavy. Sinking.

Something jerked the back of my vest. Then a hard tug at my left side. Another at my right.

The vest's air bladders inflated, and I was rising with the bubbles. Something was still pulling me, but it was pulling me up, so I didn't fight it.

I broke the surface and gasped for air, but choked on more

seawater. As I tried to find my breath, something loosened around my waist, and I wasn't being dragged down so hard. A wave crashed into me, but I didn't stay under as long this time. The rifle's strap was no longer digging into my shoulder. The dead weight of the gun was gone.

Beside me, someone coughed and sputtered.

"Rhodes?"

"Stay with me, MA2." Rhodes's teeth were chattering. "Help is coming."

"What the . . ." Words. Couldn't . . . too cold. Too much pain. Where was the boat? It was going to hit us again. Wasn't it? Still not enough air. Everything was spinning and doubling and blurring, and my mouth tasted like copper and salt as I tried to ask what the fuck was happening.

A wave rolled us again. As I came up this time, I inhaled a mouthful of icy saltwater, and my stomach lurched. I puked so hard it hurt my guts and my violently throbbing head, and before I could take a breath, the freezing ocean pulled us under again.

The waves kept tossing us. The vests kept us more or less afloat, but the ocean was trying like hell to gain the upper hand.

Distantly, there was a rumble I thought were boat engines, but every time I broke the surface, things made less sense . . . came into fuzzier focus . . . doubled . . . tripled . . . cold . . . numb . . .

"MA2, come on! Stay with me!"

And once again . . .

Darkness.

CHAPTER 2

CHRIS

The distress call came in, and before the transmission had even ended, me and MA3 Powers were on our feet and running. Several other MAs joined us, boots thumping as we sprinted down the pier. We vaulted onto the fast boat, and I stumbled on the wind-tossed deck. The water had been rough as hell when we'd gone out, and it was worse now. The wind wasn't just whistling—it was screaming, battering boats against the pier and rocking this one so violently I could barely find my footing.

My heart was in my throat as we scrambled to pull in lines and get the boat out on the water. Cold as it was, we couldn't afford to waste a second, especially not with the daylight running out and when we didn't know how bad the situation really was. In the chaos, I hadn't heard who was in the water, only that someone had gone overboard. There were only three people on that boat, and as much as I disliked MA1 Anderson, I wasn't praying for him to be the one in the drink. I just prayed like hell we'd heard the report wrong and everyone was safe, warm, and dry.

But I could see from here that the boat was outside the harbor gate. From the looks of it, even though it was getting tossed by the swells, it was stationary. Which meant it was caught on something.

Fuck. A crippled boat and at least one person in the storm-tossed water. In February. Soon to be in the dark.

MA2 Simmons took the helm of our boat. She was only Level I coxswain-qualified, but I didn't argue. I knew from experience she was competent as fuck. Let her drive—I wanted my hands and focus free to get whoever it was out of the water.

As she drove, I gripped the side of the boat and squinted up ahead. The already shitty visibility was worsening fast, but I could see the crippled boat, plus a red and white Zodiac marked *Coast Guard* that was speeding toward it from the north.

I was sick at the sight of the patrol boat. The larger craft I was on could cope with seas like this, and even it would be tossed around plenty once we hit the open water. Of course, the powers that be wouldn't let us use this thing for routine patrolling because it cost more to fuel and maintain, but at least we had it handy in the event the patrol boat needed a rescue.

Which it wouldn't have if Dalton had been driving. I winced. MA1 Anderson had no business driving a boat at all, and no one had any business taking a glorified fucking dinghy out into storm-tossed open seas. There was no way in hell they'd have gone past the harbor gate if Dalton had been at the helm. None. And now people could be in very real danger.

I drummed my fingers and murmured, "C'mon, c'mon," as we sped through the whitecaps and growing swells toward the floundering boat.

So help me, Anderson, if Dalton or Rhodes are fucked up . . .

I gritted my teeth and tried not to imagine. Not because I disliked the idea of kicking that jackwagon's sorry ass, but because that scenario would mean something had happened to Dalton or Rhodes. That wasn't something I could think about. Not now.

The closer we got, the clearer the situation was. The boat wasn't just idling in the water. It was stopped dead. As stopped as anything could be in seas like this—the waves were still tossing it relentlessly, threatening each time to capsize it, but it wasn't going forward. Every time a wave tried to push it, the bow bucked and the boat snapped backward like something was holding it in place. It reminded me of an animal with a foot in a trap—trying like hell to escape, but inescapably restrained.

"Looks like they snagged on a fishnet," Powers shouted.

I nodded. It had happened before. Civilian fishermen loved setting up nets near the mouth of the harbor, and it was just far enough out of our jurisdiction that we couldn't stop them. The Coast Guard and Fish & Wildlife tried their damnedest, but the nets were still a very real hazard for us. Somewhere in my mind, I wondered how we were supposed to untangle the net from the props in this weather, but that could wait until after I knew my shipmates—my best friend—were safe.

My heart beat faster the closer we got to the boat. I craned my neck and squinted, trying to make sense of things. From here, all I could see was MA1 Anderson. He was out on the port bow, gesturing frantically at the Coast Guard boat, the water, then boat again.

There was no one else on the deck with him. As far as I could tell, no one on the boat. The coxswain's seat was empty. Just MA1 Anderson.

Oh no.

No. No, no, no . . .

The Zodiac was already there, shining a spotlight over the scene. As our driver cut the engines, two Coasties in full thermal gear jumped feet first into the stormy waters. We came around the side of the floundering patrol boat, and I leaned over the side, trying to focus against the salt spray.

When my eyes finally focused, my heart dropped.

Dalton and MA3 Rhodes were dead ahead in the spotlight's glow, the orange-clad Coasties fighting the waves to get to them. Rhodes was conscious but visibly shivering. She must've known how difficult they were to see in their blue camouflage, because she waved a light for one of the swimmers to see.

Her other arm was securely around Dalton. Under his armpit. Around the front of his chest.

And Dalton . . .

Oh God.

My stomach turned to lead. I'd sometimes teased him about being white enough to be used as a signaling device, but now he was *white*, and it wasn't just the eerie blanched light coming from the Zodiac. Even his lips were nearly translucent. His eyes were half-open, head lolling to the side.

Then the churning water turned him and Rhodes, revealing the other side of his face, and . . . blood. So much blood.

Dalton didn't look conscious. Maybe not even alive. Oh Christ. Were we too late?

I shook myself and focused. There was no time to assess him

now—we had to get him out of the water. If he hadn't reached severe hypothermia, he was on his way and fast, assuming whatever had cut his head hadn't done him in already.

I looked around. The Zodiac was getting tossed as badly as we were. Another Coast Guard boat was on its way out, but it wouldn't be here for a few minutes yet.

Beside us, the patrol boat swung on its lines, nearly colliding with the Zodiac. In an effort to avoid the crippled boat, the Zodiac almost ended up on the rocks, and the driver had to pull it away to regain control. They took the spotlight with them, leaving the swimmers and victims with nothing but the weak glow from the patrol boat. We turned ours on, but they didn't help much.

The swimmers looked around, probably trying to orient themselves to the Zodiac.

I did the same and realized my vessel was closer. It was also bigger and had more room on the deck.

"Hey!" I shouted down to the swimmer. He didn't respond, so I whistled. When he looked up, squinting against the light coming from over my head, I beckoned and gestured at the deck beneath my feet. He nodded. He shouted something I couldn't hear at Rhodes, and she too nodded. Then he took Dalton from her and started toward my boat. Later, there might be some bullshit about jurisdiction and the swimmer needing to get Dalton and Rhodes onto the Coast Guard boat instead of ours, but right now, politics and regulations didn't matter. All that mattered was getting the two MAs out of that cold water.

I barked orders to the people on my boat, sending them scrambling to be ready to pull up Dalton and Rhodes, and as I did, I shed my police belt. "When he gets on board," I shouted, "he's going to need skin-to-skin to regain some body heat." I quickly started unbuttoning my blouse. "Get a space blanket ready, and tell the medics onshore we've got one, possibly two Sailors with severe hypothermia."

No one protested. This was what we trained for, and everyone threw themselves into their tasks with practiced ease.

As I was kicking off my boots, my crewmen hauled Dalton onto the deck. I nearly froze. His body was limp, and holy shit, he was even paler up close. His lips had started turning blue. The blood running down one side of his head and onto the C-collar someone had put on him made his pallor even more terrifying.

The barely audible groan that escaped his lips almost knocked me to my knees. He was alive. Maybe hanging on by his fingernails, but *alive*. I scrambled even faster to get out of my clothes so I could warm him up.

MA3 Powers started cutting away Dalton's soaked uniform. Someone had already taken off his vest and police belt, thank God.

As soon as his blouse and T-shirt had been cut away, I lay beside him on the deck and pressed up against him, gasping at just how icy cold his skin really was. While Powers worked at Dalton's boots, I covered as much of Dalton's cold torso as I could.

Powers cut away the rest of Dalton's clothes, then put the space blanket over us. Hopefully Dalton would be able to pull enough heat from me, and the blanket would help him retain it.

My teeth chattered, but I kept holding his cold, limp body against mine. Someone handed me a wadded-up towel, which I pressed against the bloody wound on his head. He didn't even flinch.

"C'mon, Dalton," I murmured. "Stay with me, man. C'mon."

Another faint groan escaped his nearly white lips.

"Dalton?" I tapped his face gently. "You with me? Can you hear me? C'mon, Dalton."

His eyelids fluttered. He moaned again, head lolling.

"Is he conscious?" Powers asked, leaning over us.

"Don't know. Kind of." I looked up at him. "Is Rhodes out of the water?"

"I'm over here," she said through violently chattering teeth. She was wrapped in a gray blanket, hunched over against the side of the boat. Her blouse and shirt were in a puddle on the deck, and she was huddled against MA3 Simmons under a gray blanket. Rhodes was almost as pale as Dalton, but she was conscious and coherent. Thank God.

Dalton murmured again, squirming weakly.

I touched his cheek. "Dalton? You with me?"

More fluttering. Then, with what seemed like a ton of effort, his eyes opened about halfway. "Chris?" A sleepy, kind of drunken grin appeared on his pale lips. "Heeey, you."

I laughed, just relieved to see him coming around, and held his cold body tighter, as much to hug him as to get him warm.

Then his icy hand slid up my chest before it clumsily curved behind my neck, and as he started to draw me in, he slurred something I didn't understand.

"Hey, hey." I gently pried his hand off and hugged him a bit tighter. "Take it easy, man."

His eyes rolled a bit, then shut them, and he was silent again.

I almost laughed. It figured—the one time he tried to come on to me, and it was while he was hypothermic, concussed, and delirious.

But he was alive. Not out of the woods yet, but a damn sight better than when they'd pulled him from the water. Relieved as I was, I had to fight the urge to press a kiss to his forehead.

I just shut my eyes and held him tight.

I couldn't sit still. As much as I was pacing by the fish tank in Coastal General's ER waiting room, I was probably making the colorful fish nervous.

I'd been here almost an hour, and no one had said a word about Dalton. Was he okay? Was this place even equipped to handle him? Fuck, I probably would've been more comfortable if we were at a military hospital, and some of those were sketchy as hell.

Naval Air Station Adams was too small to have its own hospital, though, and Anchor Point wasn't a big town. Not surprisingly, the emergency room at Coastal General wasn't teeming with activity, but it wasn't exactly a Level I trauma center either. What the hell was *taking* so long?

All the way to the hospital, even half an hour after we'd pulled him from the water, Dalton had stayed semiconscious. Sometimes his eyes had fluttered open and he'd babbled incoherently. Once, he'd asked where his shoes were. Most of the time, though, he'd been quiet and still, and that had scared the shit out of me.

The EMTs had assured me over and over in the ambulance that extreme fatigue was par for the course with his degree of hypothermia, but they also kept checking him for responsiveness. Checking his eyes with a pen light. Asking him questions he couldn't answer. Frowning over his vitals. He'd been semiconscious. Not awake enough to know who or where he was, but definitely awake enough to swear or cry out when they jabbed his side or his ribs.

When we'd arrived, they'd jogged the stretcher in through the red-striped automatic doors. There'd been no sitting in the waiting room. Which I'd expected. A head injury? Significant hypothermia? All kinds of potential for neck trauma? Yeah, that was an express ticket to the front of the line.

A nurse had taken down my name and sent me to the waiting room, assuring me Dalton was in good hands. He was going straight back for X-rays and a CT scan. I was almost surprised this facility had the equipment for a CT scan. Nothing about this place screamed state-of-the-art to me. The tiny waiting area looked like a regular doctor's office, complete with tattered magazines, brightly colored plastic kids' toys, and the obligatory fish tank. The gray-haired triage nurse looked as worn and tired as the cracked linoleum, and I wondered if she'd been here as long as the yellowing wallpaper and dull pastel pink paint. Maybe I'd been spoiled with the high tech hospitals I'd gone to as a kid, but this place reminded me of a veterinary clinic in a strip mall. Did they even know how to handle someone in his condition?

Of course they did. Over and over, I reminded myself this *was* a hospital, these *were* medical professionals, and they *did* know what they were doing. Hopefully.

While I waited, I fielded texts from our coworkers and our chain of command, assuring everyone I'd update them when I could. Technically, Chief Lasby should have been here, but I'd assured him I'd wait for Dalton so he could deal with our crippled boat. And whatever issue had prompted Anderson to leave the harbor. Another disabled vessel, I thought I'd heard. Chief Lasby would handle everything back at HPU, I'd keep everyone posted about Dalton, and MA2 Simmons said she'd stay with MA3 Rhodes until her husband came.

I also texted Dalton's roommate to see about getting him some clothes. What was left of his uniform was probably still on the deck of the boat. Not half an hour later, AT3 Jay Stockton strode into the waiting room with a pair of sneakers and a plastic grocery sack full of folded clothes.

"How is he?" he asked as he handed everything over. His eyes were wide—he was a younger Sailor, probably only a couple of years past boot camp, and it was entirely possible this was his first brush with the scary shit that could happen in the military.

Wait till you get deployed, kid.

I swallowed. "I don't know. I haven't heard anything. The EMTs thought he'd be okay, but he's been back there a while."

Stockton pursed his lips, glancing toward the doors leading into the rest of the emergency room. "Well, this place can be slow as fuck. Buddy of mine came in with a sprained ankle and he was here almost six hours."

I exhaled. As much as I didn't like the idea of being here all damn night, I found some comfort in knowing the hospital was notorious for taking their sweet time. I'd stay here for days if it meant Dalton was all right. "I'll send you a text when I know something. Between the hypothermia and the concussion, he's probably—"

"Concussion?" Stockton's eyes widened. "Shit, what happened? I thought he just went in the water."

"No idea. He was bleeding pretty good from one side of his head, though, and one of the EMTs said something about a concussion, so . . ." I shrugged.

"But you think he'll be all right?"

"I sure hope so."

Stockton glanced toward the doors again. "Definitely keep me up to date. Even if it's at crazy thirty in the morning. I want to know he's okay."

"I will. And thanks again." I held up the clothes he'd brought.

"Don't mention it." He paused. "You know, I can go crash at my girlfriend's place tonight. He could probably use the peace and quiet."

"Someone might need to stay with him. If you don't mind me hanging out in your barracks room, I'll stick around and keep an eye on him."

Stockton nodded. "Awesome. Does he have his keys?"

"I don't know, actually."

He took out his own and pulled one off the ring. "I've got a spare in the car."

"Perfect. Thanks." As I pocketed the key, I added, "We'll get this one back to you ASAP. If Dalton doesn't have his on him, and he didn't drop them in the water, they're probably in the security building."

"Whatever." He shrugged. "Long as he's got a place to—"

"Mr. Ingram?" a woman's voice called.

I spun around. "Yeah, that's me."

She smiled and waved for me to come with her. I glanced at Stockton, and he practically shoved me. "*Go*. Text me when you know something."

I nodded and beat feet after her, and my heart sped up as we headed down the hall. "How's he doing?"

"He might not be much of a conversationalist for a while, but he's awake."

Relief hit me so hard, I just about stumbled over my own boots. He was awake. I didn't think I'd ever heard better news.

At the end of the hall, she stopped and leaned into an open door. "Mr. Taylor? You've got a visitor." Then she gestured for me to go in.

Dalton was under a pile of heated blankets, semi-reclined in a hospital bed with an IV in one arm, white tape covering one side of his head, EKG pads all over him, and wires sticking out from under the blankets and the collar of his hospital gown. His eyelids were heavy, his skin was still pale, and damn if he didn't look better than anything I'd ever seen.

"Hey." I smiled as I stepped closer. "How are you feeling?"

He swallowed like it took some work, and his eyelids slid closed again. "Fucking hurts."

My heart jumped. "Hurts? What hurts?" In all the chaos, we hadn't even had time to check him for injuries. Aside from stabilizing his neck and trying to staunch the bleeding on his head, anyway.

He licked his lips slowly. "My fucking head. And . . ." He made a heavy, weak gesture toward his side and winced. "Kind of feel like someone ran me through the washing machine."

I barked a laugh and dragged a chair over with my foot. As I sat, I remembered the bag and sneakers in my hand. "I've got some clothes for you, by the way. So you don't have to wear that thing home."

A weak smile pulled at his pale lips. "I don't know, man," he slurred softly. "It's the latest fashion."

I snorted. "Yeah, okay. Well when you get your fashion sense back, these will be waiting for you." I twisted around to put them on the counter.

"Where'd you get them, anyway?"

"Stockton came by."

"Oh. Awesome."

The nurse cleared her throat, reminding me she was still in the room. "We're waiting on Mr. Taylor's CT scan results, and the doctor *might* want to get another X-ray of those ribs, but I think he's leaning toward releasing him."

"Are they broken?" Dalton asked, voice faintly slurred.

"They don't appear to be." She fiddled with one of the leads disappearing under the top of his rumpled gown. "Dr. Engle thinks you pulled some muscles. Probably on the way out of the water."

I shuddered at the memory of Dalton being hauled onto the deck like a ragdoll. They'd been as careful as possible in case his back had been fucked up, and they'd had a C-collar on him, but the decision had been made to pull him out as quickly as they could. His neck had probably been knocked around when he'd hit his head, but apparently they hadn't been concerned about his back. Or at least, not concerned enough to risk keeping him in the water—which was tossing him around anyway—long enough to put him on a backboard. So no, I wasn't surprised he had some pulled muscles. Probably some bruises too.

Dalton asked the nurse a few more questions. When he was done, she offered me a motherly smile. "I'll send the doctor in as soon as he's free. You're welcome to keep him company until then."

I nodded. "Thanks." Then she left the room, and I turned back to Dalton. "You really got knocked around, didn't you?"

Eyes closed, he gave a slow, subtle nod. He didn't speak, though. As his breathing slowed, I realized he was drifting off. Wait, didn't he have a concussion? Should I let him sleep? I glanced back and forth between him and the door, then decided my best bet was to check with one of the nurses.

I stepped outside the room. The nurses' station was a few feet away, and a tall white guy with wire-rim glasses and thinning blond hair sat at the desk.

"Hi," I said as I approached. When he looked up, I gestured

at Dalton's room. "Listen, my friend is here with a head injury and hypothermia. Is it . . . if he starts going to sleep, do I let him? Or should I wake him up because of the concussion and all?"

The man pursed his lips. "Are you family?"

"Yeah." I rolled my eyes. "I'm his brother. I just go to the tanning salon more often."

He scowled up at me. "Well, I can't disclose his medical information to anyone except his family or designated emergency contacts."

I fought the urge to roll my eyes again. "I'm not asking for his medical information." I jabbed my thumb over my shoulder. "I'm just asking if I should wake him up or let him sleep."

The scowl deepened, and it was followed by a long-suffering sigh as the man got up. He strolled to Dalton's room, and I silently followed him inside.

He glared at the screen, eyes moving side to side as he read what I assumed was Dalton's chart. After a moment, he said, "Your friend is fine to sleep."

"Okay. Thanks."

The man didn't offer anything further. He left, and once again, it was just me and Dalton. I took my seat beside the bed, not sure what to do except wait for someone to come in and give me news. Or, well, give Dalton news. When he was awake.

He was still asleep when the other nurse came back in. She typed something into the computer, checked his vitals on the monitor, and turned to go.

"Wait," I said. "Is he . . ." I chewed the inside of my cheek. "Look, I know you can't tell me anything because I'm not family, but can you at least tell me if he's gonna be okay?"

She hesitated, regarding him silently, but she finally nodded. "He'll probably sleep for several hours when he gets home, and then be very tired tomorrow, but he'll be fine."

"And it's really okay for him to sleep like that? With a concussion?" I didn't trust that other dickbag.

The nurse smiled. "Yes. Someone will need to stay with him for the next twenty-four hours at least—ideally forty-eight—but he can sleep."

I released a breath. "Okay. Thanks." I felt like an idiot for being so hung up on whether or not Dalton could sleep, but I was terrified of him suddenly taking a turn for the worse. Especially if it was something I might be able to prevent. Fuck, I hated being this useless.

As I watched him sleeping peacefully, my brain kept darting back to the ambulance ride. When Dalton had come around enough to moan when the medics had prodded him just right. I'd imagined all kinds of horrible injuries that might've been causing the pain in his side. Busted ribs? Internal bleeding?

Fortunately, it turned out to be some pulled muscles. Probably from struggling to stay afloat, or maybe they'd happened in the process of hauling him onto the boat. Dalton wouldn't be comfortable for a few says, but given the alternatives, I didn't figure he'd be complaining.

Neither was I. He was alive, and it looked like he was going to be okay. That was all I needed right now.

The Coastal General emergency room stayed pretty quiet as near as I could tell, but it was another solid three hours before the doctor came in. Dalton was starting to come around, and when he heard the words "preparing your discharge papers," he perked right up.

"So I can leave?" he asked.

"As soon as your paperwork is finished, yes." The bald doctor smiled. "Remember, get as much rest as you can, and check in with your primary care doctor in the next forty-eight hours."

Dalton nodded. "Will do."

The doctor left, and I helped Dalton sit up.

"How do you feel?" I asked.

He groaned, rubbing his forehead. After a moment, he exhaled as he lowered his hand. "I'm okay. Just really, really tired." He paused. "And the room keeps . . ." He made a gesture like a boat pitching on the waves.

"It probably will for a while. You need a hand?" I motioned toward his clothes. "Getting dressed?"

Some color bloomed in his cheeks. Even if it was out of shyness, I had to admit it was good to see him getting pink around the edges.

Anything to remind me he was alive.

"No, I'm good." He gingerly stepped down off the bed and took his time getting all the way up. "My head is fucking *killing* me, though."

"Yeah, I believe it. Looks like you took a pretty hard hit." I paused. "What *did* you hit, anyway?"

"I didn't hit anything," he said dryly. "The boat hit me."

I blinked. "Come again?"

"After I went overboard, a wave threw the boat, and—" He gestured at the bandage. "Didn't get out of the way fast enough."

My blood turned as cold as the water we'd pulled him out of. That boat wasn't big enough to handle seas like that, but it wasn't exactly an inflatable dinghy. Tossed around by waves that strong, it could've killed him as easily as a speeding truck.

Oblivious to the worst case scenarios bouncing around in my head, Dalton wrinkled his nose and licked his lips. "Man, I could really use some water. My mouth still tastes like the fucking ocean."

I was on my feet before he'd finished speaking. "Sit tight. I think there's a vending machine down the hall."

"You need cash?" He looked around. "Shit, where's my wallet?"

"Hopefully in your locker." I took out my own wallet and gestured with it. "I got you, though. I'll be back in a second."

It took a while to find a machine that *didn't* require exact change and *did* have something besides Diet Coke, but I eventually found one down the hall from the ER's waiting room. By the time I came back with the water, he was dressed and sitting on the bed, pulling on his shoes. When he looked up, his gaze went straight to the water, and his eyes lit up like I'd just brought him a winning lottery ticket. Not surprisingly, he downed the first bottle in two gulps.

"Holy fuck," he said as he lowered it. "I needed that."

"I'll bet you did."

He closed his eyes and exhaled slowly. "What a crazy fucking night. I swear I can still feel the ocean."

"Not gonna get seasick on me, are you?"

"Not making any promises." He was silent for a moment, eyes closed, but he seemed alert. Still sitting upright, his fingers idly turning the bottlecap over and over. Then his eyes flew open. "Shit! Rhodes!" His voice was full of panic. "Is she okay? Is she—"

"Hey, hey." I touched his arm. "Take it easy. She's fine. Her husband already took her home. In fact, she texted me a little while ago to make sure *you* were okay."

He released a relieved breath. "Oh thank God. She went in with me."

"I think she went in *after* you."

His eyes unfocused. When he finally nodded, he looked dazed. "Yeah. I think . . . I think I remember that. Sort of." He squirmed like he was trying not to shiver. "I'd be dead if she hadn't gone in."

I blinked. The statement was so matter-of-fact. I was kind of used to that from him, but not when we were talking about how close he'd come to fucking dying in the last few hours.

His eyes flicked toward me. Then he watched himself playing with the plastic ring around the top of the water bottle. "I couldn't get a grip on the handles to inflate my vest. Then after the boat hit me, I was out for . . . I don't know. Probably a few seconds. But if she hadn't inflated it for me and hauled my ass up . . ." He shook his head, Adam's apple bobbing with a hard swallow. "I don't remember much after that."

My stomach somersaulted. In the moment, while he'd still been in that cold and violent water, I'd known Dalton had been in very real danger, but it was surreal to realize how quickly and easily he could've died. He could've drowned long before hypothermia had become a concern. The boat crashing into him could've killed him in an instant if it had hit him hard enough. Ice filled my veins as it dawned on me that while I'd been begging my boat to get me to him faster, it could have easily been too late already.

He rolled his shoulders and tilted his head to one side, then the other. As he shifted around, he winced, holding his side gingerly.

"How you feeling?" I asked. "In general?"

"Better than when I was in the water."

I laughed and couldn't resist giving his forearm a little squeeze. "I think we all feel better than when you were in the water."

He turned to me, eyebrows up.

"You scared us, man." I squeezed again before taking my hand back. "When they pulled you out of that water . . ." I didn't think I could finish the thought. Not without puking.

Dalton studied me intently. "What?"

I held his gaze, then shook my head. "Man, I was honestly afraid you were already dead."

He shuddered. So did I.

Then he looked around. "Let's chase down that nurse with my discharge papers. I'm ready to get out of here."

I couldn't agree more.

My car was still on base, so I called us a cab. Fortunately, Dalton's waterproof ID case had been in a lanyard around his neck, and that had survived the chaotic night, so he had his military ID when we approached the base gate. I was pretty sure the sentries would have let us on anyway, though. They knew us, and they probably all knew what had happened.

On the way into the barracks, Dalton could walk, but his balance didn't seem to be so hot, so I kept an arm around his shoulders. He didn't protest. In fact, he leaned into me as we walked, and he still wobbled a bit.

"You okay?" I asked. "Dizzy?"

"A bit. Everything's kind of . . ." He gestured like the walls were tilting from side to side.

"Just keep leaning on me, okay?"

"I will. Thanks."

As we continued down the hall, a few guys poked their heads out of their rooms. Everyone wore concerned expressions, so word must have gotten around about what had happened. Fortunately, they also seemed to realize that neither of us was in any mood to deal with questions, and no one said anything to us.

I let us into his room with the key his roommate had left with me. Dalton was definitely still unsteady, using the bedposts and the walls to stay upright as he moved around the room.

"You need a hand with anything?" I asked.

"Nah, I'm good."

"Okay. I'm just going to step out for a second and get my bag out of the car.

"Your—" He paused, holding himself up with the bathroom door frame. "You staying here?"

I nodded. "Doc says you can't be alone. Your roommate's staying at his girlfriend's house tonight, so I guess you're stuck with me."

To my surprise, that got a smile out of him. The first real one I'd seen since he'd gone out on the boat earlier tonight. "You don't mind?"

My heart did things I couldn't even describe, and it was all I could do to play it cool. "Nah, man. Someone's gotta keep an eye on you."

The smile warmed. He looked exhausted, queasy, and in a lot of pain, but he still smiled, and it still made my stomach flutter. "Thanks, Chris. For staying with me in the ER and here."

"Don't mention it." I gestured at the door. "I'll be right back."

I always kept a shaving kit and change of clothes in my car for those times when I was sweaty, salty, and gross after a long shift. It only took me two minutes to get out there, grab my bag, and get back to Dalton's barracks room, but that was two minutes of imagining all kinds of disasters. What if he passed out? What if he fell? Hadn't the doctor said a concussion like that could result in a brain hemorrhage?

By the time I keyed myself back into the room, I was out of breath from the sprint and the borderline panic.

And Dalton was fine. He'd changed into a pair of blue sweatpants with NAVY in gold lettering on one thigh, and he was standing shirtless at the bathroom sink with his toothbrush in his mouth.

Any other time, I probably would've grabbed the opportunity to ogle the fuck out of his lean body and smooth abs, but right then, I was just relieved he was still upright and conscious. Even the angry scrapes and mottled bruises couldn't undermine the fact that *Dalton was okay.*

He wasn't upright or conscious for long, though. In the time it took me to brush my teeth and put on a pair of gym shorts, he got into bed, and he was out like a light. I'd finally started taking the nurses and doc at their word that he could sleep, so I didn't freak. Instead, I sat on the edge of Stockton's bed for a minute and just watched him.

He was still pale. The stark white bandage over the gash on his temple should've made him look like he had some color, but he really was that pale, especially next to all the scrapes and bruises. At least he wasn't as ghostly as he'd been when the swimmers had fished him out of the water. That was a scary shade of white I hoped I *never* saw again.

I shuddered, fought back the urge to caress his face just to make sure he was really there, and killed the light. As I climbed into the bed, I was more drained than I ever remembered being. I should have collapsed facedown in a pillow and passed out for a few hours.

But every time I closed my eyes, I saw Dalton in the water or on the deck. I saw all the ways tonight could have played out, but miraculously hadn't.

So instead of sleeping, I stared at Dalton's profile in the darkness. Every time he took a breath, the fear in my chest settled a tiny bit more. He was okay. He was going to feel like shit for a while, but he was okay.

And damn but I owed MA3 Rhodes one hell of a hug. And for that matter, the command owed her medals. Like, big medals. Not just a Navy Achievement Medal, which everyone involved in the rescue would probably get. No, she deserved one of those medals that practically got you an automatic promotion when someone saw it on your brag sheet. That woman had put herself in serious danger to save Dalton, and if our command tried to drop an award to a letter of commendation or some watered down shit like that, there would be hell to pay.

My throat tightened. *She saved Dalton. Dalton almost died.*

I held my breath as I watched his silhouette. My stomach roiled and my eyes stung as reality sank in deeper than it had since I'd heard that distress call.

I almost lost you tonight.
What would I do without you?

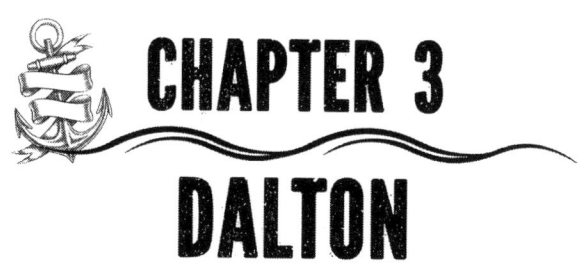

CHAPTER 3

DALTON

Long before I had any desire to be awake, my guts lurched and yanked me out of a sound sleep. I stumbled to my feet, the whole room listing and tossing around me, and by the grace of God, made it into the bathroom before I started heaving. I didn't bother turning on the light—I just braced my arms on the seat and tried to keep my head between them.

And oh, fuck, I didn't think I'd ever been so miserable. Every time I retched, I thought I was going to black out from the pain. In my head. In my sides. In my stomach. Everything hurt anyway, and my digestive system shifting into violent reverse did not help with the pulled muscles in my torso or the splitting pain in the side of my skull. And it just kept coming. One deep, violent heave after another until I was damn near sobbing in between trying to breathe.

Finally, it stopped. Even the dry heaving stopped. I spat a couple of times, fumbled for the handle to flush the toilet, then dropped back against the wall, still sitting on the cold floor. Elbow propped on my knees, I rubbed my forehead as if that might quell some of the vicious throbbing. If I just didn't move, didn't think, didn't make a sound, the pain would back off. Or at least not get worse. *Just . . . breathe . . .*

A firm hand squeezed my shoulder. "You okay?"

Chris. Chris was still here.

Relief and embarrassment mingled in my already tender stomach.

"I'm good," I croaked. "Did I wake you up?"

"It's okay."

"What time is it?"

"Almost 0700."

Ugh. Way too early for two guys on the night shift.

I groaned. I might've been trying to say something, but the pain in my stomach and my sides and my head scrambled my brain, and I decided the groan was all I'd meant to do. I kept rubbing my temples and willing myself not to get sick again. There couldn't be anything left at this point.

"Sorry," I finally muttered. "We should . . . sleep some more." I started to get up, but the room pitched so hard, I almost toppled to the floor.

Strong but gentle hands steadied me, though. "Easy. Take it slow, okay?"

As much as my pride wanted to bitch, it didn't have the energy, and its protests were nothing more than a dull mumble in the back of my mind as I nodded.

Chris carefully slung my arm around his shoulders. Slowly, he eased me to my feet, pausing when I hissed in pain. "You good?"

"Yeah." I winced and held my side as we continued upward. Once I was all the way up, I leaned against the wall and kneaded the sore muscle. "I get the feeling this is going to suck even more than the concussion."

"That bad, huh?"

I nodded, grimacing. "Hurts to breathe."

"And puke, probably."

"Ya think?"

He laughed softly and, when I was firmly on my feet, guided me out of the bathroom. The room was dark, and God bless him, he didn't turn on a light. I wasn't sure my head could handle that. I didn't even know if I was light sensitive right then—I just knew my skull felt like it was about to implode, and I didn't want to give it a reason to.

Chris helped me back onto the bed, then sat on the edge. "You need anything?"

"No. Thanks."

"Okay. Get some sleep."

I didn't know why, but I almost expected him to press a kiss to my forehead.

And when he didn't, I knew exactly why I was disappointed.

When we woke up for real, it was almost noon. Still early for us, but I was sure if I stayed in bed any longer, I was just going to get stiffer. And besides, I was hungry.

Thank God the room was dark. Jay worked nights too, so we had a double layer of blackout curtains over the window. Only the softly glowing blue numbers on the clock between the beds gave away the time.

I sat up carefully. I still hurt all over, and my stomach was pissed off and grumbling. My head throbbed furiously, probably as much from hunger as the concussion.

In the other bed, Chris was lounging against the pillows, looking at something on his phone. "Hey." He put the phone down and sat up. "How you feeling?"

I was already sure I was going to get sick of that question. "Ask me again after I've had some coffee."

"Coffee sounds good. You want to go get some breakfast and then chill for the day?"

I studied him, trying to keep him and everything else from doubling. "Don't you have to work tonight?"

Chris shook his head. "Chief knows what's up. I'm supposed to keep an eye on you for forty-eight hours. Doc's orders." He smiled uncertainly. "Nobody wants to see either of our faces at work until that time's up."

I laughed even though it hurt. "So am I S.I.Q.?" I'd only been sick-in-quarters once in my career, and the cabin fever had almost done me in.

Chris shrugged. "Yeah, probably. Even if you are, there's nothing that says you can't go out and get something to eat. You hungry?"

My stomach grumbled audibly before I could even respond.

He smiled. "Come on. Let's go feed you."

After we'd both showered and dressed, we swung by the harbor building so I could get my wallet and keys from my locker. My phone had been in my uniform, and it was done for. I'd turned up my nose at the apocalypse-proof cases everyone else had, because they were bulky and expensive. Guess the joke was on me since now I got to pay for a whole new fucking phone.

After we left the harbor building, we didn't have to go far to find food. Anchor Point was like any military town, and it had restaurants and bars clustered around the base gates. They'd finally opened up a McDonald's a few months ago, and I didn't think I'd ever seen it with fewer than five cars stacked up in the drive-thru.

Fast food really wasn't my thing, but with as wonky as my stomach had been all morning, a couple of Egg McMuffins and a Coke sounded like the safest bet. Might not taste spectacular, but if it meant avoiding a repeat of earlier this morning, I'd eat it with a smile. Good thing they served breakfast all day now.

As we stood in line, I could still feel the deck pitching under my feet while the room spun around me. It was a weird feeling, but I was starting to get used to it enough that I could at least stay upright.

At the counter, I placed my order. When the cashier gave me the total, I opened my wallet and . . . stared. I needed . . . seven dollars . . . and seven cents . . . so that meant . . .

The green bills were supposed to make sense. Couple of twenties. A ten. Some wrinkled ones. A five tangled up in there somewhere. How much did I need? What the fuck?

"Sir?" the girl prompted.

"Um . . ." Heat was suddenly rushing into my face. "I . . ."

Chris leaned past me and put his card into the credit card machine.

"Thanks," I muttered, but I was rattled. That had never happened before. I could settle up a bill and calculate the tip in my head when I was *drunk*, for God's sake.

After we'd gotten our food, we found a table. Sitting didn't even seem to help. Now my equilibrium was all fucked up again. I could stand all right, and I could sit of course, and the dizziness was becoming almost normal, but my mind was all over the place.

I hadn't been able to count out cash.

I hadn't been able to figure out how to pay for a McDonald's order.

The bills hadn't made sense, and the numbers hadn't added up, and—

"Hey." Chris's hand was a solid, anchoring presence on my arm. "You okay?"

No. I am so not okay.

He squeezed gently. "You really rang your bell last night, didn't you?" The question was light, but laced with genuine concern.

Oh. Right. My head. As if I'd forgotten about the relentless throbbing radiating from my right temple.

"Yeah." I stared down at the receipt on the tray. "Guess I did." Then I looked at him and I didn't sound like myself as I said, "I couldn't count the money."

He nodded grimly. "I know. I could tell."

"Fuck . . ."

"Relax." He gave another squeeze before releasing my arm. "The doc said you might have some trouble for a little while. Memory. Balance. Cognitive stuff."

I met his gaze. "He did? Did I . . . am I forgetting an entire conversation?"

Chris smiled gently and shrugged. "You were pretty out of it right then."

"Oh. Did he say how long this shit will last?" I gestured at my head.

He was quiet for a moment, chewing thoughtfully. After he'd washed down a bite of his McMuffin, he said, "He figured the worst of it'll last a few days, but some of it might be a few weeks."

My sandwich almost slid out of my hand. "A few *weeks*?"

"After smacking your head like that? Yes. Of course it's going to take—"

"But the E-6 exam is coming up."

Chris grimaced. "Oh shit."

"Yeah. Oh shit. If I don't make MA1 this time around . . ." I couldn't finish the thought. Didn't need to. Panic surged through me, which didn't help my balance. Good thing I was sitting down. Now how the hell was I going to sit for an exam? If I couldn't count out some cash for a damn sandwich, how was I supposed to answer multiple choice questions about my job, the Navy, military history . . .

And I couldn't just pass the exam this time. I had to blow it out of the water. Advancement was getting competitive within our rate, and either I got promoted *this year* or I got out.

"*Fuck*." I pressed the heel of my hand to my aching forehead, trying to find some relief from the pain and my thoughts.

"Take it easy, man." Chris's voice was soothing. "It hasn't even been twenty-four hours. The exam's not for like three weeks. You'll recover."

"God, I hope so." I lowered my hand, took a breath, and reached for my sandwich again.

After I had some food and caffeine in me, I did feel better. Still not exactly Einstein upstairs, but less like my body was going to quit working altogether. I'd take that.

When we were done, Chris took our trash, and I started to follow, but of course, that couldn't be uneventful and easy—

I got up and immediately had to grab the table's edge when the world wobbled.

Chris grabbed my elbow. "You okay?"

"Yeah. Just . . . forgot my balance was jacked up." I smirked despite the panicky feeling in my gut. "What does it say about my head injury when I keep forgetting I'm a wreck?"

He laughed halfheartedly but didn't let me go. I realized he still had the tray in his other hand.

"You're good at this shit," I said.

He chuckled, and then he carefully released my arm before he took a couple of steps to get rid of our trash. The whole way, he kept glancing back at me, probably making sure I didn't fall on my ass or something.

Now that I was upright, though, I wasn't too bad. Not as steady as I wanted to be, but I was finding my sea legs, which I'd never expected to need on dry land.

With a little support from Chris, I made it to his car and slid into the passenger seat. Then he went around to the other side, got in, and started the car.

I pressed my elbow against the window and kneaded my thumping forehead. "When I don't feel like shit again, you know what I'm gonna do first?"

"What's that?"

I lowered my hand and turned to Chris. "I'm gonna kick MA1 Anderson's ass."

Chris laughed humorlessly. "You make it sound like there's gonna be anything left of him by the time you're feeling better."

"Oh yeah?"

"Yep. If I don't get to him, Rhodes will." Chris shook his head. "That dude better be sleeping with one eye open."

I sat straighter. "Rhodes. She's okay, right?"

"Yeah. She texted me earlier to check on you. Says she's tired, but she's good."

"Oh." I cocked my head. "Why do I feel like you already told me that?"

"I did. But the doc says that's normal too."

"Great."

He drummed the wheel with his thumb. "So, you need anything to tide you over at the barracks?"

"I could stand to make a trip to the commissary. And I need to get a new phone." I rubbed my forehead. "Why does that all sound so fucking tiring?"

Chris laughed. "Because it's exhausting even when you haven't smacked your head on a boat." He gave my arm a gentle pat. "Come on. We'll go down to the Exchange and pick one up for you. I'll make sure they don't fuck you over on the terms or something."

"Thanks." I smiled, and I actually felt it. Everything had been on its head since last night. I couldn't even rely on myself to count out money or drive a car.

But there were constants in my world, and one of those constants was Chris. He had my back. I'd never doubted he did, but damn if he hadn't come through when it counted the most.

I owe you so big, Chris.

"I am so stealing your couch one of these days." I sprawled across Chris's amazing sofa.

He watched me from the kitchen. "You can get it out the door, it's all yours."

"Oh yeah?" I carefully laced my fingers behind my head. "Didn't fit?"

"Not without bending a few laws of physics, no." He glared at the front door and shook his head. "We had to take the goddamned door off its hinges."

I smirked. "Anyone ever told you about this thing called a measuring tape? Really helps when you're shopping for furniture."

Chris rolled his eyes. As he turned away to get something out of the fridge, he called over his shoulder, "I think I liked you better when your bell was rung."

"It's still rung," I said. "Just . . . not as much as it was."

"Great," he muttered.

I chuckled and just watched him for a few minutes. We'd come to his place so my roommate could sleep for a few hours, and Chris was rummaging around in the kitchen in the name of dinner. I didn't even know what he was making, but there wasn't much I wouldn't eat right then. It had been a couple of days since the accident, and the concussion had finally stopped fucking with my stomach.

It didn't hurt that I knew from experience what an amazing cook he was. There'd been a little barbecue outside the building where we'd done our classroom work in coxswain's school, and Chris had gotten permission to use it. Didn't matter what he threw on the grill—steaks, burgers, chicken—it was always perfectly seasoned and perfectly cooked. I might've kind of fallen a little bit in love with him the first time he'd grilled me up a steak.

My throat tightened as I watched him flitting around the kitchen. *Might've* fallen a *little bit* in love with him?

Okay, so maybe I'd been on cloud nine at that point. I'd had a flawless steak grilled to a perfect medium rare by a gorgeous man while I was on a break from learning to be a coxswain. It really didn't get any better than that.

And now that gorgeous man wouldn't leave my side while I recovered from my worst nightmare. Watching him from his couch, I caught myself physically aching to touch him. It didn't matter that he was straight. That would make me keep my hands to myself of course, but it sure as shit didn't change how I felt about him. I'd had a crush on him since day one, but right now . . . fuck, I was pretty sure the "might've" and "little bit" ships had sailed a long time ago.

I let my mind wander back to coxswain's school. It had only been a couple of weeks long, but it goddamn, those had been a couple of amazing weeks. Careening around the water, learning how to maneuver at blistering speeds during combat maneuvers, and . . .

Chris.

The very first day, I'd taken one look at that tall, dark-skinned guy with the playful smile and the dancing eyes, and that had been it. Instant crush.

Then I got to know him. Found out we had the same sense of humor. Found out he loved Taylor Swift and Britney Spears—something he'd only told me after I'd admitted to knowing every lyric from every boy band song since the dawn of time. Found out he could cook and light up a room with a joke and drive a boat like he was born to do it and . . . God. Everything. Every time I'd found out some new detail about him, I'd wanted him more. I hadn't been surprised to find out he was straight, but the disappointment had hit me hard.

Just because I couldn't have him didn't mean I couldn't want him, though, so I'd let myself swoon over him. And even if I couldn't have him as a boyfriend or whatever, I had him as a friend. A damn good friend. I could live with that.

We'd both gone back to our respective commands on opposite sides of the country, but we'd stayed in touch. I'd had to tweak my cell phone plan because we'd been texting and messaging so much. We'd chatted constantly, even while he'd been deployed, and his texts and IMs had quickly become the highlights of my day. As soon as my crew and I would finish a patrol, I'd hurry to my locker to check my phone, and I'd grin like an idiot when I had a message from him.

Then Chris had transferred to NAS Adams, and shortly after that, I'd gotten orders to the same base. I had literally jumped up out of my chair and shouted when I saw REPORT TO NAS ADAMS on my screen. My coworkers had thought I'd lost my mind, but I didn't care. And a few weeks later, I was here. And he was here. And every single fucking day, I got to see him. And—

"You don't mind it a little spicy, do you?"

Chris's voice jarred me back into the present. I blinked a few times, hoping he would blame my space-out on my rattled skull.

"Spicy? What?"

He held up a jar of some kind of bright red powder. "The chicken. I was going to put some chili powder on it. That okay?"

"Yeah. Of course." I smiled. "It's all good."

He smiled back, sending a zing of *holy fuck* right through me.

And while he sprinkled chili powder and God knew what else on the chicken, I just stared.

Damn you for being straight, Chris, because I think I fell for you long before I ever fell out of that boat.

A couple of days later, while Chris was at work, Chief Lasby called me into his office. I was on medical leave, and he told me I could wear civvies, so at least that meant I wasn't getting my ass chewed or something. If anything, he probably just wanted to make sure I was doing all right. My new phone had been ringing like crazy with people checking up on me, so I figured he was doing the same.

I just didn't want to talk to him. The only person I wanted to talk to less was MA1 Anderson.

Professionalism and military bearing demanded I suck it up, though, so I put on a decent pair of jeans and a Huskers sweatshirt. I still wasn't steady enough to drive, so I called a buddy on patrol and had him come get me at the barracks.

"How you feeling?" MA2 James asked as I slid into the passenger seat.

"I've been better, believe me."

"I'll bet. And I always knew MA3 Rhodes was tough, but goddamn." He whistled, shaking his head. "Takes some serious balls to jump in water like that."

"No kidding. Thank God she did it." I shuddered. There was no doubt in my mind I would have drowned if she hadn't come in after me. None. "You know if she's back at work? Or did they give her some time off too?" We'd texted back and forth a little, and she'd insisted she was all right, but I'd wondered if that was just to keep me from worrying.

He shook his head again. "Don't know. I saw her and her husband at the Exchange last night, and she said she was pretty sore and tired, but she didn't say anything about coming back to work."

Well, at least she was up and about. Maybe still tired thanks to the hypothermia, but she must not have been too fucked up. Thank God for that. I had enough trouble sleeping with it on my conscience that she'd gone in after me at all.

MA2 James dropped me off at the security building. Chief Lasby's office was here instead of in the harbor building, which was usually a blessing because it kept him out of our hair. Today it was a curse because security was always a lot more crowded than the HPU building, so walking through these halls meant wading through a gauntlet of people who'd heard what had happened. I appreciated the well wishes, of course, but I was exhausted. More than that, my head was still wonky after the concussion, and conversations were way harder than they should have been. I could keep up, and I could respond coherently—it just took a hell of a lot more work than usual.

Chief Jackson and Senior Chief Curtis were coming down the hall, coffee cups in hand, and stopped when they saw me.

"MA2," Jackson said. "Glad to see you on your feet."

"Thanks, Chief," I said with a smile I didn't feel. That wasn't his fault, though. I actually liked Jackson and Curtis. The fact that they were both openly gay didn't hurt, but they were also good guys. They weren't like those assholes who let their ranks go to their heads and threw their weight around. Shame Curtis was transferring out soon; his replacement would probably be an insufferable dickhead.

"How are you feeling?" Curtis asked, genuine concern creasing his forehead.

"Like I should hold off on swimming again until the weather warms up."

They both laughed, and I managed to do the same. It was hard to plaster on smiles today, though. I felt like shit. I just wanted to go back to the barracks, burrow under the covers, and fucking *sleep*.

Fortunately, they kept the conversation short, and after some more well wishes, we continued in separate directions. A moment later, I tapped on Chief Lasby's door.

When he opened it, he smiled. "MA2." He shook my hand and clasped the other one over the back of it. "Good to see you up and around. I hear the other night was a bit eventful."

"Yeah, you could say that."

"Why don't you have a seat?" He tapped the back of one of his guest chairs.

"Thanks, Chief." I sat down, grateful for the chance to let the chair deal with keeping me upright. Standing for any length of time without falling still took more effort than I liked to think about.

On the other side of the desk, Lasby sat back in his chair, hands folded under the paunch the Navy apparently issued to everyone as soon as they made Chief. Well almost everyone. Chief Jackson was ripped. So was Senior Chief Curtis. In fact, I'd seen him and his husband at the base gym a few times, and I was pretty sure Senior was getting close to a six-pack. Man, if I ever made senior chief, I hoped I stayed in as good of shape as—

"MA2?" Chief Lasby's voice made me jump.

I blinked my eyes into focus. "Sorry, Chief."

His brow furrowed with obvious concern. "You really did take a nasty blow, didn't you?"

I touched the bandage, which was almost as annoying as the throbbing gash underneath it. "Yeah. Boat, one. My head, zero."

He laughed humorlessly. "Well, I'm glad to see it didn't do more damage than it did."

"Me too, Chief."

He took in a breath. "Listen, the reason I brought you in here is I wanted to give you a heads up. There *is* going to be an investigation." He scowled, rolling his eyes. "That's the Navy for you these days—any time there's an incident, they have to investigate it."

I shifted uneasily, not sure what to say. MA1 Anderson had almost gotten me killed, so yeah, there'd damn well *better* be an investigation.

Lasby gave a heavy sigh. "You're going to need to give a statement as soon as you can."

"Okay. I can do that while I'm here." I gestured over my shoulder with my thumb. "I'll just go—"

"No, no." He patted the air. "You had your bell rung pretty good, and I want you to have some time to recuperate."

"I'd rather give the statement sooner than later. While the details are still fresh." The details I could remember, anyway.

He watched me, his expression unreadable. Finally, he shrugged. "Suit yourself. I'm confident the investigation will be . . ." He paused, then waved dismissively. "You understand how it is, MA2. We have our procedures and protocols, but in the heat of the moment, sometimes we have to bend or even break those protocols. Especially when there are lives on the line."

I nodded, but I wasn't following, and I couldn't decide if the concussion had anything to do with it.

"So when MA1 Anderson believed there was someone in distress," Lasby went on, "I think the investigators will agree he was doing his duty as a master-at-arms to take care of the situation."

I blinked. "Huh?"

He looked me right in the eye. "You can understand MA1 Anderson's motives, can't you?"

"Uh . . ." I swallowed. "With all due respect, Chief, his actions put myself and MA3 Rhodes in danger of—"

"And according to Anderson, you weren't taking appropriate safety precautions when the incident occurred." He sat up, folded hands landing on top of his blotter. "Is that correct, MA2?" He spat out the "two," as if to subtly—or not—remind me of my position on the totem pole.

My mouth had gone dry. "When we hit the nets, I was on my way into the cabin to advise him that we needed to turn back. Before that, I was watching the bow. Checking for objects in the water."

His eyes narrowed. "And after you turned away, the screws tangled in a fish net, correct?"

It took a moment for the accusatory tone to sink into my brain. For me to put the pieces together and realize what he was implying.

Sitting straighter, I struggled to hold his gaze. "I didn't see any nets."

His eyebrow arched. "You weren't looking when the bow passed over them."

Ice water spread through my veins. I fought the urge to fidget nervously, but failed. "The nets were under the surface, Chief. The visibility was barely a few inches, plus the seas were rough and the light was fading. Even if I *had* been looking over the bow right then, I wouldn't have seen them."

Eyes hard, he shook his head. "MA1 Anderson was relying on *you* to make sure there were no hazards in the water," he said coldly. "I suggest you remember that when you issue your statement."

I opened my mouth to speak, but he cut me off with a terse, "Dismissed, MA2."

Without another word, I got up and left. As soon as I'd gone around the corner, I stopped to lean against the wall, not sure how much of this dizziness was from my concussion and how much was my mind reeling after the conversation. My head hadn't spun this fast at the ER the other night. What the fuck? *What the fuck?*

I'd come in here thinking he just wanted to check in and make sure I was all right. Instead, Lasby had all but told me he was going to do everything he could to paint MA1 Anderson as a hero. Someone who'd broken protocol in the name of potentially saving lives. The damage to government property—the boat, MA3 Rhodes, and myself—wasn't because he'd stupidly taken us out of the harbor. It was because I'd been derelict in my duty of watching for hazards.

What. The. Fuck?

Technically, watching for hazards hadn't been my job, but I knew how easily it could be spun that way. By going onto the bow like I had, I'd tacitly assured Anderson I was keeping an eye out for hazards. In the seconds my attention had been off the water—when I'd been heading for the coxswain's seat to argue with Anderson—the nets had slipped past the bow and under the hull to snag the screws, crippling us and catapulting me into the drink.

I wanted to roll my eyes and remind myself he couldn't make up rules like that, and this couldn't come back and bite me as hard as he wanted me to think it could. Unfortunately, I'd been in the Navy—the Master-at-Arms rate in particular—long enough to know that was bullshit. He couldn't string me up for dereliction of duty when "watching for flotsam, jetsam, and fishnets" wasn't actually my duty, but he could make sure this followed me to the end of my career. I already knew all too well how true that was—my single trip to Captain's Mast had been following me around for a damn decade. Some scuttlebutt among the chiefs' mess could kill my chances of advancement, and without advancing, my career was over in under two years anyway. And if MA1 Anderson was not only cleared but branded as a hero who'd been trying to save some civilians only to get hung up on a fishnet thanks to me being insubordinate . . .

I blew out a breath.

And my stomach picked just that moment to lurch. I clapped a hand over my mouth. I still didn't know if it was the concussion, the conversation, or both, but it didn't matter because I had about three seconds to get to the men's room.

I made it.

Barely.

CHAPTER 4

CHRIS

"Oh hey." MA2 Powers snorted, leaning into the patrol boat's cabin. "Look at that—they're finally working on the Metal Shark."

Sure enough—there was a crew from Port Ops working on the larger vessel as I steered us back in off watch. The boat Anderson had been driving the other night was out of commission pending the investigation—the entire boat was considered evidence—so there'd been no choice but to let us take out the bigger boat for patrols, and apparently that had been enough to light the fire under Port Ops' ass. After all, if this boat broke down, we were dead in the water.

Christ. Was that *really* what it took to get a boat fixed around here?

I pulled my gaze away from the repairs-in-progress and focused on parking my vessel in its usual slip. I was eager to get off the boat and text Dalton to make sure he was doing okay. He'd been pretty steady on his feet, but still. I didn't even like leaving him to come to work. Unfortunately, the doc had only wanted someone to keep an eye on him for forty-eight hours. So this afternoon, after making sure my number was programmed into his new phone, I'd left him in the barracks and headed to work.

On my way up the pier after parking the boat, I sent Dalton a quick *Are you doing okay?* text. As I lowered my phone and looked up, I just about tripped over my own boot. What the fuck was MA1 Anderson doing in uniform and anywhere near the HPU building?

Standing outside and having a cigarette, that was what. He wasn't armed, so he was probably on some sort of desk detail until the investigation was over. Didn't that just figure—motherfucker causes a disaster and gets cake work for a while.

When I failed to kill him with my mind, I continued walking toward the building—and him—and looked him up and down. He looked like he hadn't slept in a month. I hoped he didn't sleep any time soon. Reckless motherfucker.

Except, the more I watched him, the more something didn't sit right. As he brought his cigarette up to his mouth, his hand was shaky, and I almost felt bad for thinking he was such a dick. He looked genuinely upset. A few shades whiter than usual. Keeping his eyes down. His usual bravado annoyed the crap out of me, but now that it was gone, he looked like someone who might drop if a fly landed on him with too much force. The guy was obviously rattled, and even if he deserved to be, I couldn't help a little bit of sympathy. It wasn't like he'd *set out* to nearly kill my best friend.

Okay, so maybe I wasn't feeling as charitable as I thought.

He glanced at me but quickly cut his eyes away as he sucked in some smoke. I picked up the pace so I could go inside, do turnover for the oncoming watch, and—

"Hey, MA2."

Damn it.

I stopped, but I didn't speak.

He swallowed hard, focusing on crushing his cigarette under his boot heel. "Is, uh, MA2 Taylor doing okay?"

No thanks to you.

I tightened my jaw. "He's hanging in there, MA1."

"Good. Good." He nodded, releasing a breath, and I resented the shit out of his relief. He had no right to be anything but stressed out and anxious right now. In an uncharacteristically quiet voice, he added, "Give him my best, okay? We're all worried about him."

"Yeah. Sure, man."

He glared at me, and I figured he was weighing if it was worth jumping my shit for not calling him MA1. He must've realized that now was not the time and I didn't give a fuck about military bearing, because he let it go.

I continued walking, not feeling the least bit guilty about how I'd addressed him. It wasn't like I made a habit of that shit—I was practically born with a sense of military bearing. You didn't grow up in a house with two active duty parents and not develop a deep-seated respect for rank.

So I decided I could be forgiven for some subtle disrespect toward an MA1 who'd very nearly killed my best friend. He was lucky a little side-eye and a snide tone was all he was getting from me.

After I'd finished doing turnover, I went into the main office where we all hung out between watches. It was half office, half break room—desks and computers along the walls, a large table in the middle, and a fridge and coffeepot by the window that overlooked the harbor. Since the rest of my section had gone up to the Navy Exchange in search of dinner, and the other section was out on patrol, it was deserted except for—

I did a double take. What the fuck was MA3 Rhodes doing back in uniform?

"MA3." I blinked. "I didn't think you'd be back at work yet."

She looked up from making a cup of coffee, and shrugged. "I didn't get hurt. Just some wicked hypothermia. I'm on light duty until I get a psych eval, but yeah, I'm here." She didn't sound happy about it. I didn't blame her.

She wasn't carrying a weapon, of course, and being on light duty meant she wasn't going out on the water. Dalton would be under the same restrictions once he came back, and there'd be a psych eval for him too. Odds were good neither of them would be off dry land for several months at least. Up to a year, depending on how the Navy handled things.

As I started pouring myself some coffee, I said, "Friend to friend, are you doing okay?"

She pressed her lips together and stared at the floor, chipped purple mug held tight in both hands. "I'm good. Or . . . will be. Anyway." She shook herself and paused for a sip of coffee. "I'd be a lot better if Chief wasn't being such a dick."

I bristled. "What's he doing?"

She exhaled so hard, her shoulders sagged. "Trying to act like I'm the one who fucked up."

"He . . . come again?"

Rhodes pressed her lips together for a second, her expression tight with barely contained rage. "I swear to God they're more worried about me losing Taylor's rifle than the fact that I kept his ass from drowning."

I had to replay her comment in my head three times before I was sure she'd said what I thought she'd said. "What?"

She scowled. "They're all pissy about me going in the water instead of tossing in a life ring, *and* threatening to hem me up for losing Dalton's rifle. I mean, what was I supposed to do? It was already ruined as soon as it went in the water, and it was going to pull both of us down if I didn't take it off him." She threw up her hands. "I guess they don't like the idea that someone could find it and . . . I don't know, copy it? Like it's not easier to just pull the schematics off the internet and build it from scratch instead of prying barnacles off one that's been marinating in saltwater. But now they have to send divers in after it and replace it because even if it does work, it's evidence now. And—"

"Hold up, hold up." I inclined my head. "They should be pissed at Anderson. You didn't just toss a gun in overboard for kicks."

"I know, right?" she growled. "But that's an expensive gun, and going in after it is expensive and moderately dangerous, so . . ." She growled a few curses.

"For fuck's sake. If you hadn't taken it off him, they'd be sending in divers to recover more than a goddamned gun."

We both flinched. I hadn't even thought before I'd said it, and now that the words were out, I was cold all over. Rhodes looked like she was going to be sick. And that cold in my veins was quickly replaced with hot fury. She was the reason he had survived. Quite possibly the *only* reason. And they were threatening her over protocols and a fucking *rifle*?

Before I could go off on a tirade, though, Rhodes released a long, tired sigh. "How is he doing, anyway? I mean, he's been texting me, but . . ." She bit her lip, looking worried.

"But what?"

"Well he's . . ." She hesitated. "Like, he's coherent, but either his autocorrect is turned off, or . . ."

The pieces clicked, and I nodded. "Yeah, the concussion fucked him up a bit. The doc thinks it's temporary, though." *God, I hope it's temporary.*

"Good. I'm glad. I . . ." She lowered her gaze and fidgeted.

Silence stretched out. She obviously had something on her mind, so I nudged her gently. "Come on. Spill it."

"Well, I . . ." She kept her gaze down, and some color bloomed in her cheeks.

"What's up?"

Rhodes took a deep breath. "Is it true what I heard from Powers?" she asked in almost a whisper. "That Dalton, like, tried to kiss you or something on the boat?"

Heat rushed into my face, and I cleared my throat. "He was delirious." Every time I had to clarify that—to myself, mostly—it stung a little more.

She scowled. "Damn. I was hoping it was just a rumor."

"What? Why?"

"Because you know how everyone is in this command." Rhodes rolled her eyes. "They'll never let either of you hear the end of it."

My stomach roiled. "Fuck. You don't think anyone will get violent, do you? Toward him?"

"No, no. I think people are more worried that you will. Getting hit on by a gay guy and all."

I grimaced. She was right about our shipmates probably not letting it go. Back in Norfolk, a buddy of mine had been involved in rescuing some people after a small vessel had capsized. One of the women he'd pulled from the water had glommed onto him, flirting shamelessly and trying to get in his pants right there on the boat.

We all knew it was because she'd nearly drowned, and we'd all known his obvious hard-on had just been a physical reaction to a girl's hand on his junk. Survivors grabbing onto rescuers and temporarily falling in love with them was as close to normal as anything was in those situations.

That hadn't stopped people from ribbing him about it relentlessly until he'd transferred to a ship. From his social media posts, I gathered someone had passed the rumor on to his new command, and though the jokes weren't quite as often, it wasn't unusual for someone to take a potshot at him about damsels in distress.

I could only imagine how much worse it would be for me and Dalton because we were both men. Especially since nobody knew we were both gay. And that made me feel even worse. Dalton was out and proud. He was going to get endless shit for making a pass at a straight guy, while I'd probably get a mixture of jabs and sympathy. If they only knew.

I winced at my own thought. It was bad enough I'd never come out to Dalton. I didn't even know why I hadn't. He was my best friend, and we'd been pretty open about everything else, but I'd never been able to show that card. And now he was going to get shit for coming on to a straight dude.

I wouldn't tell Dalton about what was coming from our shipmates. Not quite yet. I'd give him a heads up before he came back to work, though. No way in hell would I let him be blindsided by that shit, especially since he might not remember what had happened.

Right now, though, he needed to focus on recovering.

Rhodes left to drive up to the security building for something, and I sat at the table with my coffee, a couple of Twinkies from the communal cabinet, and a maintenance request form. The boat we were using while the little one was out of commission had some odd noises coming from one of the engines. Might've been nothing—boats were always rattling and clicking and grumbling—but with our tiny fleet already being down another boat, I wasn't taking chances.

At the other end of the hall, the locker room door thudded shut, and some boots headed in my direction. I turned to see who was coming—more out of bored curiosity than anything—and did my second double take of the night. "What the fuck are you doing here?"

Dalton smiled, but it didn't look like he felt it. He gestured over his shoulder. "Just came by to get some shit out of my locker."

"That all?"

He dropped his gaze and the smile vanished. What *was* he doing here? He was in civvies, but still—wobbly as he'd been lately, he had no business coming to work. And the way he avoided my eyes made the hair on my neck stand up.

"How did you even get here?" I asked.

"Patrol dropped me off." He motioned toward the door, still not looking at me. "They're waiting outside, so I gotta go in a minute."

"Okay." I rose and stepped closer. "What's up, though?"

He sighed, running his hand through his short hair. "Lasby

called me down to his office. Said he wanted to talk to me about what happened."

"Yeah? What did he say?"

Dalton avoided my gaze for an uncomfortably long moment. I was about to prod him when he blurted out, "I think they're investigating me and Rhodes along with Anderson."

My blood turned cold as the calm water outside. "You're shitting me."

Sighing again, Dalton pressed his shoulder against the wall, and it suddenly seemed like that wall was the only thing keeping him from sinking to the floor. He had more color than the night we'd pulled him out of the ocean, but there were dark circles under his eyes and his cheeks seemed gaunt. How the hell much damage could a man rack up in three days? Had he slept at *all*?

He scratched his neck. "Chief told me there's going to be an investigation. Which . . . no shit. But he wants me and Rhodes to play it like Anderson was totally doing the right thing by going out to help that other boat. And . . ." He closed his eyes, releasing a breath like it was just too hard to hold onto. Finally, he muttered, "Lasby's trying to protect his golden boy, and he's going to throw us under the bus to do it. If we don't agree that Anderson was in the right—"

"But there's no way an investigation will show you or Rhodes being the negligent ones."

Dalton scowled. "No, but I don't trust anyone running this investigation any further than I can throw them."

"I don't see how you or anyone else would."

"Not that it makes a difference. They're in charge. They're running this whole fucking thing, and even if Lasby can't punish us on paper for letting Anderson take the fall, there are things he *can* do." Dalton sounded more tired and demoralized than I'd ever heard him. "Fuck. Why do I get the feeling the worst of this hasn't even started yet?"

I didn't respond.

Because damn if I didn't feel the same.

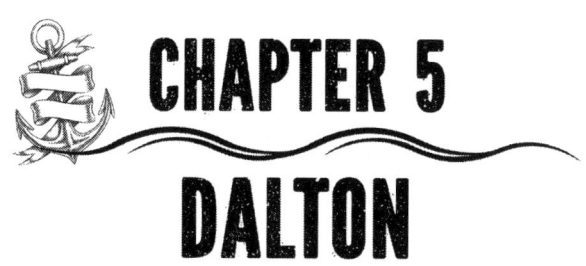

CHAPTER 5

DALTON

After a few days on medical leave, I was getting stir crazy from taking it easy. Chris was working, and my roommate was too, and I was fucking *bored*. Being agitated about the investigation wasn't helping, and I didn't think I'd ever been this restless in my life. I needed to get the fuck out of the barracks.

I still hadn't been cleared to drive, but I was steady enough to walk to the Exchange and grab a cab to take me off-base. I had the driver take me past the main gate, and he was annoyed when I handed him my credit card, but he took it without saying anything. I felt like an idiot, too. I had plenty of cash in my wallet—I was just too rattled from the other day at McDonald's and the fact that numbers and words were *still* getting scrambled in my brain. At least a credit card just meant a signature. No counting out cash. No fighting through my new dyslexia to enter my PIN. A squiggle that sort of looked like my name, and we were good.

As the cab drove off, a familiar beat-up black Toyota pickup took its place. The driver rolled down the window and barked something at me in rapid fire Spanish.

I smirked. "What'd you say about my grandma, pendejo?"

My buddy Diego laughed and motioned for me to get in. When I was in the passenger seat, he leaned across to give me a gentle hug and kiss my cheek. "How you feeling?"

"Like I got run over by the patrol boat."

He laughed, but his eyes were full of sympathy as he returned to the driver seat. "So you want to go down to the pier and ride the new roller coaster?"

I flipped him off. "Puto."

"That's cold, amigo!" He laughed again and put the truck in gear. "Why did I let you talk me into teaching you to swear in Spanish?"

"You tell me."

As we rolled away from the gate, he stole a venomous glance at the base in the rearview before focusing on the road again. With NAS Adams fading behind us, he glanced at me, this time serious and with concern etched all over his face. "So what happened, anyway?"

I took a breath and explained everything. The parts I could remember, anyway.

"Dios mio." His brown eyes were wide now. "I thought that getting run over by the patrol boat thing was a joke."

"Well it didn't run me over. It just . . . smacked me upside the head."

"Shit. And the water is fucking cold this time of year."

"You don't say."

"Doc say when your balls will come back down?"

"Shut up. Unless you're volunteering to check?"

We exchanged glances and chuckled. Not too long ago, he *would've* volunteered, and I would've let him. Things had mostly cooled between us, though, and I liked that we could still joke about it without getting awkward.

"So, you're on the mend, right?" Diego's usually playful voice was laced with real concern. "You'll be okay?"

"Yeah, yeah." I waved a hand. "Just some medical leave until my head's back on straight, and then I'll be on light duty for a while. Mostly I'm just bored." I paused. "It gave me an excuse to hang out with Chris, though, so I guess there's that."

Diego glanced at me. "Oh yeah?"

"Yeah. Doc said someone had to stay with me for forty-eight hours. Make sure I didn't keel over or something. Since Chris was with me at the ER, he took me home and just didn't leave."

When Diego glanced at me this time, he was grinning, if a bit nervously. "Damn. You should get smacked over the head more often."

I laughed, face burning. "No kidding. Too bad the guy's straight."

"Yeah," he said with a quiet chuckle. "Too bad."

He continued down the road toward his place, and I let myself steal a few glances at him. Even if we weren't still hooking up, I wasn't exactly above checking him out.

I'd met Diego last year at the High and Tight, the gay bar just off-base. He was a bartender there, and he was smoking hot. The accent had grabbed my attention, the stunning brown eyes and beautiful smile had reeled me in, and the tanned, sculpted body had finished the job.

Sometimes I missed hooking up with him. The sex had been spectacular—filthy, athletic, bruising—but I wasn't big on casual sex and Diego absolutely did not date military men. After a couple of months, we'd decided to cool it, and it had been almost six since we'd screwed around. Well, aside from the New Year's party at the High and Tight a few weeks ago, but in my defense, he'd been dressed like James Bond. Slicked back hair, tux, and all. Fuck yeah, I'd hooked up with him that night.

But *besides* that, we were just friends now. That didn't mean I wasn't still attracted to the man.

Fifteen minutes after he'd met me outside the base, Diego pulled up in front of the house where he rented a room, and I followed him up the walk to the back door.

It was basically a studio apartment that had once been a rec room. He got a good deal on it, and as long as he helped out around the yard and the rest of the house, his landlady cut him slack if he was a few days late on the rent. "You want something to drink?" he asked.

"Nah. I'm good. Thanks." I paused. "So what's new at the club?"

He gave an unhappy grunt, and as he hung up his keys by the door, he muttered, "Same shit, different day."

"Yeah?" I took a seat on the couch. "Tell me."

Diego crossed the room and flopped down on the other cushion. "Well, couple nights ago there was this guy who thought he was all that . . ."

I struggled to focus on what he was saying, which was weird because I fucking loved listening to Diego talk. He was funny and animated, and he swore enough in both languages to make most Sailors blush. The gorgeous Mexican accent didn't hurt, either. The way some sounds were sharper and others were smoother—I could listen to him for hours. His voice was low and a little raspy, too, like he'd smoked at some point in his life, and it was sexy as hell. Especially since he'd talked dirty in bed like no man I'd ever been with. Even when he was saying something completely benign, it was hard not to hear him whispering, *holy fuck, you feel good*, or, *shit, yeah, you make me crazy*—or even better, when it was all Spanish and gasping—while we'd fucked.

Today, even that hypnotic voice and sexy accent couldn't keep my train of thought on the rails. Nothing could. This wandering brain thing had been happening almost constantly since the other night, and it scared the hell out of me. It also bothered me that he wasn't making my pulse race like he usually did.

Probably because I still felt like shit from the other night. Nobody was piquing my libido's interest because my libido was pretty much MIA.

Then why were you looking at Chris like that yesterday?

The thought made me shiver, and I shifted on the couch to try to hide it from Diego.

Chris had spent part of yesterday afternoon stretched out on my roommate's bed while we'd watched a movie. My head hadn't wanted to focus on the screen or follow the plot, so that was the excuse I'd used to steal glances at him.

Okay, so maybe my libido wasn't completely MIA, because there'd definitely been a stir of something every time I'd looked at him. Not enough to make me think I was ready to get on Grindr and start hooking up with anyone—still not *that* recovered yet—but enough to send some blood rushing south.

So I could still ogle Chris, but not Diego? My straight friend, but not the man I *knew* was dynamite in bed? Huh. Especially since I couldn't have said which of the two I was more attracted to. Not usually, anyway. The only reason my lust for Diego had ever had any edge over the same feelings for Chris was that I'd actually slept with Diego. I knew what he was capable of in bed. Chris? That was never going to happen unless my fairy gay mother showed up and gave him a taste for dick.

Was I just hot for him right now because I couldn't have him? And Diego was suddenly old news because we'd slept together so many times? No way in hell. So, what? A knock on the head and suddenly I only wanted Chris?

Man, my brain really was fucked up.

It needed to get *un*fucked in a hurry, and not just because I didn't want to get caught drooling over my straight best friend. A knot coiled beneath my ribs. The exam. The goddamned advancement exam. I was still scared shitless over that thing. I couldn't afford anything other than a spectacular score, and even before I'd hit my head, Chris and I had both been panicking about how few chances we had left to advance if we didn't want to get kicked out.

Now I wasn't just nervous. I was scared shitless because the exam was less than a month away. What if my head wasn't back in the game by then? I still had to work at it to count out change, for God's sake. I'd been using my credit card for everything the last few days just to avoid anyone realizing how much trouble I had doing simple things like counting money or entering my PIN.

If I was still like this on the day of the exam, I was fucked.

"Hey." Diego nudged me. "You still here?"

"Yeah. Just . . ." *Freaking out about getting promoted.* Totally something I needed to go on about to a man who'd have sold his soul to still be in the Navy at all. We so needed this right now—a reminder of just how happy the Navy was to chew people up and spit them out.

"Sorry." I fought the urge to shake my head. It might rattle my brain back into place, but it would also hurt, if the throbbing in my temples was any indication. My surroundings—Diego's tiny apartment—came back into focus.

From the other end of the couch, he watched me skeptically. "You didn't hear my question, did you?"

"No, sorry."

"I asked what the Navy's going to do about that asshole who almost killed you."

I sighed, rubbing my forehead. "*Allegedly*, they're investigating. But since this is Chief's golden boy . . ." I flailed my hand.

Diego scowled, draping his arm along the back of the couch. "You're not going to cover for him, are you?"

Frowning, I avoided his gaze.

"Dalton." He nudged my arm. "Dude, you're not—"

"I gotta play ball, you know?" I carefully ran a hand through my hair, avoiding the goose egg and the stitches on the right side. "If I don't toe the line . . . I mean, the MA1 who was driving the night I went in the water? He does my eval. And since he's got his nose between Chief's ass cheeks, if I make any noise about throwing him under the bus for what happened, I'm fucked."

"You gotta do whatever's good for *you*. Nobody else will have your back."

"It *is* good for me to do what they tell me. Unless I want to get booted for not getting promoted."

Diego frowned.

I winced. "Sorry. I—"

"No, it's okay." He waved a hand. "Nobody knows better than I do that the Navy will kick your ass to the curb over dumb shit."

Scowling, I nodded. The Navy had worked him over hard, and even though it had been several years, who could blame him for still being bitter? That job had been his life. His whole world. Then along came Perform-to-Serve.

PTS had been a short-lived program where algorithms were created to analyze Sailors based on test scores and God knew what else. If you scored a certain number, you were good. Score below that, and you couldn't reenlist. I'd been fairly new to the Navy during that time, but I'd seen a few people go down because of it. Good solid Sailors, too. Total fuck-ups passed with flying colors. The good ones inexplicably missed the mark, and when it came time to reenlist, they were shit out of luck.

Diego had been a stellar Sailor if there'd ever been one. Eight years. Three Navy Achievement Medals. Two combat deployments. A Purple goddammed Heart.

And somehow, the numbers hadn't been good enough. While a coworker who'd been to Captain's Mast and never seen combat reenlisted for a fat bonus, Diego was discharged with nothing but some scars, a hell of a knee injury, and a wicked case of PTSD. Now he was a civilian, stuck in this town with nowhere else to go and still no idea what he was supposed to do with himself. I'd have been bitter too.

I cleared my throat. "I really don't know what to do now. I can't just lie and tell them Anderson didn't do anything wrong, but . . ."

"But you don't want to get fucked."

"Exactly."

"Man." He whistled, shaking his head. "That is not a fun spot to be in."

"No, it's not."

We were quiet for a while before Diego twisted toward me, facing me fully, and asked, "So you've been spending a lot of time with Chris? Since what happened?" There was a note of caution in his voice. Like he was uneasy with the subject but didn't want to let it show.

I nodded. "He's practically been glued to my side, literally since they pulled me out of the water."

Diego cocked his head, lips tightening slightly.

I explained everything, from the way Chris had helped me regulate my body temperature to him being at my bedside in the ER to sticking with me after I was released.

Diego sighed something in Spanish, sounding *almost* melodramatic. "Shame the guy's straight. Sounds like he's got boyfriend material written all over him."

"I know, right?"

He paused, watching me for a moment. "And you're *sure* he's straight, right?"

"Yep. I'm sure."

Diego laughed, but it was a taut, not entirely comfortable sound. And I knew why. I knew damn well Diego didn't like hearing about Chris. He was well aware that I had a thing for Chris, and he'd probably be outright jealous if Chris were actually a threat. But Chris was straight and Diego and I had figured out we couldn't make it work, so that was the end of it. He probably didn't even realize he was letting that subtle insecurity show whenever Chris came up in conversation.

I didn't mind it. Sometimes I thought his thinly-veiled possessiveness was kind of cute. If he ever got nasty with Chris or actually tried to sabotage a relationship with someone, that would be another story. But his barely noticeable teeth-grinding was . . . okay, it *was* flattering as long as it stayed harmless like this.

And Chris was definitely pulling my attention away from Diego. My mind went to him, and my heart did all the things it hadn't been doing for Diego today. What the fuck?

"You're blushing." Diego's voice was soft, without a trace of jealousy. "You're really hung up on him right now, aren't you?"

"Yeah. Ever since the other night, I . . ." Shit. How much did I want to tell Diego? I didn't want to make things awkward between us. Before I could stop myself, though, I blurted out, "Is it weird that I suddenly want to tell him how bad I want him?"

Diego blinked. He didn't quite flinch, but the corner of his lips twitched slightly. He seemed to consider the question for a moment. Then he shrugged. "I don't think it's weird, but it might not be a good idea. If he was bi or something, maybe. But the dude's straight." I took his advice at face value. Diego wasn't one to bullshit me. I knew him—no matter how he felt about me or anyone else, if he thought someone should make a move, he'd tell them. It was one of the things I loved about him. He'd tell you the truth and give you honest advice even if it wasn't what he wanted you to hear.

I sighed. "Yeah. I know. And it's . . . I mean, the way I want him—it's not even just sexual, you know?"

"Yeah, I know." Diego nodded slowly. "But before you go and tell him that, keep in mind how many straight guys you probably know that could listen to a gay guy tell him that and *not* assume it's sexual." He held up a hand, thumb and forefinger making a circle as he mouthed *zero*.

He had a point. I wanted to argue that Chris was different, but *was* he? Hadn't I had some straight friends who'd been cool with me right up until they'd caught a whiff of attraction?

Yeah, Diego was right. Telling Chris I was more attached to him than just as a friend—that would only make things weird. I sure as hell wouldn't gain anything besides an awkward conversation.

And the fact was, I needed Chris right now. If things went south at work like I had a feeling they would, I needed my closest ally. So I'd keep my mouth shut and keep my best friend.

No matter how much the silence was starting to eat me alive.

CHAPTER 6
CHRIS

The water seemed clearer than usual. The Pacific was almost always an opaque green, but today, it was practically transparent. Rocks I'd never seen before were visible as the boat cut across the calm water toward the open seas. The small boat. Which I was driving. Wait, when had we gotten the smaller boat back? Was the investigation finished already?

Well, it didn't matter—the boat was back and I was at the helm.

On the other side of the salty windshield, Dalton stood at the bow, his broad shoulders emphasized by the black vest and the rifle strap angled across his back.

He turned around and met my gaze. God, he was sexy in that uniform. So fucking hot. I hated the blue camouflage, but it would be a shame when NAS Adams finally made the switch to green.

Dalton turned around, and when our eyes met, he smiled. A lopsided little smile, like we were exchanging a secret. The way his eyes narrowed—was he flirting? Or thinking about flirting? Or maybe—

Out of nowhere, a swell crashed into the port side. Dalton stumbled. He grabbed for the rail at the same time I tried to steer and recover.

Everything seemed to slow down.

The boat listed hard.

Dalton's fingers closed.

Missed the rail.

And he was gone.

I spun the boat around and doubled back to the place he'd gone over. Then I was at the side and looking over.

The water was calm again. Clear. Perfectly clear, straight to the bottom.

And he was sinking, weighed down by boots and a rifle and trauma plates.

"Dalton!" I shouted. "Fuck! *Dalton!*"

I threw off my own vest.

Vaulted over the railing.

And just kept falling. And falling. And falling.

And Dalton kept sinking. And sinking. And sinking.

My eyes flew open and I sucked in air.

Dark. Bedroom. Sheets.

Home.

Safe.

I exhaled slowly. One of these days, I'd wake up from that stupid nightmare without feeling like it was the first time it had ever happened. Maybe I'd even stop mid-dream and go, *Hey brain, enough with the bullshit reruns.*

So far, no dice. This must've been the third time since I'd gone to bed, and according to my phone, it was only 0915. So that was three times in two hours. Fuck.

I rolled onto my back and rubbed a hand over my face. Kind of felt like I should take a shower. My skin was sticky with sweat, and it was crawling. But I really needed to sleep, and a shower would just wake me up. Plus, I'd just have that stupid dream again anyway.

I dropped my hand onto the bed beside me. Staring up at the ceiling, I let the fragments of the dream flicker through my brain. The details changed every time, but the gist was the same—watching Dalton go overboard and not being able to save him. Watching him sink or float away. My skin prickled and my stomach twisted. Was this some kind of PTSD or something? Shit, maybe I needed a psych eval. And if I was this messed up, how the hell were Dalton or Rhodes sleeping? Or Anderson? Much as I didn't like the guy, I couldn't imagine he'd walked away from all that without a mental scratch. I wondered if the only person who could sleep anymore was Chief Lasby, because I sure as shit doubted anything kept him awake. A man would need a conscience for that.

I sighed and closed my eyes. I could worry about all this shit later. Right now, I needed to sleep, or I'd be a worse coxswain than Anderson on my shift tonight.

I just hoped I didn't dream again.

But of course . . . I did.

By the time I dragged my bleary-eyed ass out of bed, it was almost 1400. Shame I only felt like I'd only slept about fifteen minutes.

I had a text from Dalton, though, and that was enough to wake me up and make me feel a bit less shitty. Partly because it meant that stupid dream had just been a dream, and partly because . . . I had a text from Dalton.

You want to grab something to eat? #CabinFever

I chuckled. He still wasn't driving yet, and the walls of that little barracks room would've closed in on me after the first day. *Just got up. Give me twenty.*

Okay, so it turned out to be more like twenty-five, but I got there. As I pulled up in front of the barracks, Dalton came outside. He was wearing a red Huskers hoodie and some snug jeans, and goddamn, he looked good. As if he ever didn't look good.

He eased himself into the passenger seat. "Thanks. I was getting stir crazy again."

"Any time. Where do you want to go?"

Dalton shrugged. "You're driving. Long as they have coffee and food and more coffee, I'm game."

"Junkie." I chuckled and pulled out of the barracks parking lot.

We found a little diner not too far from the base. Anchor Point was full of places like this. The kind of restaurant that was probably run by a family and had recipes someone had taken out of Grandma's box of handwritten note cards. Sometimes I thought about opening a place like this after I retired. God knew I had plenty of recipes from Grandma and all the ones my parents had picked up from other families at the bases where they'd been stationed over the years.

But then I'd take one look at the tired people running the joint and reconsider. As the sleepy-eyed lady took us to a table today, I was definitely thinking twice about my own restaurant. I was tired enough in my job right now, so yeah, maybe not. Just what I needed—a job where I worried about somebody getting food poisoning or choking on a meatball.

She sat us down and handed us a couple of faded laminated menus. I hadn't been here before, but I didn't bother reading the whole thing. I knew what I was in the mood for, so I scanned over the pages until I found the omelets. A meat lover's omelet? With steak instead of ground beef? Oh fuck yeah. Sign me up.

Dalton was still perusing the menu, so I drank my coffee while I waited for him to order. The coffee was strong too. Good. I was going to need it today.

I watched him surreptitiously and wondered if he'd been able to sleep. A week after the incident, he still hadn't gained back all his color, so I guessed not. Or maybe he'd just been getting pastier like he always did when our section worked nights. He and Powers both lost a few shades of tan when we were on nights, and it didn't help that this was the dead of winter. Come summer, they'd both step outside and fry in the sun.

I snickered to myself.

Dalton's eyes flicked up. "What?"

"Nothing." I shook my head, then went for my coffee.

He watched me like he wasn't convinced.

After I'd taken a sip, I set down my coffee. "So, how do the docs think you're healing?"

He narrowed his eyes a little, probably not fooled by the subject change, but he went with it. "Well, I go back to work tomorrow."

"*Already?*"

He nodded. "Light duty. It'll be good to get back to something normal." He laughed like he didn't really feel it. "Better than sitting around with my dick in my hand."

"Any idea when they'll put you back on the water?"

Dalton squirmed, avoiding my eyes. "Don't know. I'm not sure I *want* to go back out for a while."

"Don't blame you. How's your head doing?"

"Eh." His lip curled. "God knows how long it's going to take to unfuck itself."

"Yeah?"

He nodded. "I can think a bit clearer, so there's that. Actually managed to count out money at the Exchange last night, and I can walk in a straight line." He laughed self-consciously. "Just *think* what I'll be able to do in another *week* or two."

The sarcasm was almost heart-breaking. I could only imagine how much he hated being a stranger to his own brain. It could've been a lot worse—he could've had to learn to walk or talk again—but it had to be frustrating as hell for him.

"It hasn't been that long, remember that. And I mean, you got hit by a boat. My sister clocked me in the head with a book when I was nine and I felt that shit for ages."

Dalton laughed. "A book, huh? What'd you do to deserve that?"

"Hey!"

"What?" He shrugged, grinning. "Or did she just throw it at you for no reason?"

"Maybe."

"Uh-huh." He chuckled, but then he sighed and rubbed his forehead. "I just want to feel normal. Like, I can't wait until I can *drive* again."

"Any idea how long that'll be?"

"The doc says I should be okay in a few more days. He just wants to make sure the double vision is really gone."

"Seems legit. Seeing double while you're driving doesn't sound safe."

"Isn't safe while I'm walking, either." He gestured at his shoulder. "Tried to walk through the wrong bathroom door last night, and clipped the frame. You wouldn't think something like that would hurt that much, but Jesus *fuck*."

"Want me to put some bubble wrap on the frame for—"

"Shut up." He took a playful swing at me and laughed.

I chuckled. Right then, the waitress showed up with our food. One sniff of the meats in my omelet and the French toast he'd ordered, and I decided this place was a winner. No way in hell food could smell that good but taste bad.

Sure enough, it was amazing. I didn't think I'd ever had a meat lover's omelet where the cook had actually nailed a perfect medium on the steak. Add in the sausage and diced ham? Fuck yeah.

We ate in silence for a little while, and as we did, I watched him. Ever since that distress call had come in the other night, I'd had this weird panicky feeling that just wouldn't go away. It reminded me of that feeling when I was walking down some stairs and missed the last one. That jittery, heart-racing, *that-could-have-been-so-bad* feeling.

That usually wore off in a minute or two, though. It wouldn't budge this time. And the panic-inducing moment didn't seem to be over yet. Like another shoe still needed to drop. Like I still needed to do something so it wouldn't be a disaster. The investigation? Was that what I was stressing about? Probably. Except that didn't explain why every time I looked at him . . . *I almost lost you. Forever.*

And the familiar feeling would surge to the surface, and I'd be right back out on the water with him unconscious and me scared out of my mind.

If things had happened a little differently, you wouldn't be here.

I swallowed past the lump in my throat. It didn't matter how many times I had that thought, it was a punch to the gut each and every time. My best friend. The man I'd been secretly wanting since day one. And he'd almost slipped away. What if the rescue had fallen apart? What if the boat had hit him harder? What if I'd fucked up and made things worse instead of helping raise his body temperature? What if—

It doesn't matter. He made it. He's fine.

So why was I still a breath away from panicking over something that had, given the circumstances, pretty much played out in the best way possible?

That goddamned dream hadn't helped. Especially since I kept having it. Not every night—though there was always *some* kind of nightmare—but when it came, it didn't stop. Over and over, several times a night, I saw him falling and sinking, and each time I couldn't get to him.

Suddenly I had this almost uncontrollable need to tell him how I felt, but . . . good God, the man was still recovering from one hell of a traumatic night. He didn't need this on top of that. What if it made things weird between us? What if he was pissed off that I'd never bothered to tell him I was gay? What if—

Fuck. Way too many *what ifs*. Maybe I'd tell him eventually, but for the moment, it could wait.

But what if something else happens?

"Hey." He nudged my foot with his. "You okay? You seem tense."

I met his blue eyes across the table.

You're the most amazing person I've ever met.

I cleared my throat.

What if you never know?

He watched me. Curious. Waiting.

What if I tell you and it fucks things up? What if telling you that means this *is over?*

That crackly, jittery panicked feeling skittered under my skin, and I quickly said, "I'm all right. Guess I'm still rattled from the other night."

Dalton laughed so softly it was almost inaudible. "Yeah. Tell me about it."

I managed to laugh too, and it might've even sounded like I felt it. Folding my hands to keep from reaching out and putting one on his arm, I said, "We should check in with Rhodes. See how she's doing."

Dalton instantly sobered. "Yeah. Good idea." He took out his phone. "I'll text her. Maybe she and her husband are up for grabbing something to eat."

"Cool."

While he texted Rhodes, I silently ordered myself to pull it together. Maybe I was a coward for not saying anything, but keeping quiet meant not making things weird between us. It meant I still had Dalton.

So I kept my thoughts to myself.

And I wondered if I'd have that dream again tonight.

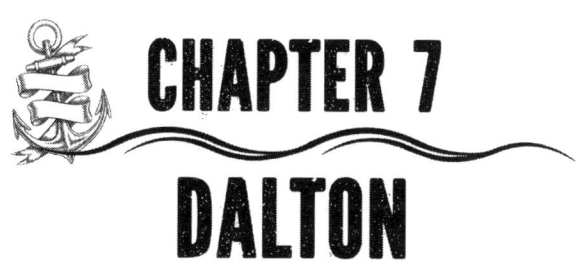

CHAPTER 7
DALTON

The water was calm today, the tiny ripples sparkling in the afternoon sun. Beyond the harbor, the waves were stronger, but there wasn't a whitecap in sight.

And just looking at it all, I thought I was going to be sick.

Standing beside the HPU building, looking out at the familiar harbor and open seas, I willed my stomach to stay put and my heart to stop pounding, but it wasn't happening. Fact was, for the first time in my life, the thought of going out on the water terrified me.

Not that it would be an issue today. I was still on medical leave. Starting tomorrow, I'd be on light duty pending a psych eval and a final all-clear from medical, so I was staying landside for the time being.

On one hand, that grated on me. I was restless and eager to get back to my normal job and my normal life. My brain didn't seem to have quite as many screws loose, though it would be a while before I was completely back to myself. I'd started going on walks a few times a day, not just to combat cabin fever but to enjoy my mostly-restored equilibrium. Never thought I'd ever find it a novelty to be able to walk in a straight line, but here I was.

The more I recovered, the more restless I became. This must've been what grounded pilots and benched athletes felt like—chomping at the bit to get back in the game.

At the same time, as I gazed out at the water, I decided it was just as well. My confidence was trashed. I didn't trust my balance on land, so I sure as shit didn't trust my sea legs, and anyway, I was terrified of leaving shore.

I told myself the sting in my eyes was because of the sun reflecting off the water's sleek surface, but that didn't explain the lump in my throat.

Being afraid of the water was as foreign as marveling at my ability to walk. It felt a lot like being scared of the family dog who'd been perfectly behaved for years and then bit you. It didn't feel right to shy away, but it felt stupid not to.

So what the hell did I do now? Boats were what I was good at. First time at the helm, it had been like I'd found my calling. Working as an MA had always felt a bit like trying to do someone else's job in a pair of boots that didn't quite fit. I'd always assumed that was just how it felt to work. It was a job. You did it, you went home, you got paid, and you did it again.

The second I'd stepped on that rickety-ass patrol boat back at Little Creek, though . . . it had been like slipping into my own skin for the first time. Perfect. Everything about it.

And now this. Now it scared me, and being scared of the water made about as much sense as not being able to count out money at McDonald's.

Except I understood why. It was no different than when my oldest brother had struggled to get behind the wheel for months after that car crash that had nearly killed him. Didn't matter that he'd been confidently driving for years or that the odds of another wreck like that were slim—the wreck had left him scared to make the five-minute drive down a thirty-five mile-an-hour road to the grocery store.

He'd recovered, though. He was driving again, full of all the confidence he'd had back when he'd taught me to drive. Maybe I needed to call him. We didn't talk nearly as much as we should have anyway, but I could definitely use some advice. Or at least some reassurance. Even if I wasn't sure I wanted to know how long it had really taken him to recover.

"MA2." Chief Lasby's cheerful voice came from behind me and sent a prickle of dread down my spine. "Just the man I was looking for."

Oh, shit.

I summoned as much military bearing as I could, schooled my expression, and turned around. Funny how the sight of my chief made me queasier than the sight of the ocean right then. "Yes, Chief?"

"We need to have a chat."

Of course we do.

I nodded mutely.

He stopped beside me, looking out at the water for a moment while the uneasiness settled in. Then he turned to me. "When do you think you'll be fit to be on a boat again?"

My throat tightened and a prickle of straight-up fear climbed my spine.

On a boat? On the water? *Oh fuck.*

The obvious answer was that that was up to medical, and that I should probably be behind a desk indefinitely like MA1 Anderson. But something about Lasby's tone made me think we weren't talking about when doctors and regulations said I could do my job again. "I'm not sure."

He scowled. I avoided his gaze, watching a seagull trying to yank a Doritos bag out of a trashcan while I wondered what Lasby had up his sleeve.

The chief studied me for a long, uncomfortable moment. "Listen, MA2. On paper, I can't send you back out on the water until you've had a full psych eval. But if you *want* to get back to it sooner, and you think you're fit for that detail, I can't stop you."

Technically, he could. And by all rights, he should, at least until my psych eval, but there was no point. We both knew the outcome of the eval depended on me. On what I said. On how I answered the questions. If I wanted to go back on the water, I knew exactly what to say and how to say it so the evaluator would sign off and let me get back to work. In a command where qualified coxswains were in short supply, nobody was going to object to my miraculously speedy recovery and ability to return to the helm. It wasn't like I had a broken bone or anything. A nice gash in my head, but nothing that would objectively disqualify me from duty.

TBI and PTSD? Those couldn't be measured. Not the same way, at least. Concussions and psychological traumas affected different people in different ways. If I said I was fit to work, and the evaluation reflected that, there was no reason to argue. That was how the military saw it, anyway. I was an expensively trained tool for a high-demand job. They didn't want me on the bench a minute longer than I absolutely had to be, and nobody would protest if I said I was good to go.

I tried not to fidget. "What do you recommend?"

"That depends—how bad do you want to make MA1?"

My stomach flipped. "I need to. Either this cycle or the next."

He nodded slowly. "Uh-huh. And it's not going to look good on your eval if you're tucked behind a desk somewhere instead of leading Sailors."

I gritted my teeth. "So I'm going to be punished for—"

"No, you're not being punished for anything. But other Sailors are going to be *rewarded* for what *they're* doing." He paused. "Here's the deal, MA2. You can't be penalized for recovering or convalescing." He put up a finger. "But your shipmates who aren't convalescing or recovering will have more bullet points on their evals. They'll have more examples of leading Sailors and functioning as someone who should be an MA1. So even though you won't have anything on your eval that can be used against you, you *also* won't have anything that can be used in your *favor*." He grimaced sympathetically. "I don't want you out on the boat before you're ready, but you need to keep this in mind. As competitive as it's getting in the MA rate, you need all the edge you can get. Particularly with that missing Good Conduct medal on your brag sheet."

I winced. Once again, the stupidity of my youth—that one trip to Captain's Mast—was coming back to haunt me. I should have had three Good Conduct medals by now. I had two. People noticed. Fuck.

Still watching the seagull—it was now mutilating the Doritos bag—I spoke quietly. "So what you're saying is I don't have a choice."

"You have a choice. As with any choice, whatever decision you make will have consequences of some sort."

I swallowed, wondering when my mouth had gone dry. And why I swore I could taste saltwater in the back of my throat again. I fidgeted and shrugged away the panicky feeling that skittered around under my skin. More and more, I'd felt like my career was balanced on a knife's edge, and that edge just seemed to be getting sharper and sharper.

And now, today, when I could still barely handle driving a car or counting out change, I had two choices that could make or break my entire career—go back on the water or don't.

I knew damn well it was ethically wrong for anyone to even

suggest I go near the water right now. That proper protocol dictated I be behind a desk like MA1 Anderson—pending medical clearance, not disciplinary action—until the investigation was over and my psych eval completed.

But just because it was wrong in black and white didn't mean it was wrong in practice, and no matter how I sliced it, Chief was right. If I wanted to get promoted, I had to arm up and start working as a coxswain again. Sitting at a desk pushing paperwork would do me no favors, not even if it was the best thing for my physical and psychological recovery.

Yeah, whatever decision I made would have consequences, and whether I liked it or not, there was only one set of acceptable consequences. Right or wrong, an extended period of downtime for any reason would hurt my chances. The Sailors who'd done their jobs continuously for the entire eval cycle would get better scores than I would. Fact was, I wasn't getting a coveted EP—Early Promote—eval unless I was doing my job, and without that EP . . .

I cleared my throat. I tried and failed to look Chief Lasby in the eye as I spoke:

"Okay. My psych eval is tomorrow. After that, put me back out on the boat."

"You're *what?*" Chris stared at me, his voice echoing off the HPU building next to us and probably audible all the way down onto the pier. He wasn't angry, but I'd definitely caught him off guard.

Sighing, I slid my hands into the pockets of my jeans. "I'm coming off light duty next week. And I'm . . ." I swallowed before quietly repeating what I'd just told him: "I'll be going back on the water."

"Already?" His jaw was hanging open. "Dalton . . . they can't make you. That's—"

"They're not," I said softly. "I, uh, volunteered."

An eyebrow rose. "You volunteered like you volunteered, or like you were volun*told?*"

I avoided his gaze.

"Dude." Chris sighed. "You're not ready to drive the boat. You can barely drive your car!"

"I don't have to drive," I said, sounding pathetic. "I was the gunner most of the time anyway."

"And Lasby wants you out there as a coxswain. You'll be driving."

I shuddered.

"You really ready for that?"

I'm so scared I can't even put it into words. "I have to be."

"No, you don't. This is bullshit, D." He looked right in my eyes. "You're not ready to go back out there."

"And what choice do I have?"

"I don't know. I don't . . ." He huffed sharply. "You know what Chief's doing, right?"

I lifted my eyebrows.

"If you're capable of going back out on the water, that'll prove that the incident didn't do any long-term damage. You're telling the investigators you've bounced back. It'll still be a Bravo class mishap, but it'll seem like less, you know?"

I pursed my lips. "And what about my promotion?"

Chris deflated, and so did my tiny bit of hope that he'd have the answer. Something to counter Lasby's plan. Instead, he quietly said, "Fuck. But still, the sooner you're back on your feet and *look like* you're functioning at a hundred percent, the less serious the whole incident will seem."

"And the outcome will be less severe for Anderson." The resignation in my own voice made me feel even worse.

"Exactly."

"But in the long run, what matters to me is how this affects *my* career." I shifted my weight, staring at the boats and the water because I couldn't look at him. "What good does it do me for Anderson to get what's coming to him if this hurts my eval enough to keep me from advancing? I'll still be out of the Navy with no retirement."

Chris swore under his breath. "Shit. I don't know. It just isn't right he's gonna get off easy."

"No kidding. But at this point, I have to protect myself."

"So you're going to throw yourself back into driving boats when you're not physically or mentally ready."

I glared at him, ready to demand to know how he knew if I was or wasn't ready. But damn it, Chris wasn't stupid. If anyone knew just how ready I wasn't, it was him.

I dropped my gaze to the gravel beneath our feet. "I need to get back on the horse that threw me. It's the only way I'll ever be able to do my job again. The longer I wait, the harder it'll be."

He didn't reply. I supposed he didn't need to. He was probably wondering who I was trying to convince, and truth be told, I wondered the same thing.

We were quiet for a little while, letting gentle waves and seagull snark fill the silence. I was about to suggest we go inside. He needed to get to work, and I figured I should go home and try studying for the advancement exam.

Before I could, though, the HPU building door opened, and MA3s Grey and Sanchez appeared, cigarette packs in hand. They'd been in mid-conversation, but they cut off when they saw us. They both smirked.

"Oh hey." Grey grinned like an idiot and gestured at us. "We interrupting? Just wanted a cigarette, but we can go someplace else if you want."

What the fuck?

"Uh, no." I shrugged. "Go ahead and smoke."

Grey and Sanchez both laughed as they lit up. I eyed Chris.

Am I missing something here?

He sighed, rolled his eyes, and motioned for me to follow. As we started walking away from the building, Sanchez muttered, "Might have more privacy down by—"

"Shut up, MA3," Chris snapped, and Sanchez shut up.

Chris and I exchanged glances. He broke eye contact first, which didn't do much to ease the tension coiling in my stomach. Then he nodded for me to follow him, and we started walking. We wandered past the HPU building, away from anyone who might eavesdrop, and continued down to the strip of sand south of the seawall. It was a small beach—maybe two hundred feet long—but it was secluded, and almost no one came out here.

On the sand, we halted. He stuffed his hands in the pockets of his uniform and gazed out at the water. "Listen, um . . ." He pushed out a breath. "Look, I know you've got enough on your plate right now, but since you're coming back to work tomorrow, I think you should hear this now. From me."

I turned to him, alarm bells ringing in my head. "What?"

He stared out at the water. "The, uh . . . the rest of the section has been making some jokes. And it's probably not going to let up when you come back."

That caught me off guard. "Jokes about what?"

"About . . ." He closed his eyes and sighed. "The thing is, when we pulled you onto the boat, priority one was getting you warm. I was the biggest guy there, so . . . I was the one to warm you up."

My throat tightened. He didn't have to spell out how he'd done that. In fact, somewhere in my rattled brain were vague flashes of being wrapped up in a bear hug—a *naked* bear hug—with him. I'd thought it was a dream or something, but apparently not.

Chris shifted nervously. "The thing is, you were . . . not quite conscious, but not quite out either."

Something in the pit of my stomach turned to ice. *Oh no. Oh fuck.* We were trained to deal with hypothermia. Knew it could make people delirious. Throw in a head injury and a latent crush on the man nakedly warming me up, and . . . *oh fuck, fuck, fuck.*

I squeezed my eyes shut. "What did I say?"

He gave a quiet little laugh, but the nervous sound told me I was very much on the right track. "You . . . well, I don't remember exactly what you said, only that you tried to kiss me."

"I . . ." Panic surged through me. This was not something any Sailor would live down. An openly gay Sailor with a few possibly homophobic coworkers? I knew better than most people just how unforgiving that environment could get when a gay man lost his filter and let something slip. It didn't matter how drunk, battered, semiconscious, delirious, feverish, or otherwise fucked up—just *hint* at being into one of your straight coworkers and you'd better learn to sleep with one eye open.

I was mortified, and I was fucking scared. I didn't have any coworkers who I'd expect to get violent, but that didn't mean they wouldn't.

And then there was Chris.

My best friend. My one confidante at this command. My *straight* best friend who would now get endless shit from our coworkers. And what did he think of me now? He'd always been totally comfortable with me, never batting an eye at me being gay, but would that change?

I covered my face with both hands and groaned. "God, I feel like such a tool."

"Why?"

Dropping my hands, I turned to him. "Dude, I made a pass at you!"

"While you were out of your head, yeah."

"Still!"

"Hey." He gave my arm a nudge. "You know me better than that. You really think I'm gonna let that—or anyone else giving us shit about it—get to me?"

I wanted to say no, but staring at the sand, I said, "Did I ever tell you why I never drink with my coworkers anymore?"

"Um. No?"

I swallowed. "Because on my first deployment, we all went out boozing in Hawaii. I got absolutely blackout fucking hammered. When I woke up . . ." I shuddered hard, the memory bringing acid to the back of my throat. "I was in my rack with a black eye and bruised ribs."

Chris sucked in a sharp breath. "What the hell?"

I stared down at my hands, willing them to stop shaking. When that didn't work, I started wringing them so at least the movements were deliberate. "Turns out I made some dumb comment to one of my guys. It wasn't even anything really offensive from what I heard—I guess I just let it slip that I thought he was hot."

"And they beat you up?"

I nodded. "After that, I promised I'd never get drunk around people I worked with again." I laughed bitterly. "Guess I never took hypothermia and a concussion into consideration."

"That isn't going to happen to you. The guys here, they'll bust our chops and that's as far as it'll go."

Why don't you sound so sure?

I kneaded the bridge of my nose, giving me an excuse to avoid his gaze. "Being out in the Navy kind of sucks sometimes. There's always straight guys who get all bent out of shape over it, and even the ones who are cool with it don't necessarily want to hang out with me." My voice was shaking, but I was too nervous to do anything about it. I dropped my hand. "I don't find people like you very often, you know? Straight guys who'll chill with me like they would with anybody else. And I'm fucking terrified that what I did that night is going to jack shit up between us." Immediately, I cringed, squeezing my eyes shut and cursing under my breath. As if things weren't already going to be awkward from here on out.

Chris was silent. My heart pounded harder with every second he didn't respond. Not far from us, the tide lapped at the beach, and I begged the temperamental seas to reach out, grab me, and drag me and my shame down to Davy Jones's locker where we belonged.

Finally, Chris spoke, his voice soft. "You're worried I'm going to beat you up because you were out of your head, didn't know who or where you were, and got flirty with me?"

Face burning and stomach roiling, I nodded. "I mean, not that you'd beat me up. Just . . ." I chewed my lip. "You're my best friend, man. I don't want to lose that because of something I did while I was fucked up."

"You won't."

I eyed him skeptically.

"It isn't going to make shit weird between us," he said with conviction.

I searched his eyes, wanting to believe him, but still not convinced.

"I know you were out of it that night." There was suddenly an undercurrent of something in his voice. Nerves? What the hell? "I'm not going to hold anything against you that you said after a goddamn boat slammed you in the head. But also . . ." It was his turn to avoid my eyes.

I stood straighter. "What?"

Chris looked out at the ocean, fixating on it like it held all the words he needed. "Look, I'm sorry I didn't tell you this a long time ago. And I don't even know why I didn't. I . . . really haven't told anybody. But . . ." He closed his eyes, pulled in a deep breath through his nose, and murmured, "I'm gay too."

My jaw fell open. "What?"

"I'm . . ." He faced me. "I'm gay, D."

I stared at him. Chris? Gay? The man I'd been . . . the guy I'd . . . *Chris?* "Are you serious?"

Chris nodded. It was always hard to tell because of his complexion, but I was pretty sure he was blushing.

"You never . . . I had no . . ." I sputtered, shaking my head. "*Really?*"

He laughed shyly. "Is it that hard to believe?"

"Only because I've known you this long and never suspected anything."

He chuckled again, but then the humor faded. "I'm sorry I never told you. And I don't know if that makes this whole situation better or worse, or—"

"Don't. Seriously, don't worry about it. I know it's tough to come out, even to a friend."

"Still." He blew out a breath. "Anyway. So . . . there it is. You don't have to worry that you hit on a straight guy."

"Oh. Wow. I . . . had no idea." *This changes everything. And nothing, but also . . . everything.*

He tilted his head. "So, are we, um, still cool?"

"Of course we are." I stepped closer and hugged him tight, and he hugged me right back. As much as I was glad he'd told me—and still shocked because *oh my God*—there was a whole new breed of apprehension gnawing at me. I was no longer afraid things would get weird between us because he was a straight guy I'd deliriously hit on.

Now I was terrified they'd get weird because he was a *gay* guy I wanted so bad it hurt.

CHAPTER 8

CHRIS

I t was a good thing I'd warned Dalton about our shipmates, and not just because it had given me a chance to come out. As much as I'd expected them to give us both shit, I hadn't realized just how relentless they would be.

They'd been giving me hell since a few days after the incident. The moment Dalton came back to work, it became nonstop. They were just fucking around and didn't mean any harm, and I'd sure as hell given them shit for things too, but they couldn't have known what nerves they were stepping on every time they asked one or both of us how long we'd been dating on the sly, who was the "man" in the relationship, and if it was true that once you went black you never went back.

Technically it was all sexual harassment, and technically they could all be in deep shit for any of it, but as with anything relating to Navy politics, there was what was on paper and what was in practice. On paper—harassment. In practice—well, it depended on how much paperwork, headache, stigma, ostracizing, and sandbagging a person really wanted to deal with. Considering all the scrutiny Dalton was under right now, and how badly we both needed to get promoted, we'd agreed this was a "pick your battles" moment.

Our shipmates *were* good about backing off if one of us was obviously not laughing about it—the "once you go black" one had lasted all of two days before everyone had caught on that neither of us thought it was funny. A few dirty looks established some *you just went too far* boundaries, but for the most part, we didn't have much choice except to let it roll off.

Still, within the confines of the shit-talking Dalton and I both tolerated, the jokes were as steady as the tide. Usually just a one-liner here or there. Maybe "that's what your man said" instead of "that's what she said." Sometimes subtle, sometimes not, but the constant undercurrent of snark didn't seem like it was going to stop any time soon.

It wouldn't last forever. We both knew they'd eventually find something else to play with, and there'd be some other target. Such was life among Sailors, especially MAs. It was like being on a playground, except we were all adults and actually knew how to swear.

One of the worst parts—besides seeing Dalton so uncomfortable and embarrassed—was that I knew everyone was watching us for anything they could use for a joke. Now I was more self-conscious than ever of the glances I'd steal at Dalton. It was easier when the sun was up because I could hide behind my wraparound Oakleys. Once it was too dark to justify wearing them, I had to be extra careful. The longer, brighter days of spring and summer couldn't get here fast enough.

It also didn't help that being back at work meant being back in uniform. He wasn't armed up yet, but he still had on his police belt and vest. God, he was hot. And God help me if anyone—especially him—knew I thought so.

Every time someone commented, Dalton's cheeks glowed bright red. I didn't know if it was better or worse now that he knew I was gay too, or if that made any difference at all, but he was mortified.

"They'll get over it," he'd assured me as we'd walked into the building earlier. "All it'll take is one person doing something dumb at a bar, and they'll forget all about us."

Us. I flinched every time he said that. There wasn't an *us* except in their jokes and in my mind, and it killed me to have to remember that all the time. It made me wish I could tell them to back off without anyone acting like we were being too sensitive. And maybe we were. Maybe I was. Maybe I didn't want to explain that I was afraid of Dalton finding out how many times I'd replayed that moment on the boat in my mind. It was stupid—hell, it was downright pathetic—but I'd grabbed onto what he'd said and the way he'd looked at me, and I'd tucked them into a corner of my brain so I wouldn't forget. It was the closest I'd ever get to him actually making a pass at me, so I'd take what I could.

Part of me wanted to tell him that. Just get it out there that I wished he'd meant it. But I wasn't holding my breath on that because I'd damn near puked just working up the courage to tell him I was gay. Admitting I had a thing for him? Probably not happening any time soon.

We strolled into the main office, and I knew the instant I saw Grey and Sanchez that they'd been waiting for us, jokes at the ready.

"So, spill it," Sanchez said.

"Spill what?" Dalton grumbled. "My coffee in your lap?"

Grey gave him a clap on the shoulder as Dalton walked past. "Naw, man. What did you guys do for Valentine's Day? Anything special?"

Oh fuck. Had that been this week? So much for hoping they'd forget about us any time soon.

"Eat a dick, MA3," Dalton muttered.

"What?" The asshole smirked. "You guys are such a cute couple. I'm just asking if—"

"Cute couple?" Chief Lasby's gruff voice made everyone freeze. He stepped into the doorway, cover tucked under his arm and a scowl set firmly on his ugly mug. "Someone want to tell me what's going on in here?"

"Uh." Grey cleared his throat and stood. "Just shooting the breeze, Chief."

"Uh-huh." Lasby glared at me, then Dalton. "Ingram. Taylor." He gestured sharply down the hall. "I need to talk to you two. *Now.*"

We exchanged uneasy glances, then got up and followed him. No one else said a word.

The HPU building had a generic office, and it was closer than his office back at the security building, so Chief pretty much claimed it as his own. He directed us inside and shut the door.

He didn't order us to attention, but I instinctively went to parade rest. Beside me, Dalton did the same. Hands clasped behind our backs, shoulders back, chins up, we didn't make a sound.

As he always did when he wanted to make someone uneasy, Lasby stared at us in painful silence for a long time. Long enough it always made me wonder if I was supposed to say something. Except I knew damn well he'd bite my head off if I spoke without being spoken to. So, like Chris, I stood straight and quiet, waiting for whatever had pissed

Lasby off.

After several centuries of tense silence, he finally spoke. "You boys want to tell me what all this shit's about?" He glared at us in turn. "All this shit I keep hearing about you two . . ." His nose wrinkled for a split second before he spat out, "Being a thing and getting 'lovey dovey' while MA2 Taylor was hypothermic?"

I swallowed, not sure what to say.

Dalton's boots creaked like he was shifting his weight. "I was delirious, Chief." Dalton's tone was flat and professional. "I didn't know what was going on or where I was, and apparently I made a pass at MA2 Ingram."

I gritted my teeth. It was the truth and we both knew it, but admittedly, it stung.

"I don't remember what happened, Chief," he went on, "but it was on me. Not MA2 Ingram."

"MA2 Taylor was understandably delirious, Chief," I said. "He was in a state of severe hypothermia, and he was barely conscious at that point." *He had no idea what he was doing, or how much it's killing me that it wasn't real.*

The chief's eyes darted back and forth between us. "I don't think I need to spell out to either of you gentlemen that you're both in precarious positions. You're second class petty officers who've been in longer than some first classes."

We both winced. As if either of us was unaware of the fact that we'd been lapped by some younger Sailors. There were even chiefs who hadn't been in as long as we had.

"So," Chief Lasby went on, "I would suggest the two of you keep yourselves in line and focus on your careers. You've each got two advancement cycles left before you hit high-year tenure, which means neither of you can afford less than flawless evals, never mind any black marks."

I clenched my teeth.

"I don't want this"—he gestured at each of us, subtly wrinkling his nose—"killing your careers."

Yeah. Sure you don't. Your motives are obviously a hundred percent altruistic.

In a low growl, he went on. "And whatever is or isn't going on between you, I don't want that shit flying around my HPU. I can't tell you what to do in your off time, but as long as you're on duty in my harbor unit, I better not hear another goddamned word about this bullshit. Not from you and not from any of them." He pointed sharply in the direction of the main room where our peers were probably still shooting the breeze. "Shut it the fuck down. Am I clear?"

"Yes, Chief," we said in unison.

"Get out of my office."

We left without another word. There were too many people in the main room, so I headed for the locker room. Dalton did too. I didn't know if he was avoiding them or sticking with me—or maybe both—and I didn't ask.

As soon as the locker room door thudded behind us, we both exhaled. We wandered into the alcove between a bank of lockers, and for the longest time, neither of us spoke. He was probably doing the same thing I was—mentally debriefing. Replaying everything Chief Lasby had said to us. Wondering how much was homophobic bluster and how much could actually hurt us.

Thing was, even if we were together, Lasby couldn't discipline us for dating. DADT was history, and Dalton and I were peers. Neither of us had any kind of authority over the other. We were both enlisted. There were other couples on this base, even within our command. Whether Lasby liked it or not, he couldn't order us not to date.

But whether *we* liked it or not, there were other ways a supervisor could fuck with us. It wasn't unheard of—or even that uncommon—for perfectly squared away Sailors to get dinged on their evals for bullshit like unsat leadership and a bad attitude when their only sins were having political views that clashed with their superiors. A female Sailor who turned down a highly inappropriate—and impossible to prove—sexual advance from a superior could find herself struggling to get even a passable eval. God help her if she started dating someone else.

At one of my previous commands, my supervisor had been barely subtle enough—*just* enough to avoid any actual consequences—about being a racist fucking bastard. How could we prove our evals were racially motivated when he had documentation to back him up that me and two other Sailors had been occasionally late, moderately insubordinate, and completely unmotivated? The fact that he'd never written up our paler peers just meant that on paper—which was where things counted in the military—they'd never done anything wrong. In the end, I couldn't prove a thing, I didn't get promoted, and nothing ever happened to him.

Chief Lasby didn't seem to be a racist, but he was sure as shit a homophobe, and I knew all too well he could use his prejudices against us. Just the fact that he thought we were dating was more than enough to stain his views of us. Since he was buddy-buddy with MA1 Anderson, who would be writing our evals . . . yeah, Chief Lasby's opinion of us did fucking matter.

At the end of the day, it didn't make a difference that Dalton and I weren't dating. Or that I wasn't out as gay. If Lasby so much as *thought* there was any truth to the joking and rumors, he could do plenty of damage to our careers.

It also dawned on me that Chief Lasby had never asked us to confirm or deny if we were dating. I wasn't sure what to make of that. My only guess was that he knew he couldn't tell us not to date—only that he didn't want to hear heads or tails of it in his command.

"Fuck, that was some bullshit." Dalton's voice startled me. Apparently too restless to stand still, he started pacing beside the bank of lockers. "I can't believe he said all that shit."

I chewed my lip. "You can't? This is Lasby we're talking about."

He gave a quiet grunt as he kept pacing, boots thunking hard on the concrete floor. "Someone needs to give him the memo that DADT is gone."

I grunted quietly. "He doesn't give a shit. The son of a bitch is trying to get us to say MA1 Anderson didn't fuck up and almost get you killed. Making our lives hell for being gay isn't exactly below him."

Silence again. Nothing but Dalton's boots on the floor. Then, he stopped pacing. Back to me, he rubbed his neck. "I'm sorry about what happened out there. What those idiots have been saying. You were saving my ass, and I—"

"It's nothing doing. You said yourself you were out of it. Didn't know what was going on or what you were saying."

Dalton's posture tensed. His knuckles turned whiter as he kneaded his neck harder. He was silent, though. I could feel some sort of unspoken thought radiating off him like a fever, but he didn't speak.

"Talk to me." I stepped a little closer. "What's going on?"

Slowly, Dalton faced me, and I couldn't read his expression. It was hard to tell if he'd actually gone pale, or if it was just the harsh fluorescent lights over our heads.

"You sure you're okay, man?"

He swallowed hard. "What I said on the boat, yeah—I was delirious. I don't even remember it. But . . ." He dropped his gaze, and his cheeks colored. Speaking so softly his voice was almost lost in the buzz of the lights, he said, "But that doesn't mean it wasn't . . ."

My heart sped up. "It wasn't . . . what?"

He chewed his lip but kept his eyes down and said nothing.

I took a step closer. "Dalton. Look at me."

His spine straightened a little. Then, slowly, he raised his head. The panic in his eyes made my breath hitch.

Fighting the urge to put a hand on his shoulder, I said, "Come on. Talk to me. It's just us. Whatever it is, tell it to me straight."

He held my gaze, and he started and stopped a few times, but never got more than a syllable out. I swore I could feel his pulse accelerating with each false start. Or maybe that was mine.

Then he muttered, "Fuck it."

Crossed the space between us.

And kissed me.

For a single second, I was too stunned to respond. My brain caught up, though, and realized I had Dalton's lips against mine, and I came back to life, wrapping my arms around his solid torso. A soft moan vibrated between us. Whose? Who cared? I cradled the back of his head as Dalton teased the corner of my mouth with the tip of his tongue.

The kiss deepened. We both staggered a little, and I pushed him up against the lockers for support. He wrapped his arms around my neck, tilted his head, and let a soft moan escape as he kissed me hungrily. Oh God. Oh *God*. All my fantasies about kissing Dalton were pathetic compared to the real thing. I hadn't imagined his fingers trembling against my scalp or my neck. It hadn't crossed my mind how hard it would be to breathe with him against my chest and his mouth claiming mine. Or how little I'd care about oxygen. Or how fucking frustrating it would be to have our police vests and both our bulky utility belts keeping us so far apart. Oh God oh God oh God.

The need for air finally forced me to break the kiss, and I drew back enough to meet his eyes. Panting, we stared at each other in disbelief. Was he shaking? Because I was shaking. And I was pretty sure he was shaking.

Holy fuck—what just happened?

Dalton slowly ran his tongue along the inside of his bottom lip. "What I did on the boat," he whispered unsteadily, "I might've been out of it, but it wasn't fake."

"Y-yeah." I licked my lips. "I'm getting that impression."

"I've been wanting to do that forever," he breathed.

"Me too." My heart thudded so hard, I wouldn't have been surprised if he could feel it. God knew we were pressed close enough together.

Dalton kissed me again, and this time, he didn't hold back. He slid his tongue past my lips and encouraged me to do the same. He moaned—damn near purred—into my kiss, sliding his hands up my back and pressing his body against mine. He could be almost timid sometimes, especially for a cop, but wind him up and turn him loose like this? Holy fuck. I could only imagine what he'd be like when we were alone and—

The locker room door swung open, and we jerked apart. We each casually adjusted our uniform pants. A second later, MA3 Switzer appeared at the end of the aisle. He gave us a curt nod and continued toward another bank of lockers without a word.

We stood there in annoyed silence, both craning our necks as Switzer opened his locker, riffled around, and closed it again. There was some rustling and movement. Then more footsteps.

Switzer walked past, focusing on his phone, and a moment later, the locker room door swung shut with a heavy thud.

Dalton faced me, and a shy grin played at his lips. "We're going to get caught if we keep making out in here."

I laughed. "And Lasby will shit himself."

Dalton smirked. "That would *almost* be worth it." We both chuckled and he stepped closer. He slid his hands up the front of my blouse, a finger catching on the embroidered police badge. "Any chance we can pick this up after our shift is over?"

"I'll be lucky if I last that long."

His playful grin made my legs shake.

He pushed himself up and kissed me lightly. "We should get to work."

"Yeah, I know." I wrapped an arm around his waist. "Just a second, though."

And I kissed him again.

No shift in the history of the Navy ever dragged on as long as ours did that night. There was next to nothing going on, and our shipmates had been—whenever Lasby was out of earshot—relentless as usual. They'd caught on that our chief wasn't having it, so at least they were discreet, but it was still fucking irritating. There was a whole new level of annoying to the whole thing too. They weren't just ribbing us about some imaginary thing anymore. Every time they made a comment, it was all I could do to keep my focus off all the things I needed to be doing to Dalton right then. Making out for five minutes against a locker just wasn't cutting it.

Finally, at 0630, half an hour after I came in from my last watch, turnover was done and we got the hell out of there. Neither of us said a word to each other. We'd texted while I'd been on the boat, and we already had a plan. Dalton would shower at the HPU building while I headed home. When he left, he'd go through a different gate just to make sure none of the sentries caught on—sentries were usually bored senseless this time of night after all—and he'd meet me at my apartment off-base. If anyone saw his car there, well, they'd either gossip or they wouldn't. I was too horny to worry about any more cloak-and-dagger shit like hiding his car at another complex or something.

At my apartment, I had just enough time to strip out of my uniform, grab a shower, and throw on some gym shorts before he showed up.

When I opened the door, our eyes locked, and his grin made my whole body heat up. He was insanely hot anyway, and standing there in the hallway, dressed in some black shorts and a black UnderArmour shirt that fit him just right, with a *we're about to fuck* grin on his face? Holy shit.

I waved him inside. As soon as the door was closed, Dalton's arms were around me and his mouth was against mine. I staggered back, hitting the door and letting it support me while we picked up where we'd left off earlier. Except this wasn't where we'd left off earlier. There were no police belts between us anymore. No thick uniforms. No one who might bust in and catch us. Just some thin shorts, one shirt, and not a damn thing else. When my hands slid over his clothes, the heat of his skin radiated right through the fabric and into my palms. God, he might as well have been naked. He needed to be naked. Like, now.

I nudged him back and took his hand. "Come on."

As I started to lead him toward the bedroom, Dalton wobbled slightly, putting his free hand on the wall for balance. I stopped, my gut clenching. Was it too soon for us to be doing this? It hadn't been that long since he'd fucked up his head.

"You sure you're up for this?" I asked.

"I'm good." He reeled me in and kissed me softly. "Might not be quite a hundred percent yet, but I am definitely up for this." He pressed his erection against me, emphasizing the double meaning of his comment.

"Just don't want to push you too far." Except . . . how far *was* too far when a guy'd had his bell rung like he had? "You sure you're . . ." I kissed him lightly. "I don't want to go too fast with all this."

"Chris." He smiled, trailing his fingers down my cheek. "Do I look like a blushing virgin to you?"

I dusted a kiss across his lips. "No, but it hasn't been that long since a damn boat hit you upside the head."

"I'm fine," he whispered.

"But your head. Are you—"

He kissed me, gripping the back of my neck tightly. Then, still holding onto my nape, he panted, "Yeah, my head still hurts sometimes. Yeah, I still get dizzy." He trailed his thumb along my lower lip. "But I've been wanting you for way too long to wait."

"Likewise, but I also want you to enjoy it. If you're hurting . . ."

Dalton held my gaze, and to my surprise, he deflated a little. "Okay, so maybe we can't get too rough or anything quite yet. But I'm good with that if you are."

"Yeah, of course." *I just want you. I want you so bad I can barely stand up. No throwing each other around? Roger that. As long as I've got you in my bed tonight.*

"We just have to take it a little easy for now. That's all." Dalton licked his lips. "Another week or two, and we can get as rough as you want."

My whole body responded to that mental image, and I gasped as I shuddered under him. "You say the word when you're ready for that."

He moaned as he brushed his lips across mine. "I so will."

"Good," I murmured. "When your head stops acting like a dick, I'm going to make you come so hard you feel it for days." Instant embarrassment heated my face—I wasn't usually one for talking dirty—but the soft little groan that slipped past his lips made my blood rush.

Pressing his erection against mine, he growled, "I am so looking forward to that. Now let's get to the part we *can* do right now."

"Good idea." I led him the rest of the way to my bedroom.

The second we were through that door, everything ratcheted up. We kissed harder. Deeper. I peeled off his shirt. He toed off his shoes. The waistbands of our shorts snagged on our dicks, but only for a second, and finally those were out of the way too. Before I knew it, I was on my back with Dalton—naked, hard, and hot—stretched out on top of me.

Fucking Christ, he was definitely not one of those guys who looked better with clothes on. He spent a lot of time at the gym, and it showed in the smooth muscles and gorgeous contours.

He had a tattoo on his back. An eagle. I'd seen it before in the locker room, but now the lines were subtly raised under my fingers. Because I was touching him. I had my hands on his bare, warm skin.

I shivered under him and held him tighter and kissed him harder. How the fuck was this *real*?

Didn't matter. It was.

Dalton broke the kiss with a gasp. "Fuck."

"What's wrong?"

"Nothing. Nothing." He shook his head, then grinned. "I've just been wanting this forever, and . . . fuck, I'm horny." The sheer desperation in his voice brought a moan out of me, and I almost melted when he whispered, "You have condoms?"

"Uh-huh."

"Okay. Get . . . get one. Like now." He closed his eyes, shuddering as he rubbed his dick against me. "Tell me you top."

I just about lost my damned mind. "You better believe I do."

Dalton whimpered, then got up off me. "Condom."

I pushed myself up and reached for the bedside table. I fumbled around, found the pack, and tore off one rubber. Then I paused and squinted at it.

"Looking for the directions?" Dalton teased.

I glanced up at him, cheeks burning. "Just, uh, checking the expiration date."

He slid a hand up my thigh. "Been a while?"

"You could say that." I found the expiration date, and thank God, it was still a few months off. "So." I tore the wrapper with my teeth. "How do you like it?" I was already breathless. All it would take was one stroke inside him and I was going to pass out, I just knew it.

Dalton watched me rolling on the condom, gazing at my hands like the motions hypnotized him. "Doesn't matter. Just want you to fuck me."

"Hmm . . ." I reached for the lube. As I slicked up my cock, I could think of a hundred different ways I'd like to ride this man's gorgeous ass, but I wanted to be careful. How much he could handle and how much he'd *say* he could handle might not be the same thing, and I'd feel like hell if I hurt him. Probably better to let him be in control at first.

So I rolled onto my back. "Why don't you get on top?"

Dalton grinned. "I like where this is going." He straddled me. Biting my lip, I steadied my cock and guided him down, and *oh my God is this really happening?*

Uh-huh. It was. Dalton was naked and hard and over me and just needed to relax a little more so he could—

"Oh, yeah," he whimpered as the head of my cock slipped into him. "Fuck . . ." He lifted up a little, and as he eased himself down, his head fell back and he released the sexiest groan I'd ever heard. "Oh God, Chris . . ."

"Jesus," I whispered.

Dalton swept his tongue across his lips. His eyes slid closed, and they stayed that way as he continued taking me slowly. When I was buried to the hilt, he stopped for a couple of seconds. Then he started moving. Slowly at first, rocking, letting me slide almost all the way out before he'd start coming down again, and then taking every inch until I had nothing left to give him.

I rested my hands on his hips and didn't—couldn't—make a sound. He was so tight and hot, but it was the sight of him that drove me wild. He looked so good like that, sitting up over me, impaling himself as ecstasy played out on his features. The pale skin of his neck and chest were starting to flush, and sweat gleamed on his face. His cock jutted out between us, fully hard with pre-cum gleaming on the tip.

I'm doing this to him? I get to see him like this and have him like this? Whoa.

Another shiver ran through me, and my hips bucked, pushing me into him. That involuntary movement made him curse, so I did it on purpose this time, and he said something soft, incomprehensible, but definitely profane.

I had to hold my breath as my orgasm nearly broke loose without warning. No way in hell was I coming yet. This was too good to rush.

Gripping his hips a little tighter, I willed myself to stay in control. "I never thought I'd be thankful we're using condoms," I ground out. "But goddamn, I'd have come already if we weren't."

Dalton laughed, and it sounded free and relaxed. Almost delirious with pleasure. God, yeah. I hadn't thought it was possible for him to be any more attractive, but there he was. Holy crap.

He slowed abruptly, squeezing his eyes shut, and a subtle wince flickered across his face.

I put a hand on his hip. "You okay? Getting dizzy?"

"No." He licked his lips and looked down at me, laughing softly. "Quads are getting tired."

"Already?"

"Hey, shut up." He rolled his eyes. Leaning on his hands, he started riding me again, a little slower this time. "I'm the one doing all the work, you know."

"Yeah." I slid my palms up his chest, catching slightly on his sweaty skin. "Maybe we should switch."

Dalton grinned. "Mmm, maybe. I like this, but something tells me it would be a seriously good ride with you in control."

"Only one way to find out?"

His grin got bigger. He leaned down for a long kiss, then groaned as he lifted himself off my cock. "How do you want me?"

"On your stomach."

Dalton bit his lip, and I thought he might've been trying to suppress a shiver. We switched positions, and we both sighed as I pushed back into him.

"Oh God," he murmured into the pillow. "That's . . ." He trailed off into a happy, wordless noise. "Fuck . . ."

I buried my face in his neck, barely keeping myself from sinking my teeth into his skin, and groaned as I thrust harder.

"Oh yeah, baby," he breathed. "Yeah, that's . . . that's so good . . ." His moans sounded so deliciously and perfectly helpless, they just about made me come, and I held my breath as I fucked him as hard as I could in this position.

Then his entire body tensed. He clenched around me and his muscles seemed to turn to steel under me, and he choked on something that sounded like, "Don't stop," so I didn't stop, and then he jerked under me, nearly levitating both of us off the mattress as his release reverberated through him.

That was all I could take. My rhythm went out of the window, and nothing mattered except getting as deep as he could take me, and his neck muffled my cry as I came inside him.

I pulled out and dropped onto the mattress beside him, gasping not only because I was out of breath, but from the sudden absence of his hot skin against mine. "Holy . . ."

"Uh-huh." Dalton was boneless next to me, still flat on his stomach and breathing hard. I ran a hand down his back and rested it on his ass just because I could. All that time spent imagining how he'd look and feel naked, and here he was.

I managed to find my legs long enough to get up and toss the condom and clean myself up. By the time I came back, Dalton had rolled onto his back, and I offered him a towel. Then we were back right where we'd fallen—lying on my bed, completely spent.

Any other night, a sort-of-quickie like that would've been the first of two or three rounds. Maybe more if I'd eaten my Wheaties. But after a long shift? This was as good as it was going to get. And I wasn't about to complain because damn, it *was* good.

Dalton felt around blindly before he found my hand. When he did, he laced our fingers together and gripped tightly. "Well," he slurred, "there goes all the fantasies I've been jerking off to."

"What? Why?"

He turned to me, grinning sleepily. "Turned out the real thing is *way* better."

I chuckled and rolled closer to him. Draping an arm over his belly, I gave him a quick kiss. "But you know, if you want more fodder for the pornos in your brain, I'm happy to do a few recording sessions."

Dalton burst out laughing, and holy fuck if that wasn't the sexiest thing ever. Dalton Taylor, naked in my bed *and* laughing the way he always did when he was relaxed and happy. Corners of his eyes crinkling, lips pulled into a wide, lopsided smile.

I was in bed with my best friend. And it was perfect.

You are the most beautiful man I've ever seen, and now I can touch you.

I smoothed his ruffled, sweaty hair. "Any chance I can talk you into staying here tonight?"

He licked his lips. "You really want me to stay?"

"What the fuck kind of question is that?" I slid a hand up his bare chest. "I don't even want to let you leave for work tomorrow."

Dalton chuckled. "Too bad we can't call in sick, right?"

"No kidding."

"Damn Navy." He laughed again, but then turned more serious. "Lasby will lose his mind if he finds out about this."

"Technically, he already knows."

"Still . . ."

I nodded, heart sinking a bit. "I know."

"Hey." Dalton touched my face and held my gaze. "We're going to have to keep it on the down-low. Doesn't mean we have to stop."

"I know. I'm just . . ." I chewed my lip. "I mean, careers aside, what if we screw *this* up?" I gestured at him, then myself. "I've been wanting you for a long time, but that's what held me back. I didn't want to fuck up our friendship, you know? What if we—"

He cut me off with a soft kiss, and when he pulled back, his smile melted my heart. "I don't think we have to worry about fucking up this part. We're friends and we're good at fucking."

I laughed, sliding a hand up into his hair. "Yeah we are."

"Exactly. So let's just take things as they come. We've been friends for a while, and this only has to be as complicated as we make it."

"And as complicated as work makes it."

"Yeah." He rolled his eyes. "Fucking Lasby."

"Seriously."

He cuddled up closer to me. "We'll figure shit out with him. Right now, I'm too tired and feel way too good to even think about that jackass."

"You and me both." I kissed his temple, then closed my eyes and just enjoyed the warmth of his body pressed to mine. I still couldn't believe things had turned out this way, but they had. Somehow, after Lasby had threatened us over a relationship that didn't even exist, this had happened, and now we were here. In my bed.

And with Dalton wrapped up in my arms, I drifted off to sleep.

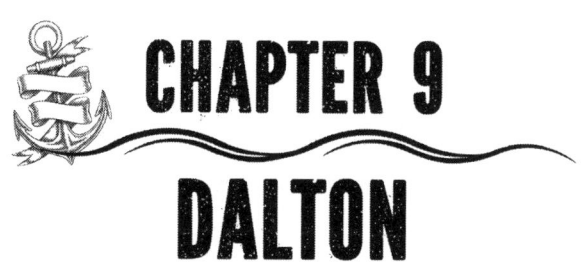

CHAPTER 9
DALTON

Eyes still closed, I rubbed my temples. There was a dull throb behind my forehead, but it wasn't the same headache I'd had almost every morning since the incident. This wasn't the aftermath of a concussion that promised to fuck with me for weeks or months to come—just the benign if annoying craving for some coffee. Which meant I must've slept later than I'd intended.

I opened my eyes so I could hunt down my phone and check the time.

And froze.

Where the . . .

The room was dark, though there were some telltale light leaks around the edges of the blackout curtains. Which meant I wasn't in the barracks. Jay and I had our blackout curtains sealed so tight no natural light made it into the room at all.

A flutter of panic ran through me before my brain caught up.

Oh. Right.

Figuring out where I was took a few seconds longer than I would've liked to admit. I hated being disoriented, and I felt like an idiot for forgetting—even momentarily while I was semiconscious—about last night.

Chris. I was with Chris. I was naked in bed with Chris.

Headache aside, I couldn't help grinning like an idiot. I didn't even care about the time anymore. Chris's alarm would go off when we needed to get ready for work.

I rolled over to drink in the sight of my best friend in the bed beside me. In the almost nonexistent light, it was hard to find the edges of his dark skin against the navy blue sheets, but as my eyes adjusted, the contours became clearer.

Good God, he was gorgeous. He was sprawled on his stomach, face buried in the pillow and an arm draped over the edge of the mattress. With the way the sheets were draped across his hips, I barely had to imagine the gorgeous ass.

The memories of last night brought a grin to my lips and sent goose bumps prickling down my back. I could only guess how hot it was going to be when I was back to a hundred percent. And hell, I felt a lot better just knowing I'd been able to handle last night. That I'd wanted it. That meant I was definitely on the road to recovery. I wasn't quite up to the level of wild sex I usually liked, but I wanted to be. A week ago, the thought of sex had actually nauseated me—my head had still been messed up enough that any kind of exertion registered as something that might make my skull explode. Up until a few days ago, I hadn't even been able to jerk off. Hadn't had any desire whatsoever to touch my own dick, never mind let someone else.

But I was getting better. The headaches were getting fewer and farther between. My equilibrium was better. I could think more clearly. I could even count out cash without feeling like someone had replaced my brain with seagull shit. More and more, I was me again, and the thought of sex had some appeal again.

Especially now that sex *with Chris* was a thing.

I drank in the sight of his dark, muscular frame. Oh yeah, sex definitely had some appeal now. When I was recovered enough to go all out, Chris was in for a hell of a ride.

I shivered, grinning as I slid closer. As much as I didn't want to wake him up, I couldn't resist cuddling against him.

"Mmff," he said into the pillow, but it didn't sound like "get off" or "let me sleep," so I didn't pull away.

I kissed the side of his neck. "Is it considered prostitution to blow you for coffee?"

He laughed and turned his head a little. "I don't know if it is or not, but it'll definitely get you some coffee."

"For the record, I'm not above prostituting myself for coffee."

"I know you're not."

"Hey!" I playfully swatted his ass through the sheets.

He laughed into the pillow, then rolled over and smiled sleepily up at me. "Hey you."

"Hey yourself." I dropped a light kiss on his lips. Enough to be affectionate without inflicting any morning breath on him.

He ran his fingers through my hair. "You want to share a shower? It's not huge, but there's room for both of us."

"Is that a sneaky way of asking if I want to have sex in your shower?"

Chris grinned, sliding a hand down my side. "Kind of don't feel like I need to be sneaky, you horndog."

I laughed and leaned down to kiss his neck. "Didn't hear you complaining last night about me being a horndog."

"Oh, you won't hear me complaining about that." He squirmed as I nipped gently. "It's gonna make our shifts *really* long though."

"Don't remind me."

He chuckled. "C'mon. Let's go get that shower."

He wasn't even subtle about bringing a condom in with us, so I had no doubt how this shower was going to play out. A little Scope to kill the morning breath, and it was game on—under the hot water, we kissed and groped and sort of made an effort to get clean. His skin was slick against mine, and I loved the feel of our rock hard cocks trapped between our bodies. Wasn't like he was the first guy I'd ever been naked with, but damn he turned me on. More than anyone else. Probably because I'd been wanting him for so long and hadn't ever believed I had a shot at him.

I slid a hand between us to stroke him with wet fingers, and Chris groaned. He let his head fall back, and I kissed his neck as I stroked his dick. When a shudder almost knocked him off his feet, he braced one hand on my shoulder and the other on the wall, and then he started rocking his hips to fuck my fist.

"Jesus, D," he breathed. "Why didn't we start doing this sooner?"

"Because you were asleep?"

He laughed, and I couldn't tell if he was rolling his eyes at my comment or if he was just getting into what I was doing with my hand. Quite possible the second option, judging by how his hips started moving faster. "I meant . . . I meant this. Hooking up."

I grinned, adding a little twist to my strokes and watching him shiver. "Don't know, but I'm glad we're doing it now."

"Uh-huh. Me . . . me too." He let his head fall back, and his low groan *just* carried above the rush of water. "God that's so good."

"Good. And since you promised me coffee . . ." I carefully went to my knees. "Couldn't hurt to earn it, right?" I didn't give him a chance to respond. As I took his thick cock between my lips, Chris groaned, the sound echoing in the small shower. His fingers were immediately in my hair. Not that it was long enough to really grab onto, but he managed to find some, and I loved the scrape of his nails against my scalp. His hips were still moving, pushing his dick into my throat, and I couldn't help moaning around him. I stroked him with one hand, and slid the other up his thigh and around to his ass cheek. When I gripped it, he got the message and thrust harder, fucking my face, and I couldn't tell who was moaning with more enthusiasm.

"Goddamn." He sucked in a breath. "Oh, that's good." His fingers twitched in my short hair. "Fuck, I'm gonna come. I'm . . . D, I'm gonna come." A second later, he whimpered, and he came harder than I expected, but I managed to swallow it without choking and keep stroking him until he nudged my hand away. Then—carefully since my balance was still iffy these days—I stood.

As soon as I was on my feet, Chris had an arm around my waist and a hand around my cock. He kissed me so hard it was almost violent, and I damn near came just from that alone. With the way he was pumping my cock like he was the one desperate to get off, I didn't last long. In seconds, I was sagging against him, hips jerking as I came all over his hand and his stomach, and then we were both panting and shaking and doing our level best to hold each other upright.

"When you're ready for it," he growled against my lips, "I'm going to fuck you into the mattress until you cry."

A whimper escaped my lips. "Gonna hold you to that," I murmured between kisses.

"Mmm, guess I should stock up on rubbers, then."

That gave me pause. I glanced at the condom we hadn't used. "Do . . . do we *need* them?"

Chris pulled back and met my gaze. "Uh . . ."

"I mean . . ." I slid my palm up the smooth, dark skin of his chest. "I have to go to medical this week anyway. I can have them test me while I'm at it."

He seemed to mull that over for a minute, then shrugged. "Wouldn't take much for me to swing in and do the same."

"So then assuming everything's all clear and it's just us . . ." I paused. "I mean, is it just us?"

Chris touched my face. "Can't think of any reason I wouldn't want it to be."

"Me neither." We exchanged smiles, and I added, "So we don't really need condoms, do we?"

He shook his head. "No, I guess we don't. Just until everything comes back clear, right?"

"I'm good with that."

"And I can't wait." He cupped my ass and squeezed. "The minute we get the all clear, it's game on."

I shivered, grinning. "Hell yeah." I kissed him, and we both let it go on for a while. The hot water was still raining down on both of us, and his water bill would probably be insane this month, but he didn't seem to be in any hurry to get out of the shower, so neither was I. It was still too novel and amazing to be standing here naked with my gorgeous best friend, still feeling every thrust from last night and tingling from the orgasm I'd just had.

Chris drew back and met my eyes. "You know, what happened on the boat fucking sucked." He grinned, running his hands up my back. "But I think this might count as a silver lining."

I returned the grin. "I think you're right. At least *something* good came out of all that."

"Something real good," he purred and kissed me again.

I couldn't argue with him. That incident out on the water had turned my whole life on its head, but the fallout wasn't *all* bad. If that hadn't happened, God knew when Chris and I would've ever gotten around to this.

I wasn't about to say I was glad I'd gone overboard. The headaches, the investigation, the PTSD, the general fucked-upedness the incident had left in its wake—I'd have sawed off a limb to have all that go away.

But if I *had* to go through all that shit, winding up in Chris's bed was definitely, as he'd said, a silver lining.

A week after Chris and I started getting physical, three weeks after I'd taken an unexpected swim in the Pacific, I was fully cleared to go back to work. No more light duty.

Which meant today, I was going back out on the water.

It didn't matter that I wasn't ready. HPU was desperate for manning, especially with MA1 Anderson still pushing a desk back at the security building, which was where he'd stay until the investigation was over. And no one had heard a peep about that in a while, so God only knew where it was going. The silence on that end made me nervous. Were they just letting it drop? Sweeping it under the rug? I hadn't even had to talk to anyone outside of our command, so maybe Big Navy wasn't going to look into it after all. Which was . . . weird. There should've been someone out here from Regional to interview everyone, but nothing had happened. Not yet. So maybe it wasn't going to?

Nice to know they follow up when a Sailor almost gets killed.

Maybe they'd decided it wasn't a big deal after I'd gotten the all-clear to go back on the water. Especially so soon after an incident like that. Technically, I should've been behind a desk just like Anderson for at least a few months, if not a year, to make absolutely sure I didn't have permanent physical or psychological damage.

And the fact that I wasn't behind a desk was more my fault than any medical professional's. I didn't like it, but I knew Chief Lasby was right that staying off the water would damage my eval and kill my chances at getting a promotion. So I'd glossed over my answers. Nightmares? No. Confusion? Not anymore. Memory loss? None at all. Balance issues? Nope. Pain? Just an occasional mild headache.

Either the doctor hadn't seen through my act or he hadn't cared enough to look, but he believed me, and on paper, I'd had a quick and full recovery. So maybe that told Big Navy the incident hadn't been as serious as the initial reports had stated. Hell, they were probably more concerned with the costs of unfucking the patrol boat—the fish nets had done a number on its propellers—and getting the Metal Shark back online.

Whatever was going on, we hadn't heard anything about the investigation, and no one seemed to object to me coming back to work. Nice to know the Navy was willing to let a guy carry a weapon so soon after he lost a head-butting contest with a boat.

Physically, I *did* feel pretty damn good. I'd been sleeping better, which may or may not have had something to do with spending almost every night in Chris's bed. Between his warm, solid presence beside me and the orgasms he gave me before we went to sleep, it was impossible not to knock out. Even the times when a nasty headache kept us from fooling around, just having him next to me was enough to relax me and let me sleep.

"Hey." Chris elbowed me from the driver's seat of his car. "Still awake?"

I shook myself, wondering how long I'd been zoned out. Long enough to get from his apartment to the HPU building, apparently. Had I even taken my ID out for the sentry? No, my wallet was still in my pocket. Or had I put it back?

"D?"

I cleared my throat. "Sorry. Just . . . thinking about being back on the water, I guess."

He grimaced as he killed the engine. "You sure you're ready for that?"

Not even a little.

"I'll be fine." My voice was almost a croak. Yeah, I sounded totally sure of myself. "Now let's go get some coffee before I pass out."

He laughed, not quite hiding the uneasiness in his tone, but he let it go. We'd talked circles around this for over a week. What more was there to say?

We went into the HPU building and upstairs to the main office. I made a beeline for the coffeepot and used it to fill my travel mug.

"Oh, coffee. Come to Daddy." I sipped it carefully to test it, then gave a happy little groan as I drank some more.

Chris laughed. "Anyone ever tell you you're an addict?"

I flipped him the bird as I took a deeper swallow. "Let's see how perky *you'd* be if we cut you off the caffeine for a week or—"

"All right, all right." He put up his hands in surrender. "Ain't no need to get crazy."

"That's what I thought. And for the record, you show me an MA who isn't addicted to caffeine, and I will show you a *liar*."

Chris nearly choked on his own coffee. "You're not wrong."

I chuckled.

He watched me for a second, head cocked. "You really ready for this? Going back on the boat?"

I gulped, staring out at the water. It was calm right now. The boats on the pier were barely rocking at all, and the flags were sagging alongside the poles. If there was a good day to try going on the boat, this was it. Turning back to Chris, I nodded. "Yeah. I told you I need to get back on the horse that threw me."

He didn't look convinced. His lips tightened and his eyebrow arched. "They say you can wait to get back on that horse until you're actually healed, you know."

"I'm *fine*. Especially with the weather being like this." I tilted my coffee cup toward the view. "Can't ask for a better day to go back out, you know?"

He studied me before releasing a resigned sigh. "All right. But you're coming out on watch with me, and if I think you need to come back in, we're coming back in. Got it?"

I blinked, then chuckled. "You already sound like an MA1."

He rolled his eyes. "Yeah right. But I'm serious."

"I know." I sobered, nodding slowly. "And . . . thanks. For looking out for me."

"Don't mention it. You know I always got your back."

Our eyes locked, and we both smiled.

Then he cleared his throat. "Anyway. I'm going to go have a look at the boat reports. See if there's anything we need to ping Port Ops about."

"Yeah. God forbid day shift actually put in the call when they find the problem."

Chris snorted. "I know, right? Lazy assholes."

We both chuckled, and then he left to go downstairs. It was kind of an ongoing joke between days and nights. They'd find a problem and dutifully put it in the boat reports but never seemed to think about actually calling Port Ops and getting it taken care of. Somehow that was always on us even though Port Ops didn't usually answer their phones at night. When the shifts switched and we went to days, I had a feeling the *report it but don't call it in* thing wouldn't go over quite as well.

My good-if-nervous mood lasted until I was refilling my coffee a while later, and Lasby materialized next to me. "How are you feeling, MA2?"

I focused on topping off my travel mug. "Good. Better."

"That's what I like to hear." He paused. "Listen, you're not officially on watch. Not yet. You're not arming up, either—just going out with the watch standers to work on getting your sea legs back."

I nodded, pretending I didn't already feel seasick. And I was relieved they weren't giving me a weapon after all. I felt like my head was mostly back together, but my gut said I wasn't ready for that. As I screwed the lid on the mug, I said, "Okay. Can do." *Right?*

"For the next week, I just want you on the water. Making sure you can handle it. If there aren't any issues or incidents, I'll advise the LPO that you can act as gunner or coxswain again."

I pursed my lips. "Who *is* the LPO right now, anyway?"

Lasby stiffened, eyes narrowing slightly. "MA1 Anderson is still the LPO. He'll continue writing up the watch bills."

That didn't seem right. If he was under investigation, he shouldn't have been anywhere near HPU. Not even in an administrative capacity. Somehow knowing he was still writing the watch bills didn't do much to fill me with confidence that the incident was being properly investigated.

Pick your battles, MA2.

So I just said, "Understood, Chief."

None of us had to carry a rifle today because we were on the Metal Shark, which was both functional *and* had a mounted machine gun.

"So all we had to do to get this thing running again was throw somebody overboard?" I muttered on the way down the pier.

MA3 Powers laughed. "Guess so."

Chris glanced at me, but he didn't seem to find it as funny. He didn't comment, though.

We did turnover with the previous watch—signing off boat reports, getting an update on any mechanical issues, being briefed on anything suspicious they'd seen during their patrol. Of course there was nothing. The Metal Shark was in working order, so unlike the boat we'd been using before, there wasn't a laundry list of *this is leaking* and *that's making weird noises*. Having a fully operational boat really was something else.

And the Oregon coast wasn't exactly a hotbed of terrorist activity, so the "suspicious shit" list consisted of a pleasure boat that had gotten a little too close to the harbor, some tourist taking pictures of the base from the north end of the seawall, and a couple of curious sea lions barking at them near the harbor gate.

"We saw Bill today too." MA3 Switzer nodded toward the ocean. "Hadn't seen him in a while, so we thought something might've happened to him."

Chris grinned. "Might have to grab some fish from the bait shop. See if we can get him to play catch again."

I chuckled. Bill was the ballsiest of the sea lions. He'd come right up to the boat sometimes, and he'd bark until we fed him. We weren't supposed to—Fish & Wildlife would have a *fit* if they knew—but he had those big puppy dog eyes and none of us could say no. Last summer, the whiteboard in the main office had even had *Bill Has/Has Not Been Fed Today* written in one corner. No one had seen heads or tails of him recently, and we'd all been afraid something had happened to him, but apparently he was back. At least there was *some* goodness around here.

When we were done with turnover, we boarded. I helped Powers pull in the lines, and Chris steered the boat out of its slip.

Part of me wanted to stay in the cabin, but I knew better. I didn't want Chris to be distracted by me trying not to freak out, and anyway, I needed to keep the horizon at least in my peripheral vision or I'd get seasick. That was what I told myself. I hadn't needed to worry about seasickness in years. I could read a book in my rack on an aircraft carrier while the ship rocked hard enough to nearly tumble me out of bed, and I wouldn't get the least bit nauseated.

But tonight, just looking at the water made me a different kind of sick. One that didn't seem to be much better than seasickness. This didn't start in my stomach. It started somewhere deeper than that. Like in my damn bones.

I gripped the railing with both hands, focusing on the cold, smooth surface and how solid it was, reminding myself that as long as I was holding this, I wasn't going anywhere. If the boat pitched or rolled, I just had to *hold on.*

Except the boat wasn't doing any pitching or rolling. I felt like a fucking idiot, breaking out in a sweat when the water was so gentle the boat barely rocked or bobbed at all.

I closed my eyes and took a few slow, deep breaths. The psychologist had given me a few coping methods for PTSD even though I'd told her it wasn't necessary, and I tried to recall them now. Grabbing onto something cold had been one of them. Shit, no wonder I had a death grip on the railing. I slid my hand to the side, finding a spot that hadn't been warmed by my skin, and concentrated on the chilly metal. I opened my eyes. Focused on the railing. The water—no, not a good idea. The deck. A solitary white cloud in the distance.

Heavy boots clomped on the deck behind me. Then a hand came to rest between my shoulders. "Hey. You okay?" Chris. I'd known it was him, but somehow the sound of his voice surprised me. In a good way.

Keep talking. You don't know how soothing it is.

"You still with me, Dalton?"

It was a stupid question. Of course I was still here. Where else would I be?

Except . . .

Why did I suddenly feel like I'd just come back to the here and now? And why did I feel like I'd been gone . . . a *while*?

I didn't know what it meant, only that it wasn't good. Swallowing the nausea, I turned to face him. "I don't think I'm ready to be back on the water."

"Want us to take the boat back in?"

My pride and my stomach warred with each other. "Fuck . . ."

Chris twisted around and called out to Powers. "MA3, take her back pierside."

A moment later, the deck listed slightly as the boat began the wide arc of a U-turn. It wasn't even the motion that made my stomach lurch—it was the defeat. The shame. The sense of complete and utter failure.

I'm a coxswain. I'm a Level II fucking coxswain. And I can't handle being out on glass-smooth water?

"Hey. Look at me." When I met his eyes, Chris said, "This doesn't mean you won't get back on the water. It's a process."

"I know, but I feel like such a . . . fuck, I don't even know. I mean, we've got guys here who've been to combat, and I've got PTSD from falling off a fucking boat a million miles away from—"

"Dalton." Chris squeezed my shoulder. "It doesn't matter that we're not in a warzone. You could have been killed. You understand me?"

I chewed my lip, avoiding his eyes.

"Anyone would have PTSD from that shit," he went on. "You better believe Rhodes is fucked up too. Hell *I've* had nightmares about it."

I jerked upright and met his gaze. "You have?"

"Are you kidding?" he whispered, shaking his head. "When we got to you after you'd gone in, I took one look at you and thought we were already too late." A shudder rippled through him and his fingers twitched on my shoulders. Chris swallowed hard. "I thought you were dead, Dalton. I thought—" It was his turn to break eye contact. "I thought I'd lost you."

Queasiness burned in my throat. "I'm still here."

"I know. And I want you to stay that way." He looked in my eyes. "I want you to be okay too. Like . . ." He tapped his temple. "So, we'll take it in today, and we'll try again when you're ready. You'll get there. I promise."

I nodded, but I didn't say anything.

A few minutes later, we were back at the pier. MA2 Simmons was waiting, and after I'd gone ashore, she took my place on the boat. Before I'd even made it back to dry land, the Metal Shark was headed back out onto the calm water, silhouetted by the slowly setting sun. I tried not to think about how that seemed like a metaphor for my career—sailing away without me.

"Why aren't you out on that boat?" Lasby's voice made my teeth snap together.

I turned away from the fading boat and saw him heading down from the HPU building with a cigarette between his fingers. He didn't look pleased.

I took a breath. "Chief, I think I need to stay onshore for a while."

He glared at me. "We talked about this, MA2. It's not going to look good on—"

"And neither will me having a flashback or something while I'm out there."

"A flashback?" He blinked. "All your paperwork said you've recovered completely."

"Yeah, it does, but . . . I don't know. Maybe I need more time after all." *Maybe I lied to the psychologist because I was afraid of losing my career.*

Lasby eyed me, his expression a mix of impatience and annoyance. Then he sighed heavily and shrugged. "It's your call, MA2. But remember what we talked about."

"I know. I remember."

"Good." He took a deep drag and blew out some smoke. "You keep me updated, all right?"

"Will do, Chief."

He gave a curt nod, then turned to go back inside. I stared at his back, watching him go just like I'd watched the Metal Shark a few minutes earlier. I doubted he actually wanted me to get promoted. And it wouldn't exactly reflect badly on him if I wasn't working at full capacity because everyone knew I'd been injured.

Which left only one option as far as I was concerned—Chris's theory that Lasby wanted me back at a hundred percent because it would make the incident look less serious. Or more to the point, make it easier to sweep under the rug.

Only problem was, I couldn't prove it.

I couldn't prove it, and whether I liked it or not, I needed that promotion more than I needed to be right about Lasby.

So one way or the other, I was getting back out on that water.

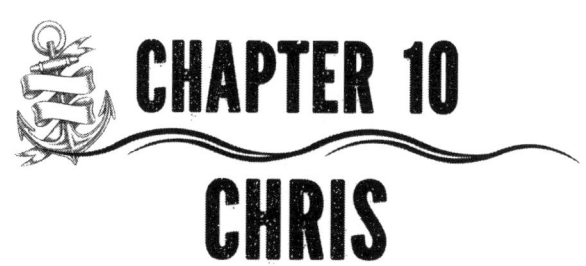

CHAPTER 10

CHRIS

It was early March, and spring was sort of thinking about showing up, so the sun was shining and the weather was . . . not warm, but not as violently cold as February could get. Since Dalton and I had a few hours before we had to be at work, we wandered down to the beach a few miles north of NAS Adams. We'd started doing that lately, so it was no surprise whenever we ended up here.

In fact, it had kind of become our routine, now that I thought about it. In the couple of weeks since that kiss in the locker room, we were always either in bed, at a restaurant, or right here—sitting in the sand or leaning against a log of driftwood, one of us resting his head on the other's chest. If it was warm enough, our sneakers would be a few feet away with our socks tucked into them while we dug our toes into the sand. And regardless of the temperature, there was always the faint scent of sunscreen rising over the salt of the sea; apparently Dalton had experienced a second degree sunburn once as a teenager and did *not* take chances now.

The whole scene was becoming as familiar as my apartment or my uniform, but not monotonous or boring by any means. I loved this. Today, with three hours before we had to muster at work, I was propped up against a log with Dalton cuddled up against me. In another month or so, when summer started to set in, it would probably be too hot for this. Right now, though, it was perfectly comfortable.

Except for the stiffness in Dalton's muscles. Tension had been radiating off him all day. Hell, even since last night. He'd shake it off when we were screwing around, and after he came he'd be boneless and satisfied for a little while, but it wouldn't take long before he started to tense up again.

I combed my fingers through his hair. "What's wrong?"

"Hmm?" He twitched slightly, then twisted around enough to glance up at me, almost like he'd forgotten I was even here. "What?"

"You've been wound up lately. What's going on?"

Dalton sighed and leaned back against me. "Just worrying about work."

"The investigation? Or being on the water?"

He shuddered. "Both."

That was no surprise. He was getting better about the boat. Mostly, he'd go aboard to do boat reports, and he'd help clean even when the MA3s were handling most of it. Just being on the boat while it was tied to the pier was helping him get his legs under him again. Going out on patrol still shook him up, but he was doing better. Lasting longer before he'd finally ask me to take him back to the pier.

Fortunately, aside from Chief Lasby, everyone was endlessly patient with him. I'd briefed them all while he'd been out of the room and let them know it was going to be a slow process. Everyone had understood. No one had so much as batted an eye. A few more weeks, I figured, and Dalton would be as confident on the boat—even at the helm—as he'd been before Anderson had fucked up his world. As a bonus, the guys had apparently caught on that Dalton wasn't in a good place mentally, and they'd backed off about him and me.

Leaning against me on the beach, Dalton exhaled. "Is it just me, or has the investigation gone quiet?"

I frowned. "No, it's not just you. I haven't heard anything. Neither has Rhodes."

Dalton absently ran his thumb back and forth along the inside of my knee. "I don't know how I feel about that. Like maybe it means Anderson's going to get off scot free, but maybe it also means they're not going to come after Rhodes for all that bullshit about the rifle."

I rolled my eyes. Word had trickled down a few days ago that the divers had pulled up the rifle. No surprise—it was completely destroyed. I supposed now it was just a question of whether the investigators would realize it had been fucked the moment it went into the water, or if they'd try to insist it could have been salvaged if Rhodes had held onto it. "Maybe someone back at Big Navy is testing how long it took for the water to fuck up the rifle. So they know whether to blame you or Rhodes."

Dalton snorted. "You know, I wouldn't put it past anyone."

I laughed but didn't really feel it.

He sighed, letting his head rest against my shoulder.

After a while, I quietly said, "Can I ask you something?"

Dalton turned his head a little so he could look up at me again, but he didn't lift it off my shoulder. "What's up?"

"You don't have to answer, but I've always been curious—why did you go to Captain's Mast?"

He sighed heavily, shifting his gaze to the sky. "Because I was a young, stupid, defiant little shit who picked the wrong time to act like a young, stupid, defiant little shit."

"You might have to narrow that down."

Dalton chuckled. "The official charge was failure to obey a lawful order and regulation, dereliction of duty, and . . . um . . . drunk on duty."

"Drunk on duty?" I blinked. "You?" I wasn't being sarcastic—this was a guy who almost never drank at all, never mind around our coworkers.

Sighing again, he nodded. "This was back when I used to party a lot more. We were deployed in the Med, and basically, I was going out and getting hammered during port calls even when I had to stand watch the next day. My LPO and my chief kept warning me that if I showed up to muster with a hangover again, they'd fuck my world up." He sighed, wiping a hand over his face. "I just didn't think they actually would."

I grimaced. "What happened?"

"I showed up hung over. I'm not sure my section leader even noticed, so I thought I was in the clear . . . until I fell asleep during watch."

"Oh shit. Dude. *Dude.*"

"I know, right? And of course the goddamned Master Chief caught me." He groaned, covering his eyes.

"Express ticket to Captain's Mast?"

"*Oh* yeah." He gazed out at the water, but his eyes didn't seem focused on anything. "Honestly, even though the whole thing has still been a headache for the last ten years, it's probably the best thing that ever happened to me."

"Yeah? How's that?"

"Because it was the first time in my life something ever had *real* consequences." He turned slightly so he was looking up at me. "You know, besides an ass-chewing or a threat for a punishment that never happened."

"Your dad wasn't strict?"

Dalton shrugged, facing the water. "I was the youngest of four being raised by a stressed-out grieving widower. Everyone felt sorry for us kids, especially me because I never knew my mom, so they kind of spoiled us. Or were just too exhausted or whatever to put in the effort, you know?"

I nodded.

"So when we screwed up, it didn't matter. Or it didn't matter as much as it should have. That was why I had to go into the Navy in the first place. My grades were so bad I only graduated by the skin of my teeth, and about the only thing I had going for me was that I had no criminal record and could run." He gave a soft, sheepish laugh. "Those last two things are, uh, not exactly unrelated."

I laughed louder than I intended and clapped a hand over my mouth. The mental image of a young punk version of Dalton running like hell to evade some small town pudgy-ass Midwestern cop was a lot funnier than I'd expected.

He elbowed me playfully. "It's not *that* funny."

"Actually, it is. It really is."

"Shut up." He was chuckling too, though. After a moment, he went on. "So yeah—I spent my whole life convinced that rules were suggestions or outright challenges. Then I fucked up good and found myself standing at attention in front of the CO. And I mean, it's one thing to get chewed out by your dad or the principle for the hundredth time. Especially when they've reached the point where they know you're just going to do it again so they're just wasting their breath." He lifted his chin so he could look at me. "You ever been glared at by a pissed-off captain?"

"Can't say I have, no."

"That shit is intimidating. Like . . . holy fuck."

I chuckled. "I believe it. My last CO was intimidating even when he wasn't pissed off."

"Yeah, mine too. And the more I explained what I'd done and why, the more pissed he got, and the more terrified I was. And I remember standing there thinking, oh shit, there's no getting out of this one. This guy literally has the power to kick me out of the Navy if he wants to, and then what do I do?"

"So what happened?"

"I . . ." He sighed, and his cheeks turned a little pink. "I went from cocky punk asshole to scared little kid. I swear, I almost cried. And I think he saw it. So he told me in no uncertain terms that could strip me of a rank, dock my pay for a couple of months, and put me on restriction so I couldn't leave the ship when we were in port, but he understood that I obviously realized I'd fucked up, and that he had faith I would get my shit together." He paused, smirking. "And then he stripped me of a rank, docked my pay for a couple of months, and put me on restriction. Because, as he put it, he didn't have *that* much faith that I'd get my shit together."

I laughed. "That sounds like a CO."

"Yeah." Dalton chuckled. "It sucked, but it straightened me out." He sighed, and his humor faded. "Now if it would just stop biting me in the ass at every turn . . ."

"Shouldn't something like that be off your evals by now?"

"Oh it is. And no one's ever officially said that it's hurt my chances at advancement, but come on—I'm not stupid. It's just like how us being older and with more years of service without advancing shouldn't hurt us, but we know it does."

I grimaced. "Yeah. But still—how many people even know about what happened back then?"

"Too many. The MA rate is tiny and incestuous. People know about what happened, and they think if someone has ever gotten in enough trouble to lose a rank, they're not fit to be promoted." He shrugged tightly. "It is what it is. I just have to make sure my PT and exam scores are high enough to blur whatever bullshit comes through on my eval, you know?"

I nodded. It blew my mind, hearing him talk about that part of his past. It was hard for me to imagine the guy Dalton had been before. By the time we'd met, he'd already turned into the professional, focused

Sailor he was now.

Sometimes I wished we'd met sooner, because my life was so much better with him in it. On the other hand, maybe it was for the best that we'd both been quite a few years into our careers before our paths had crossed. We might not have been friends otherwise.

Watching my fingers trail up and down his arm, I thought, *We wouldn't have been* this *either.*

"You ever get in trouble since you've been in?" he asked.

I barked a laugh. "Oh, fuck no."

"What? Never?"

"No." I shook my head. "My whole life was the opposite of yours—I knew damn well if I got in trouble, I could fuck up my parents' careers."

Dalton snickered. "Did your folks use MAs to keep you in line?"

"You know they did."

He burst out laughing. "Oh, man. I would've been so much less of a dick as a kid if my dad could've done that."

"Yeah, but you wouldn't be as fun."

"Tell that to my dad. The man's almost completely gray, and I'm pretty sure I had something to do with that."

"Eh." I shrugged. "My dad says he's bald because of me and my sister."

"Thought you didn't get into trouble."

"Not the kind of trouble that got teachers or cops involved, but that don't mean we weren't a handful."

Dalton snorted. "Somehow, I'm not surprised."

"Ass."

We both laughed, and comfortable silence set in again. When his phone beeped, we both swore. Didn't even have to look to know what that was about.

Dalton took it out, turned off the alarm, and sat up. "Guess we should go get ready for work."

"Yeah. Guess so."

He stood and offered me an arm. I took it. Once I was on my feet, I put my hands on his hips and drew him in. "You going to be okay at work?"

He sighed, chewing the inside of his cheek and looking away. "I don't know. It's . . . rough, you know?" His Adam's apple jumped. "I have no idea how to deal with being afraid of the water. Part of me knows it's just a reaction to what happened and I'll get over it, but that part of me is fucking silent when I actually step out on a boat."

"I believe it." I smoothed his hair. "You gotta give yourself time, though."

"I know. But the Navy isn't going to give me much." He huffed, then quietly added, "Lasby sure as fuck isn't."

"It ain't his decision."

"It's his decision what goes in my eval."

I squeezed my eyes shut and bit back some cursing. He'd told me about the shit Lasby had put in his head. And the fucked-up thing was I couldn't tell him Chief was blowing smoke. Because he wasn't.

Dalton ran his hand up my chest. "I know I'll get over it. It's just a question of when. I mean, my brother got in a bad car accident when he was twenty. He's been driving since he was fourteen and never thought anything of it, but after that?" I shook my head. "Took him a long, long time to be comfortable on the road again."

"But he got there, right?"

Dalton nodded.

"So will you." I kissed him softly. "Just let yourself recover right now, you know? If you're off the water for months on end, yeah, it might hurt your eval. But we're probably talking a few more weeks at most. You're already getting better, so don't push yourself so hard."

"I won't. And . . . thanks. For listening. I'll be bitching about this stuff for a while, guaranteed."

"It's okay." I smirked. "If it's too much, I'll just shove my dick in your mouth."

Dalton threw his head back and laughed, the sound carrying along the deserted beach. God, I loved when he smiled like that.

Eyes sparkling, he met my gaze again. "Now I might bitch about it just to see how long it takes you to whip it out and shut me up."

"Uh-huh." I wrapped an arm around his waist and, as we started for the car, added, "I wouldn't put that past you at all."

He laughed and leaned into me, and we kept on walking.

CHAPTER 11

DALTON

We had the next day off, so when we wandered down to the beach again, there was no hurry and no alarms set on our phones to make sure we didn't stay too long. If we ended up here until the sun went down, fine. I had Chris, a gorgeous beach, and nowhere else to be. It was perfect. There was a good chance we'd wind up in his bed later too—I hadn't slept in my barracks room in days.

So why did I feel like shit?

Oh right—because the advancement exam was fucking *tomorrow*.

I shivered like a cold wind had suddenly smacked into me.

The exam. Tomorrow. Shit.

My concentration *was* improving. I had to fill out reams of paperwork as part of my job, and my brain was finally starting to level out enough to focus on those things. I could count out change without any problem. I could drive again. Chris and I had even started playing on the Xbox, and I could handle that as long as I stopped when I got a headache.

So in theory, I'd be fine tomorrow. I was just worried because so much was riding on it.

"Hey." Chris elbowed me as we walked along the high tide line. "You're somewhere else today."

"Yeah, I know." I paused to scoop up a small rock, and as we walked, I played with it, turning it over between my fingers like it might soak up some of this nervous energy. "I'm just freaking out about tomorrow, and I still don't know what to do about my job." I tossed the rock into the surf before I stopped walking and turned to Chris. "I mean, I'm a Sailor and a coxswain. It's what I *do*."

He wrapped his arm around my waist. "We talked about this.

You've got time. It hasn't even been that long."

"No, but . . ." I glanced warily at the ocean before looking up at him again. "I won't lie—I'm scared."

Chris nodded. He cupped my cheek and kissed me lightly. "Anyone would be. I'd be worried if you weren't. Yeah, it'll take some time to get used to being on the water again, but you'll get there. I know you will."

"And probably just in time for the Navy to show me to the door."

"Hey. Hey. Don't talk like that." He brushed his thumb along my cheekbone. "Your last eval was solid as fuck, your PT scores are all outstanding, and you'll nail the exam tomorrow."

I sighed and covered his hand with mine, wishing like hell some of his enthusiasm would transfer through that gentle contact.

"You'll be *fine*," he insisted. He pulled me in for a soft kiss. "Come on. Let's sit down for a bit."

I didn't protest. If there was anything that could relax me, it was sitting on the beach with Chris's arms around me. So, I sat on the sand and toed off my sneakers. It was chilly today, but not cold. Oregon didn't get cold like Nebraska did, so this was comfortable for me.

Chris took off his shoes and socks, then moved behind me. When he sat down, he was straddling me like he usually did. Sometimes he leaned on me, but this seemed to be our default setting. Worked for me, and I didn't hear him objecting.

A gentle hand tugged my shoulder back, and I leaned against his chest. Didn't matter how many times we did this—I loved it. We didn't talk for a while, and that was okay. I liked just leaning against him. His presence was warm and solid, and I loved the way his arms felt when they were loosely wrapped around me like this. Sometimes he'd run his fingers through my hair or trail one down my arm, and those little touches gave me goose bumps.

This was something I'd never had with a boyfriend before. Maybe because I'd never dated a friend. I was friends with a lot of my exes, but we'd always started out as a couple—or at least a hookup—then split up and become friends like Diego and I had. This thing with Chris . . . this was new. We were already comfortable with each other. Had been since long before I even knew he was gay or anything got physical. Segueing from friends to more than friends had been so effortless,

I couldn't explain why it hadn't happened ages ago. Everything was relaxed. We weren't self-conscious together, which was probably why the sex came easy and the cuddling seemed so normal. Why we'd gone from totally platonic to casually touching without batting an eye.

He pressed a kiss to my temple. "You'll get there, you know. Back to being confident on the water."

I closed my eyes. My thoughts had been drifting to us instead of all the reasons I didn't want to go back on the water. Not that I blamed him for pulling me back. "I know. I'm just not looking forward to what it's going to take to get there."

He gave a soft, sympathetic grunt. "It's gonna take time. I know the brass want to write it off as you just going for a swim, but something like that's traumatic. It's *going* to affect you for a while." His arm tightened subtly, almost imperceptibly, across my chest. "Like I said, I'd be worried if it *didn't* fuck you up."

I didn't reply, and we both let the subject drop. It was our day off—no point in getting worked up over shit we couldn't control. Especially not while we were lounging together on a beach.

He held me closer, and as I nestled back against him, the incident and my fear of water couldn't hold my thoughts anymore. I was too caught up in the firm, warm presence of Chris behind me. My body was obviously healing because my libido had come back in full force, and now just touching Chris was enough to get me fired up. I took a few slow breaths, hoping he didn't glance down and noticed the swelling bulge below my belt. I couldn't help it—I had Chris, and Chris turned me on, and goddamn it felt good. Even that sort-of-frustrating feeling of getting randomly horny in a place where I couldn't do anything about it.

Chris leaned down and kissed my cheek, then behind my ear. A shiver went through me, and there was no way he didn't feel it that time. When he kissed that spot again, there was something a little more deliberate about the touch. Something that was echoed in the way his arms were tightening around me. I sucked in a breath as his lips skated along my hairline.

"You have any idea," he murmured against my skin, "how hard it is not to get turned on around you?"

I guided his hand down to the front of my jeans. "Mmm, I think

I can relate."

He released a soft breath across my skin, then started kissing his way down the side of my neck while he squeezed and teased my erection through my jeans. "Can't help it. Get my hands on you, and that's all she wrote."

"Know . . . know the feeling." Goose bumps were covering every inch of my skin, and I was dizzy. The good kind of dizzy. The *I want you so bad it hurts* kind of dizzy.

Chris shifted a little to one side. I shifted to the other, so now I had my back against his thigh and was sort of facing him. Much better—now I had all kinds of access without straining my neck. Access to his mouth with my own, and also to the front of his pants with my hand. He groaned into my kiss as I started undoing his zipper. He kneaded me through my pants, and as soon as I had my fingers around his cock, he started on my zipper.

"Does this count as sex on the beach?" he asked between messy kisses.

"I don't care what it counts as." I moaned as he freed my dick from my pants. "Just don't stop."

"Stop? No way." He nipped my lower lip and started stroking me.

"Oh God." I shivered, then buried my face in his neck, kissing his skin as we pumped each other's cocks. Since when was a simple, mostly-dressed handjob this hot?

Since you got to start hooking up with Chris. That's when.

My toes curled and I moaned against his neck. That was it, wasn't it? There was sex, and there was sex with Chris, and when he was involved, we didn't have to be doing much for me to go crazy. I loved how he kissed, the things he did with his hands, the way he fucked me when we were in bed, and yeah, even just jerking each other off on a beach with our clothes on was so . . . insanely . . . *sexy*.

"Gonna come." His voice vibrated against my lips.

"M-me too." I let my teeth graze his skin, which made him shudder and grip my dick even tighter. "God, yeah . . ."

"Fuck, D . . ." He stroked me faster, and I squeezed my eyes shut, trying not to come quite yet because this felt so good and I didn't want it to be—

"Oh God!" My whole body jerked. His strokes were instantly

slick and hot, and my eyes rolled back as he kept on pumping me, and I couldn't help sinking my teeth into his shoulder and right then he was coming too, and that moan he let go was almost as hot to my ears as the thrumming was against my mouth.

We both relaxed, exhaling in unison.

"If this is going to start happening when we walk on the beach," I slurred, "I say we come down here *every* day."

"We already do." Chris laughed, nuzzling my cheek. "And I mean, we don't have to walk on the beach. Any time, any place, you just say the word."

I bit my lip and squirmed with what might've been an aftershock of that awesome orgasm. "Careful what you wish for."

He laughed. "You know," he breathed, "if we leave now, by the time we get back to my place, I'll bet we'll be ready to go again."

I grinned. "Is that a challenge?"

"No. Just a suggestion that maybe we should leave. Like *now*."

CHAPTER 12
CHRIS

I pushed Dalton up against my apartment door, and we kept right on kissing while I fumbled with my keys. It took some doing, but I got the key into the lock, turned it, and—after putting an arm around him to keep him upright—opened the door. He walked in backwards, our feet brushing but somehow not getting tangled, and I kicked the door shut behind us.

"If I'd known it would be like this," I said between kisses, "I'd have told you I was gay the day I met you."

Dalton laughed, sliding his hands over my hips. "Guess we'll just have to make up for lost time, right?"

"Mmm, I like the way you think. C'mon. Bedroom."

We separated enough to get down the hall, and we left a trail of shirts, shoes, socks, and jeans behind us. By the time we made it to the bed, there was nothing left but drawers, and those were gone about two seconds later.

Fooling around on the beach was hot. Tangling up naked on my bed? Oh fuck yeah. No clothes in the way. No one to stumble in and bust us. Just Dalton's body pressed up against mine, hands all over each other, and mouths going to town like we hadn't kissed in years.

I loved how much Dalton loved kissing. I didn't even mind the nights when we set out to fuck and wound up jerking each other off instead because getting lube and all that meant we had to stop kissing. The way he was kissing me now, I could see that happening again, except not tonight—I'd already had his hand, and now I wanted his ass.

In a minute.

Right now . . . *God*. He had a hand on the back of my head, fingers twitching against my hair, and he was teasing my tongue with his, and . . . oh Jesus, I loved this. Everything else going on in our world was messed up and wrong, but this? Fuck, this was right. So right I still couldn't help asking myself every single time why we'd taken so long to get to this point. It just made sense.

"There's still lube in that bottle, right?" he murmured between kisses.

I glanced over at the bottle we'd almost used up, and saw there was still some left. "Yeah. We'll need to get some tomorrow, though."

"Fine. Fine. Just . . . long as there's enough for right now."

"Mm-hmm. Plenty." I kissed him again. I wasn't in a hurry to get to the lube. Except I kind of was. But I wasn't. Damn, I could never decide—spend half the night on foreplay or get right to fucking him?

"C'mon, baby," he whispered, barely breaking the kiss. "Want . . . want you. Now."

Well that made the decision a hell of a lot easier. I kissed him one more time, then pushed myself up. "Turn over."

Dalton grinned. Then he turned onto his stomach, and I couldn't get the lube on quick enough. Most guys I'd been with liked switching, but Dalton seemed to love bottoming. I wasn't going to argue with him—not when he was enjoying it so much, and not when it felt so damn good to be in him. Especially since we'd gotten the all-clear from medical and didn't have to use rubbers anymore.

I positioned myself over him and guided myself to his hole. Dalton whimpered softly as I pushed in.

"You okay?" I asked.

Another whimper, this one very clearly a happy sound.

As he relaxed, taking me more easily, I stared down and watched myself slide in and out. Watched my hands on his ass cheeks, then running up his back, over his tattoo, back down, then on his ass again. I loved how it was so easy to see where one of us ended and the other started—dark as I was and light as he was, there was no mistaking who was who. Something about it—about seeing my hands on Dalton's body and my dick moving in him—was too fucking hot for words.

The muscles in his back rippled with the shudder running up his spine, and we both groaned as he tightened around me. "God, you feel good," he groaned.

"You feel amazing." I kneaded his ass as I fucked him slowly.

"I can . . ." He looked over his shoulder, hunger written all over his face. "I can take it hard."

"Yeah? You sure?"

"Uh-huh. C'mon." He rocked his hips like he could get mine to move. "*C'mon.*"

Grinning, I moved a little faster. Then faster. Then I slammed into him, and he clawed at the edge of the mattress as his back arched.

"More!" The pillow muffled his voice, but not the hunger, and I gave him more. "Don't stop," he pleaded. "Oh God, Chris, don't stop."

I gritted my teeth and fucked him as hard as I could. Hard enough it smarted every time my hips smacked into his ass. Hard enough to make him yelp and gasp—Jesus, fucking him like this brought sounds out of him I'd never heard before. Strangled, helpless moan-sobs that were *almost* curses.

And maybe some of those were coming from me because I'd never felt this good in my life. The hot, slick heat around my dick. The gorgeous man under me, begging for more. The orgasm building fast like my body had completely forgotten I'd come in the last hour. The utter fucking bliss of riding Dalton hard while he cried out and moaned like it was the most amazing thing he'd ever felt.

Then a shudder ran through him, jolting him forward and making him clench hard around me, and he sucked in a breath, shuddered again, and whimpered helplessly with the force of his second orgasm of the night. I rode it out, trying to hold my own back, but there was nothing in the world hotter than Dalton in the throes of an orgasm, especially when we both knew it was one I'd given him, and I followed him right over the edge. I roared as I forced myself as deep as he could take me, and I unloaded inside him as we both shook and moaned.

I collapsed over him. He sighed under me. I managed to pull out, but I couldn't find the willpower to get off him, though I did hold myself up enough that he could still breathe.

As he caught his breath, he murmured, "Probably good we didn't do this part out on the beach."

I laughed and burrowed against the warm skin of his neck. "We'd go to jail unless I could figure out how to keep you quiet."

His laugh was a drunken, sleepy sound. "Sounds kind of hot when you put it like that."

"Of course it does." I kissed his neck and finally managed to flop onto my back next to him. After a few more minutes of coming back down, we cleaned ourselves up, then dropped right back on the bed.

I had no idea how long we lay there, just relaxing on top of the rumpled sheets. Somehow, I didn't doze off. That was saying something, considering how relaxed I was after he'd gotten me off twice.

Eventually, Dalton rolled onto his side, facing me, and I mirrored him. I'd expected him to be half asleep, but there was something unexpectedly intense in his expression. Like he'd been deep in thought while I'd been drifting on a post-sex high.

"What's wrong?" I asked.

"Nothing. I'm just thinking."

"What about?"

He searched my eyes, biting his lip. "It's, um . . ." He hesitated, then finally draped his arm over me as he said, "I don't . . . I don't think I want just sex from you."

I swallowed. "So, like, a relationship?"

Dalton hesitated, but then he nodded, his stubble hissing across the pillowcase. "I don't usually do casual anyway, but to be honest, it kind of feels like . . ." He bit his lip.

"Like, what?" I nudged.

Pulling in a deep breath, he touched my face, and his expression was so serious, it made my heart thunder. He watched his thumb tracing my cheekbone. "Kind of feels like a relationship is what we've been doing all this time. Like we added this part as an afterthought."

I was already nodding before he'd even finished saying it. "Yeah. Yeah, I think you're right. Makes me feel like an idiot for not coming out to you sooner." I smoothed his hair. "Could've been doing this months ago."

He laughed, cuddling closer to me. "Better late than never, right?"

"True." I kissed him softly. Dalton as my boyfriend? Fuck yes. *Fuck yes!* It really did feel like we'd been doing this all along, but actually saying it out loud? Fuck. Yes.

As I settled back on the pillow, though, another thought worked its way in, and I couldn't help frowning. "This might make things kind of hairy at work if one of us gets promoted and the other doesn't."

Dalton scowled. "I know. Especially if Anderson gets kicked out of Harbor. First person to make MA1 is going to end up LPO of the duty section."

I nodded. Neither of us said it, but he knew the regs as well as I did. If we were peers, dating was no big deal. If one of us suddenly outranked the other, that got muddier. If one of us became Lead Petty Officer, that was a whole new bucket of shit. There was no way we could stay in the same duty section if that happened. Which sucked, but at least we'd be able to keep dating. All we'd have to do was swap with someone else. One of us would work nights, the other would work days, and we'd wedge in a relationship during our days off.

"We'll make it work one way or the other." I ran my hand up and down his back. "Let's get through the exam, see what happens, and go from there."

Dalton nodded. "Good idea."

"And for tonight . . ." I trailed my fingers down his side. "You want to stay here?"

Dalton grinned. "You know if I do, we'll be up half the night."

"You say that like it's a bad thing."

"It's not, but we do have the exam at ass thirty in the morning."

"Mm-hmm." I curved my hands down over his ass and gave each cheek a firm squeeze. "And we'll get some sleep. But I really want to fuck you again."

Dalton sucked in a sharp breath and squirmed against me. "Well, damn. When you put it like that . . ."

I laughed. "Thought you'd see it my way. And as long as it's lights out by 2200, we'll be fine. That gives us plenty of time."

"It does. A few hours at least."

"Mmm." I dipped my head to kiss his throat. "I think I can work with that."

Dalton laughed drunkenly, cradling the back of my head as he stretched his neck out to expose more skin. "You're gonna get me all fired up again."

"Am I?" I nipped his jaw. "What a shame."

We spent most of the evening in bed having lazy sex until neither of us could move anymore and then lying there talking or dozing. We got up long enough to hunt down something to eat. Then we wound up right back between the sheets, kissing and playing around but not getting much farther than that because holy fuck, a man could only come so many times. Once we were completely wrung out and exhausted—and we'd triple-checked our alarms were set to get us up stupidly early—we settled in to go to sleep.

He was out in no time. I stayed awake for a little while, mostly running through everything we'd talked about earlier. I was nervous about the exam and both of our chances at getting promoted, and the investigation that had inexplicably gone quiet nagged at me. But I felt better than I had recently. If there'd been evidence of wrongdoing, the investigation would've heated up. If going quiet meant Anderson was getting off with a slap on the wrist, I didn't like it, but I could live with it as long as Dalton and Rhodes could move on.

I cuddled closer to Dalton and kissed the back of his shoulder.

We'd be okay. Careers. Relationship. Dalton's injuries. Yeah—it was all good. Nothing to worry about now except getting those promotions. And we'd both been studying for that exam for months. Dalton seemed to have his head back together from the concussion. He wasn't a hundred percent yet but enough to sit for an exam he'd already taken half a dozen times and had been studying for since October.

Yeah. We'd be all right.

I kissed his shoulder again, then closed my eyes and let sleep come and get me.

And for the first time since Dalton's accident, I didn't dream.

CHAPTER 13

DALTON

Advancement exams were miserable things. It was like taking the SAT, except it was all military-related. And they were fucking cruel about it—not only did it start at 0730, even for those of us who worked nights, but they didn't let us bring in our goddamned coffee. As far as I was concerned, that was a hell of an oversight from the Geneva Convention.

There was nothing that said we couldn't load up on caffeine beforehand, though, so Chris and I swung into the Starbucks drive-thru on the way to base. Once we had our coffee, we sipped happily while we waited in the long, slow crawl to get to the gate.

The coffee hadn't even started to kick in, but I was jittery. Nerves had me almost vibrating. I couldn't decide if that meant the coffee was a good idea or a colossally bad one, but hopefully my heart could take it.

"Hey." Chris nudged me as he put his cup in the holder. "You're twitchy."

"Can't imagine why," I muttered into my own cup. "No pressure or anything, right?"

"No point in being nervous." He gave my shoulder a friendly squeeze. "You know this shit inside and out. We've been studying for months."

"Yeah, and I had my brain knocked around in my skull."

His smile faded and he looked at me with palpable concern. "I thought your head was doing better."

"It is. It's a lot better. But sometimes I still have to really think about things I *know* I know. Like how to pull up a contact on my phone or where I put my *razor* when it's right in front of me."

"Just take your time." He put his hand over mine. "You know how it is. They give us a ton of time for the exam, and we both usually finish with an hour or two to spare. There's no shame in using all that time if you need it." He glanced at me and smiled. "We got this."

I smiled back. It was tempting to lean across the console and steal a kiss, but I didn't dare. Not out here in the open, with cameras and our peers everywhere. I decided that long look would hold me over, though. Chris's smile made my spine tingle; I knew exactly how we'd be celebrating after we were done with the exam.

He parked outside the security building. Coffee in hand, we headed inside. Downstairs, signs directed anyone taking the MA1 exam to classroom three.

My nerves weren't getting any better, but I took Chris's advice to heart. We had this. We both knew our shit. Even with my bell rung, I knew this stuff, and as long as I cut myself some slack and took some extra time, I'd be okay.

We were almost to the door when a voice stopped us in our tracks. "MA2."

We both turned, as did three other MA2s loitering in the hallway, and my gut clenched at the sight of Chief Lasby. Especially since he was looking right at me.

He beckoned sharply. "Can I talk to you for a minute, Taylor?"

I chewed the inside of my lip. When a chief asked if he could talk to you, it was as good as an order to drop everything and listen. So I nodded. "Yes, Chief."

Beside me, Chris shifted his weight. I glanced at him and gave a subtle nod toward the classroom. He nodded back before he kept walking. At the door, he tossed his coffee cup in the trash, then went inside. The other MAs quickly made themselves scarce too.

And I was alone in the hallway with Chief Lasby.

"I'm glad I caught you, MA2." His eyes darted back and forth as if he wanted to make sure we were absolutely alone. Then he dropped his voice. "Listen, Big Navy wants to dig deeper into what happened. They're classifying it as a Bravo class mishap, and they want a more thorough investigation."

A chill ran through me. I was well aware of how serious the incident had been, but the Bravo class label was yet another reminder of how bad it could have been if the waves had been slightly higher or the water slightly colder or if the rescue attempts had taken even a few minutes longer. How easily the boat, the cold, or the water could've killed me or Rhodes and upgraded the whole thing one measly step to an Alpha class. I shuddered.

"Okay," I croaked, my mouth suddenly dry. "So what happens next?"

"What happens next is there's an investigator coming in who wants to talk to you, Rhodes, and Anderson."

My stomach had already been a ball of nerves because of the exam. Now it felt similar to how it had right before the concussion had had me puking my guts out. "When?"

"He flew in last night. He's expecting you today at 1100."

I very nearly launched my meager breakfast onto Chief Lasby's boots. *Today? Right after the exam?* "Uh. Oh. Okay."

"He'll be waiting for you in my office."

Good thing I was already in uniform. "Yeah. Okay. Will do, Chief."

He nodded sharply. "And remember, just tell him what happened as best you can remember." His brow pinched. "Nobody's expecting your memory to be completely clear. Not after that bang on the head."

"No, I remember clearly."

He studied me, his unspoken skepticism making my skin crawl. I did remember. Didn't I? There were bits and pieces that were hazy, but I remembered the important things. Right?

Chief Lasby put a heavy hand on my shoulder. "This is serious, MA2. Don't try to fill in gaps you don't remember clearly. Just tell them what you know *for certain*." His hand seemed heavier. "You don't want anyone taking the fall for something you *think* you remember. The Navy doesn't like to let things go as accidents, and the investigators will be looking for someone to blame."

But there is *someone to—*

My blood turned cold.

I swallowed.

"We're all on the same team, right?" Lasby went on. "Sailors look out for each other. MA1 Anderson already talked to him, and he assured me he didn't throw you or Rhodes under the bus."

"Under the—" Well apparently I didn't need any more caffeine. I was wide awake now. "With all due respect, under the bus for what?"

Lasby's features hardened and his eyes bore right into me. "We discussed this, MA2. You had a responsibility on that boat."

My jaw fell open. "And I was outranked by the coxswain."

He glared at me. "Look, if you're going to pull off being an MA1 yourself, you're going to need to learn when to step up and own your responsibility. MA1 Anderson outranks you, but as the only Level II coxswain on the boat, you had a responsibility too."

"I . . ." I gaped at him. "I told him a *dozen* times we shouldn't go out there. When we hit the nets, I was literally on my way to tell him *again*."

Lasby lifted his chin and narrowed his eyes. "So you weren't watching over the bow anymore."

"No! I couldn't see a damn thing anyway, and I was trying to tell him to take us back into the harbor so we—"

"So you weren't looking when you *could* have seen those fish nets."

I blinked. "In those conditions? Even if I'd been looking right then, we can barely see the nets in clear, calm water."

"MA1 Anderson has stated he was counting on you to see debris in the water. You turned away from your post, and the boat tangled in a net."

I stared at him, disbelieving what I was hearing. "Chief, I told you—I couldn't have seen—"

"I know what you've told me." He sighed as if I was trying his patience. "Listen. Everyone has to take responsibility for their roles in what happened out there. It was a terrible accident, but this could end a man's career. You know MA1 Anderson and his wife have a baby on the way, right? Think about them."

I swallowed, certain I could taste both seawater and bile.

What about me? I could have died. Rhodes could have died. What the fuck?

Lasby smiled and gave a slight nod as if he'd taken my stunned silence for agreement. "Anyway. The investigator will be waiting for you in my office." He clapped my shoulder and jerked his head toward the classroom. "Good luck on the exam."

"Thanks, Chief," I said automatically.

After he'd gone, I stared at the empty hallway for a full minute before I shuffled into the classroom. I dropped into the empty desk chair beside Chris, my mind reeling and my stomach doing things I really didn't need it to be doing right now.

Chris looked at me. "You okay?"

I shook my head. I didn't dare speak. God knew who else in this room was in Chief Lasby's pocket, and anyway, if I opened my mouth I was liable to get sick.

The worst feeling of *oh fuck, I'm so screwed* started settling on my shoulders like a wet, heavy blanket. I knew what was happening. The command had dragged its feet on the internal investigation. The longer it took for Big Navy to get involved and send in their own team, the more likely our memories would get cloudy. Our stories would be more easily massaged by suggestions.

Or by outright fucking gaslighting.

I knew what was happening now just like I knew what had happened out there on the water. Yeah, everything was fuzzy after I'd gone into the drink, but before that? I remembered. MA1 Anderson had nearly gotten both me and MA3 Rhodes killed, and now I was being pressured by a higher-up to lie to save Anderson's ass. So he could continue on his merry way through a career as—

The proctor silenced everyone in the room, startling me out of my thoughts. My stomach lurched again as the proctor started handing out the exams.

By the time the test began, I was still a jittery half-panicked mess. I stared down at the exam. Nothing made sense. It wasn't the concussion this time, either. Sure, the knock on the head made it harder to parse things—I had to read a little slower and give myself a bit more time to process than I was used to—but it was the chief's words echoing in my ears that jumbled everything on the page.

Oh fuck.

I am so screwed.

After the exam was over, Chris tried to get me to tell him what was going on, but I promised him I'd fill him in later. Right now, I just needed to get to Chief Lasby's office.

When I walked into the office, I was immediately uncomfortable. I knew in a heartbeat I should have asked to speak to the investigator someplace else. Neutral territory. Someplace that didn't feel so . . . biased. It was just a room—cramped, full of gunmetal gray file cabinets and a desk covered in drab green folders and picture frames—but it was *Lasby's* office. His presence and his authority and his threats hung over everything like stale cigarette smoke.

The investigator rose behind Lasby's desk. "Come on in, MA2."

Trying to hide my nausea, I shut the door, then approached the desk. The investigator was a tall commander with a shaved head and a shitload of ribbons on his white uniform. There were Iraq and Afghanistan campaign ribbons, several I didn't recognize, and a Purple Heart. He had scars on one side of his face, and there was a deep gouge in his forearm. This wasn't someone who'd skated through his career as a desk jockey.

He extended his hand across the table. "MA2, I'm Commander Worley. Just going to ask you some questions."

I shook his hand. "Okay, sir." We both sat, and I tried to will my stomach to settle while I waited for him to speak.

He skimmed over the papers in front of him before he looked right at me. "First, I'd like you to tell me everything that happened on the night in question. Starting when you went out on watch."

I moistened my lips. I could see a copy of my statement peeking out from beneath his notepad. He already knew the story, but he wanted me to repeat it anyway. I'd have done the same thing if I were on his side of the desk. It was the quickest way to refresh his memory and mine and see if there were any glaring holes in the statement I'd already made ages ago and my account today.

I took a deep breath and told him everything.

When I was done, he made some notes before meeting my gaze across Lasby's desk. "You're a Level II coxswain. MA1 Anderson is only a Level I. Rank notwithstanding, you have the qualification and with it the responsibility." He inclined his head. "There a reason why his discretion overrode yours?"

"He was the assigned coxswain for the patrol. I had to defer to him."

Worley studied me. When he furrowed his brow, some of the scars on his cheek and temple deepened, as if to remind me this was a man who'd been through hell and didn't have the patience for a dipshit like me. "According to your statement, you were on the bow before the boat snagged on the nets. When the incident occurred, you had stepped away from your position. Why?"

I swallowed. "To tell MA1 Anderson to turn back."

"But he was the assigned coxswain, as well as your superior." There was a hint of challenge in his tone. *Almost* sarcasm. My heart sank deeper than before. He'd already heard from Anderson. Worse, Chief Lasby had gotten to him. He'd given him the story the way he wanted it told. Instead of my testimony being able to stand on its own merit, everything I said was being stacked up against that of a respected— and connected—chief and his pet MA1.

I fought the urge to squirm under the commander's scrutiny. "I felt that MA1 Anderson's actions as coxswain were putting myself and MA3 Rhodes into physical danger. I made the decision to override him and take control of the boat. By force if necessary."

Worley's eyebrows shot up. "By force?"

"If necessary, yes, sir."

"What kind of force?"

"I hadn't decided yet, sir. I'd only made the decision to remove him from command of the boat."

"I see." He looked down at his notes for a painfully long moment. "I understand it's procedure for the boat's gunner to secure the weapon in rough seas." His eyes flicked up to mine. "There a reason you hadn't done so?"

"My primary concern was watching for debris or obstacles, sir."

"Were you aware that fishing nets were a possible danger?"

"Yes, sir. We've had boats get tangled in them before."

"I see." He made a note, then folded his hands on top of the pad. "Tell me about what happened after you went overboard."

I shuddered. "I don't remember much, sir."

"Tell me what you do remember."

I took a deep breath and gave myself a moment. "I remember fighting with the inflators on my vest, but I couldn't get them inflated."

"Why not?"

"They're not auto-inflators. I couldn't get my fingers around the handles. Not while I was trying to swim and keep control of the rifle."

Worley wrote something down.

When he was done, I continued. "At one point, I surfaced, and the hull of the boat hit me. I was . . ." *Darkness. Saltwater. Copper.* I shivered, the chair creaking and giving me away. "I might've been unconscious for a few seconds. Next thing I knew, the vest was inflated, the rifle and my police belt were gone, and I was at the surface."

"MA3 Rhodes was with you at this point." It wasn't a question.

I nodded. "Yes, sir."

"Did she make any attempt to throw you a life ring before getting into the water herself?"

"I don't know, sir. If she did, I didn't see it." I paused, then quickly added, "I couldn't have grabbed onto it if she had, honestly."

He wrote some more notes.

The interview continued until I was almost hoarse from answering the same questions over and over. Sometimes he'd word them differently, but it was like he was trying to find an inconsistency in my story. Which of course an investigator needed to do, but it was more like he already knew there was an inconsistency, and he was bound and determined to find it.

"*Nobody's expecting your memory to be completely clear,*" Lasby had said. "*Not after that bang on the head.*"

Icy sweat trickled down my spine. That was what he was doing, wasn't he? Looking for that slip that would kill my credibility because the TBI had scrambled my brain. Jesus.

When we were finally finished, I was sweating and shaky. Partly because I hadn't eaten in way too long, partly because I'd been up since way too early, and partly because I felt like I'd just been interrogated as a suspect, not a witness. Or a *victim*.

He dismissed me, and I went into the men's room to collect myself. Somehow I managed not to throw up, and instead I splashed some cold water on my face. Hands on the sink, I stared at a crack in the porcelain snaking toward the half-rusted drain and focused on breathing.

Commander Worley was probably a standup officer and a solid investigator. He'd probably come into this with no bias. But somehow,

Chief Lasby had gotten to him, and he'd tainted Worley's perspective.

It wasn't hard to do. I was a cop—I knew more than most people how easy it was to sway someone. There was a reason we always had the involved parties of a domestic questioned separately and by different officers. Otherwise, whoever questioned the first person was likely to be biased by their answers, and the second person wouldn't stand a chance at a fair investigation.

On paper, Worley probably wasn't supposed to have contact with anyone except Anderson, Rhodes, and myself. Maybe Chris and the others involved in the rescue. But Chief Lasby was in charge of HPU. Of course he'd speak to the investigator. All he had to do was let a few subtle comments slip to put some chinks in our credibility.

MA2 Taylor is going to make a solid leader someday. Especially once he learns to assert his authority before *a situation gets out of hand.*

Once MA3 Rhodes goes to coxswain's school, she'll be calmer. Not so quick to overreact to things.

Shame about that concussion. Really did a number on the poor kid's mind.

I sighed at the thought. That was all it would take. A few bugs in Worley's ear about me and Rhodes, and every single word we said would be filtered through a lens of bullshit. It didn't matter what I'd said in that room. Commander Worley already knew the truth. Or rather, the truth that would go into the official report on the incident.

Heart in my feet, I continued down the hall. I needed food. I needed sleep. I needed—

Chris. I definitely needed Chris.

I took out my phone and texted him. *You up for a late lunch?*

CHAPTER 14
CHRIS

"**A**re you fucking *kidding* me?" I stared at Dalton, struggling to comprehend what he'd just told me.

Dalton shook his head, pacing back and forth across my kitchen, boots clomping on linoleum. He'd stripped off his blouse, and any other day I'd have been ogling the way that dark blue T-shirt hugged his chest and the blue digicam pants showed off his ass. And even now I noticed it, but I was way too fixated on what he was telling me to even think about hauling him off to bed.

"The guy fucking interrogated me like I was the one who caused the whole thing," he went on. "And . . . I mean, fucking Lasby! He came at me right before the exam too." Dalton ran a shaking hand through his hair. "I bombed it, man. I fucking—" His voice cracked. When he looked at me, he didn't quite have tears in his eyes, but I'd have bet money he was close, especially as he whispered, "I fucking *bombed* it."

I stepped closer and wrapped him up in my arms. "I'm sorry. That was fucked up."

"I know. And . . . man, my career is riding on this." He sighed heavily and leaned his head against my shoulder. "*Fuck . . .*"

Fuck was right. Those exams were tough even when you weren't stressing about other shit.

"Jesus." I closed my eyes as I stroked his hair. "He's trying to sabotage you. Your exam and your testimony."

"No shit." He sighed. "Fuck. What do I do? It's not like I can prove anything one way or the other. And the fact that the investigator was talking to me like that . . ." He drew back and shook his head as he leaned hard against the counter. "I mean, that's the first thing they teach us, right? When a suspect thinks you're accusing him of something, he's probably getting paranoid for a reason."

"Yeah, but sometimes that reason isn't that the suspect is guilty of something—it's that they know the investigator is trying to corner them."

Dalton's shoulders sagged. "God, this is so fucked up."

"It is. But you've done everything you're supposed to do. You told the investigator the truth. What else could you do? You know damn well Anderson was in the wrong. And it's not like Lasby will hear what you said. Everything's confidential except the result of the investigation."

"Yeah, and if Anderson gets strung up, Lasby will know damn well I threw the fucker under the bus." He slouched against the counter. "And I mean, confidential or not, I don't trust the guy not to tip my hand to Lasby. I got the feeling Lasby had already buttered him up to be against me, so . . ." Dalton flailed his hand. "So they've probably already decided Anderson didn't do anything wrong, and when this is all over, he'll be back at the helm and I'll be out of the Navy because I didn't get fucking promoted."

"There's still another advancement cycle."

"And what good does that do me?" he snapped, glaring at me. "My next set of evals are going to be shit because I'm not functioning as a coxswain and I'm sure as shit not leading Sailors." As soon as he'd finished, he closed his eyes and sighed. "I'm sorry. I'm . . . This isn't your fault. I'm sorry."

"It's okay." I put a hand on his shoulder. "Listen, why don't we go get something to eat? Chill for a bit, clear our heads, and maybe . . . I don't know. Think of something."

Dalton nodded. He wrapped his arms around me and kissed me softly. "Okay. And I mean it—I'm sorry."

I kissed him, letting it go on a little longer. "Don't worry about it. Let's go."

We were both too lazy to change into civvies, so we straightened our uniforms, put our blouses back on, and left my apartment. I drove us back on-base, and we decided on the food court at the Exchange. It wasn't the greatest food on the planet, but it was close by, cheap, and there was usually something available that wasn't gross. This time of day, there wouldn't be long lines either, not even at the Taco Bell or Subway.

As we walked in, I asked, "What are you in the mood for?"

"Depends," Dalton muttered. "What can I sprinkle a few ground-up painkillers on without tasting them?"

I eyed him. "You hurting?"

"No. Just feel like getting fucked up." He was scanning the food court like he was trying to settle on a place. When he caught me staring at him, he chuckled. "I'm kidding. I'm not like that." He shook his head and looked around again. "I don't know. I'm hungry, but just thinking about eating is making me nauseous."

"Like post-concussion nauseous? Or post-Lasby bullshit nauseous?"

"Yes."

I frowned, and it was damn hard to fight the urge to wrap an arm around his waist. We were in uniform, though, so I had to be careful. I opened my mouth to say something, but someone else beat me to it.

"Hey guys." MA3 Rhodes's voice stopped me in my tracks, and we both turned around.

The instant I saw her, my stomach dropped. She was in civvies, hair pulled up in a messy ponytail, but even the Rick & Morty T-shirt and ripped jeans didn't make her look relaxed. She was about as tense as some kid who'd just gotten their ass chewed in boot camp.

"What's wrong?" Dalton asked. Apparently it wasn't just me.

Her lips pulled tighter and she looked away for a second. Folding her arms, she growled, "You get to talk to the investigator yet?"

I wasn't sure about discussing this out in the open, but the food court was just noisy enough to create a certain amount of privacy. You had to be really close to someone to actually hear what they were saying. Anyone more than a couple feet away from us wouldn't catch a thing.

Dalton kept his voice down. "Yeah. Just got back a little while ago. You?"

Rhodes's jaw was tight and she looked like she was close to either blowing up or breaking down. "I talked to him this morning." Her voice wavered and she folded her arms across her blouse. "I mean at least he didn't try to tell me what to say like Lasby did, but still."

"It's bullshit," Dalton muttered.

"Yeah it is. And it gets worse." She shifted her weight. "Right before I went in to talk to the investigator, Lasby pulled me aside and told me they're considering downgrading my award."

Dalton and I both straightened, exchanging wide-eyed glances.

"What?" he said.

She hugged herself tighter, shifting her weight. "Senior Chief Curtis put me in for a Medal of Commendation, but Lasby said that's on hold until the investigation is over. Until they decide if I should've broken protocol by jumping in with Dalton." Her arms dropped to her sides, and she exhaled hard. "And they're still hung up on whether I did the right thing letting go of that stupid rifle. The way he's talking about it, I'll be lucky to get a Navy Achievement Medal because I was just doing my job. And if MA1 Anderson goes down, I can kiss any kind of medal goodbye and go to Captain's Mast instead."

"Captain's Mast?" I sputtered. "What the fuck for?"

She pursed her lips like she was forcing them not to tremble. "He said if Anderson goes down, Taylor and I are going with him because I broke protocol and because we were all derelict in our duty." She blew out a breath. "How the fuck was I derelict in anything? Because I didn't physically wrestle Anderson to the deck and force him not to take the boat out there?" She was getting louder and more pissed off with every syllable. "Or because I let go of that stupid goddamned rifle instead of holding onto eight pounds of dead fucking weight while I was trying to keep a man twice my size afloat?"

I stared at her incredulously. "They're . . . what the . . ."

She huffed out a sharp breath. "And I mean, they said I should've thrown you a life ring. You were unconscious and sinking. How the fuck would a life ring have helped?"

Dalton visibly shuddered. So did I.

Rhodes cursed softly, staring down at her hands as she played with the hem of her T-shirt. "I'm done. My enlistment is up next year, and I'm just . . . I'm done. I'm getting out."

"Aw, shit," I said. "Man, I want to tell you to stick with it, but after all this . . ."

"No fucking way." She snorted. "I jumped into the goddamned ocean in February so my shipmate wouldn't die, and they're up my ass about a *gun*. Best case scenario, I get a NAM like everyone else because I was just doing my job, not going above and beyond."

"What the *fuck*?" Dalton snarled. "You didn't go above and beyond? That's bullshit! *And* they want to discipline you for doing exactly what any goddamned person in their right mind would have done."

"Yeah, but if they acknowledge that, then they have to admit their golden MA1 might've fucked up and put us in jeopardy in the first place. It's all . . . *fuck*." Rhodes sniffed, and she turned away for a second. She wasn't crying yet, but she was damn close, so we gave her a chance to compose herself. After a moment, she wiped her eyes, took a deep breath, and faced us again. "I mean it. Come January? I'm fucking done with the Navy." She shrugged heavily, like there was a phantom waterlogged rifle weighing her down. "I risked my neck, and the best I can hope for is to not get punished for it and maybe get the equivalent of a 'good job' sticker. I'm just done."

Dalton and I exchanged glances, both of us scowling. Rhodes was a damn fine Sailor and an excellent MA. The Navy and the MA rate were better because of her. She had some serious potential to be the kind of leader our rate desperately needed. Getting out after eight years was a hell of a shame.

But I didn't blame her. There were only so many times you could get fucked with the sandpaper condom of political games and favoritism before enough was enough.

She rolled her tense shoulders and glanced outside. "I have to go. My husband is waiting in the car." She motioned toward the doors. "I'll see you guys later."

"Okay." Dalton sighed. "And I'm sorry you're getting a shit deal on all of this. For what it's worth, the only reason I would've handled things differently in your shoes is I don't think I have the balls you do."

She eyed him uncertainly, then broke into a quiet laugh. "Nah. You'd be amazed how fast your balls drop when your friend is in trouble."

He smiled and gathered her into a hug. "Thank you again. And fuck everyone who says you didn't do the right thing."

"If I had it to do over, I wouldn't have done anything differently." As she let him go, a little smirk played at her lips. "Aside from maybe tossing Anderson over."

Dalton laughed softly. "Maybe that's why they haven't let him come back to Harbor. They know half of us would do it if we got the chance."

"Amen to that," I grumbled.

"Yeah," Rhodes said. "Okay, I have to go. I'll see you guys at work tomorrow."

My stomach lurched. Just what we all needed—another shift with all this crap hanging over our heads.

After Rhodes had gone, Dalton looked around at the food court options, and it wasn't just the fluorescent lights that made him look a bit green.

I nudged him with my elbow. "Not hungry anymore?"

"Not really, no."

"Come on." I nodded in the direction Rhodes had gone. "Let's get out of here."

When we went to work the next night, Dalton was still obviously rattled from the shit before the exam and with the interrogator. Err, investigator. Neither of us had slept much. We'd both been too wound up and pissed off.

Now, as we trudged up the walk from the HPU parking lot with coffee cups in hand, he looked about as awake as I felt. Heavy shadows under his eyes. No expression on his face. Hand shaking whenever he sipped his coffee. Shoulders down. It was probably good we didn't have to carry a rifle aboard anymore—he'd have fallen over under the damn thing's weight.

Rifle or not, I didn't like the idea of him going out on patrol tonight. He shouldn't have been on the water at all, but especially after yesterday, he had no business out there. Not until Lasby and the investigation were out of his head.

Thank God he'd mostly recovered from the concussion. The first week had been rough, but after that, he'd been a lot better. He still sometimes had to stop and think before he found a word, and his balance wasn't a hundred percent, but the worst had cleared up pretty fast. The last thing he needed was to still be untangling his brain while Lasby and the investigator circled him like goddamned sharks.

Dalton was on the first watch too. He wasn't even awake yet, but half an hour after we'd arrived, he was on his way down to the boat with Powers and Simmons.

Rhodes joined me next to the HPU building's second story window. "How's he doing?"

I sighed. "Not good."

She scowled, watching the boat move away from the pier. "I wish I knew what to do. I've thought a hundred times about going to one of the chiefs in Security, but . . ."

"Yeah. Me too. But if Lasby's getting away with monkeying with this investigation, then I don't trust any of the senior enlisted. If we take it above *their* heads, we'll just get our dicks slapped for jumping our chain of command."

"No kidding."

We watched the boat in silence for a long moment.

"Kind of funny, isn't it?" She turned around and leaned against the window. "They tell us from day one we're supposed to use our chain of command, and if someone's being sheisty, go above them until we find someone who isn't." She looked at me, and damn if she didn't have exhaustion written all over her just like Dalton did. "But we all know if we do, they'll just send us back down, and then we'll be in deep shit for going over our boss's head. Like, what's the point, you know?"

I nodded. "I know. But man, there has to be something we can do. This investigation is in violation of—"

"And the minute we do, they'll find all the protocols Dalton and I violated." She let her head fall back against the glass with a heavy *thunk*. "We can take those assholes down, but I guarantee they'll drag us right down with them."

I scowled, staring out at the boat, which was getting smaller by the minute. I wanted to argue, but she was right.

Rhodes faced the water again, scowling hard. "Sometimes I still think about going to Chief Jackson or Senior Chief Curtis. They're good guys, you know?" Deflating slowly, she shook her head. "But . . . chiefs look out for chiefs."

"Yeah. They do." I sighed. Some things were true no matter what. The tide went in and out. The sun went down in the west. And chiefs looked out for chiefs.

There was nothing we could do. We had no allies. We had no proof of wrongdoing. Nothing to show Lasby was playing favorites. Nothing we could take to the Equal Opportunity officer to nail Chief Lasby for his homophobia. No write-ups, emails, orders, or witnessed comments that could get his ass hemmed up for trying to gaslight us and sandbag our statements against Anderson.

We had nothing except he said, we said, and the word of two MA2s and an MA3 didn't hold water against a chief. Not when we were taking it up with two other chiefs.

I wished like hell we could go above Lasby's head and get the rest of our chain of command involved, but we couldn't. Not only would they back him up over us, but Chief Lasby was the most dangerous kind of chief. He knew where the lines were and exactly how to cross them in practice without crossing them on paper. He knew how to keep Rhodes and Dalton in line by making it risky for them to tell the whole truth. He knew how to order Dalton and me apart without openly *saying* he was ordering us apart. With a few benign emails, he could have us on different shifts or kick one of us out of Harbor or . . . fuck, God only knew what he could do to us or to Rhodes.

I had no idea how to fix this.

All I knew was that we were on our own.

As he came in off watch, Dalton wasn't quite steady on his feet, though he did a damn good job of trying to hide it. He walked a bit slower than usual, stepping a bit more carefully.

When he reached the landside end of the pier where I was standing, I asked, "You okay?"

He nodded. "Yeah. Just, uh . . ." He motioned toward the harbor. "We hit some waves out there, and it was . . ." He chewed his lip.

"You have a flashback or something?"

"No. Kind of. I don't know." He rolled his shoulders and shook his head. "Just kind of a panicky thing. I got a little seasick, and when

I hurled off the stern, I lost my balance, and . . ." He shuddered. "I'm all right, though."

"All right? You're getting seasick and—"

"Chris." He patted the air. "I pulled myself together. I'm fine."

"Yeah, but has this happened before?"

He thought for a few seconds, then shrugged. "Yeah, but not very often."

"Not very . . ." I stared at him. "How many times?"

Dalton sighed, shaking his head. "Relax, okay? I can handle it."

"You shouldn't have to."

"No, but I don't have much choice. It's not right, but it's not like I can do anything except move forward, you know?"

"Yeah, I know." I watched him for a moment. God, the way his shoulders were tense and heavy at the same time, how he seemed rigid and so exhausted he could barely hold himself upright, was heartbreaking. It killed me that I couldn't touch him. Not here. "I hate seeing you like this."

"I know you do." He smiled faintly. "Sorry?"

"No, no. Don't be sorry. Just . . . you sure you're gonna be okay? You're scheduled for another watch later on."

Dalton nodded, swallowing hard. "Yeah. One day at a time, am I right?"

I scowled. He was getting noticeably better every time he went out on the water, but he was still noticeably not okay.

He must've seen it in my expression because he added, "I'll be fine, Chris."

"You were fine until that fucker messed you up," I growled. "It's bullshit they're not taking care of you and keeping you onshore until—"

"Chris." He gave my arm a light squeeze. "It sucks, but it is what it is. All I can do is work on getting better. And I *am*."

You shouldn't have to get better. *You were perfect before.*

He smiled. "Relax. And don't you have to go out on watch pretty soon?"

I glanced past him. "They're refueling. I've got some time. And I need to go get my gloves anyway."

Dalton nodded. "Okay. I should probably get to work on the boat reports."

As we headed inside, I asked, "You're doing all right with the reports? With your head and all?"

"Yeah. Sometimes I have a dyslexic moment and switch digits on a timestamp or something, but I just have Rhodes check them for me."

I grunted in acknowledgment but didn't say anything. I didn't like that he still had even that much trouble, but I supposed it was better than the problems he could have had after a concussion like that.

At the top of the stairs, he headed into the main office, and I went to the locker room. I took my gloves out of my locker, shut the door, and spun the dial. As I was tucking the gloves into my belt, someone came into the room. I grinned to myself. Had Dalton followed me in here? Maybe we could steal a minute as boyfriends instead of shipmates. I wasn't in the mood for much, but a kiss or two might be enough to salvage *some* of my mood.

I stepped out of the bank of lockers and halted. "MA1." I tried to make myself sound more surprised than irritated. "Didn't expect to see you down here."

"Yeah, I know." MA1 Anderson motioned toward a bank of lockers. "Just came down to get a few things."

"Oh." It occurred to me right then that Lasby still hadn't brought in another LPO to fill Anderson's position. After what had happened, Anderson's transfer out of HPU should have been permanent, or at least long enough to warrant bringing in someone else to take over. Long enough for his locker to be reassigned.

My stomach turned to lead. Lasby hadn't replaced Anderson because he didn't think Anderson was going to stay gone. Which did nothing to instill any faith in this investigation. I completely believed Dalton about how the investigator had come at him sideways, and this cemented what we'd already figured out—that this investigation was nothing more than a formality, and that Anderson was going to get off with, at worst, a slap on the wrist. And meanwhile Dalton would be dealing with the physical, mental, and professional consequences for . . . I didn't even want to think about how long.

Anderson looked around, releasing a sigh that sounded almost nostalgic. "Man, I miss this place. Even this shitty locker room."

I gritted my teeth.

You deserve to miss this place.

"I'm sure," was all I could say.

"Hopefully not for long, though." Anderson flashed a bright, if kind of tired smile. "I'm so ready to come back to Harbor. Working in Admin is fucking boring."

"It's . . ." I blinked. "It's *boring?*"

"Yeah." Anderson laughed dryly. "Going from driving boats to pushing paperwork is—"

"Is about the best thing you could have expected after what you did out there."

It was his turn to blink in surprise. "Excuse me, MA2?"

I clenched my teeth. "You're fucking lucky all they did was dump your ass behind a desk. You almost got two Sailors *killed.*"

His eyes narrowed. I was on seriously thin ice, but right then, I just didn't care. He outranked me, but that didn't change what he'd done that night.

"You think you should come back to Harbor?" I demanded. "What the hell makes you think you have any right to be at the helm of—"

"It was an accident," Anderson snapped. "There were fishnets under the damn water. And Taylor and Rhodes are fine."

"No, MA1. They are not *fine.* They got out of the water, and thank the Lord they weren't seriously hurt, but don't you dare tell me they're *fine.*" In the back of my mind, I could hear my parents warning me about military bearing and respecting rank, but I was too far gone to rein it back in. "Do you have any idea what something like that does to someone?"

His lips tightened, but his eyes darted away for a second. Some of the bravado slipped out of his posture. "Look, I—"

"What happened out there, that has been front and center in Dalton's life ever since that night. Front and fucking center, MA1. Do—"

"And you don't think it has been for me?" He glared at me, fury filling in where the bravado had pulled back. Jabbing a finger at me, he stepped closer. "You have no idea what my life has been like since that night. None."

I shrank some more of the space between us, glaring right back at him. "Boring, from the sound of it. That's gotta be rough, pushing papers around. Man, I think that would be even worse than, I don't know, getting smacked in the goddamned head by a *boat*."

His lips peeled back. "Watch yourself, MA2."

Fresh anger flared in my chest. "Or what? You got the brass balls to complain about being bored in Admin after your reckless ass almost got two people killed." I was distantly aware of the locker room door opening and of boots on concrete, but I was too heated to stop or look. "What were you thinking out there? That boat couldn't handle open seas in those conditions, and anyone with half a fucking brain knows that. What were—"

"What else was I supposed to do?" he growled. "There was a disabled boat out there. I couldn't just—"

"You call in the fucking Coast Guard and let them handle it!" I threw up my hands. "Or did you think it was better to have *two* disabled boats out there, plus our personnel in the water, so—"

"Hey! Hey!" Dalton wedged himself into the narrow space between us. Anderson took a few steps back.

Me, I kept going. "How many SAR swimmers and coxswains did you want to put in danger, MA1? Huh? Was it *that* hard for you to listen to an MA2? Did you have to be right so bad that—"

"MA2." Dalton put a hand on my chest. "Don't. It's not worth it, and you know it."

I turned my glare on him, but the look on his face stopped me dead. His tone had been gentle, almost pleading, but his eyes were hard.

Stand the fuck down, *Chris.*

I swallowed. Then I drew back a little and exhaled.

His expression softened. His hand stayed on my chest for a few seconds, but then he drew it back.

Anderson was about to say something, but right then, the locker room door banged open. "Taylor. Ingram." Chief Lasby. Son of a bitch. "My office. Now."

I cringed. Dalton swore under his breath. There was nothing we could do except follow him into the office he'd claimed. I didn't dare steal a look at Anderson to see if he was being a smug asshole. I didn't need to.

Lasby didn't even wait to make us uncomfortable this time. He slammed the door and immediately snarled, "What did I tell you both about discussing the incident with MA1 Anderson?"

I straightened, staring right at Lasby. "We were told not to, Chief."

"Exactly. And what were you doing in the locker room?"

I swallowed. "We were discussing—"

"You were discussing the incident." He stepped closer and got right in my face. "Did I not make it abundantly fucking clear that you weren't to discuss the case, MA2?"

You've made it abundantly fucking clear you're going to do anything you can to save MA1 Anderson's ass, yes.

But I just ground out, "Yes, Chief."

"Then why the hell did I just catch you idiots arguing with him about it?" He stepped back and glared at Dalton. "You want to tell me that?"

"It won't happen again, Chief," I said.

"That doesn't answer my question." He was back in my face again. "The incident is being investigated, MA2. There are people far above your paygrade handling this. You want me to have them investigating you for misconduct and insubordination while they're at it?"

I gulped. "No, Chief."

"That's what I thought." He glared at me for a long, uncomfortable minute before he stepped back again and jabbed a finger at both of us. "I hear so much as a rumor that either of you have made a peep about the investigation or MA1 Anderson or what happened on the boat, and you'll both be at Captain's Mast. Am I clear?"

In unison, we said, "Yes, Chief."

"Dismissed."

We left his office without hesitation and, like we had the first time he'd chewed our asses, went to the locker room to cool down. Fortunately, MA1 Anderson was gone.

As soon as the door was shut, I leaned against a locker. "Fuck. That was bullshit."

"I know it was." Dalton's hands were heavy on my shoulders, and his eyes bored right into me. "And I know you're pissed. So am I. But we've got to be the cooler heads on this. Don't give the command a reason to pull their focus away from the investigation."

I closed my eyes and let my head fall back against the locker while I tried to calm myself down. Dalton was right. As much as I'd been tempted to lay Anderson out, that would've been an express ticket to me going to the brig and the boat investigation conveniently disappearing. It shouldn't have been that way, but the investigation had been shady from the start. They wanted to bust Rhodes for breaking protocol? Ha. How about all the investigation protocols that had been bent, ignored, and outright broken from day one?

Fuck. Dalton *was* right. I'd lost my temper and damn near handed Lasby and his minions a reason to let the Navy "forget" about the boat incident.

I sighed again. "I'm sorry about all that."

Dalton shook his head. "Don't be. This is stressing us both out. If I'd been in there with Anderson, I might've done more than yell at him." He smirked halfheartedly. "Remember who's the hothead here."

I chuckled. "You haven't been that way for a long time, though."

"No, but if someone sets me off . . ."

"True." I glanced at the clock on the wall and sighed. "I better go. My watch starts in ten."

"Okay. Your place after shift?"

That made me smile a bit. "Definitely."

Then I stole a quick kiss and headed out to the pier.

Well, at least I had something to look forward to tonight.

CHAPTER 15

DALTON

The bullshit in the locker room and Lasby's office were, in a weird way, kind of a blessing. They were almost enough to distract me from how nervous I was out on the water as I went out on my second watch of the night.

The sun had gone down hours ago. If not for the lights around the harbor—basically stadium lights—it would've been a big black void around the boat. I kind of wondered if that would be better than being able to see the sliver glint of waves, especially since it was windy tonight. Not as bad as the night I'd gotten hurt, but enough to keep the boat continuously rocking even inside the harbor.

I was only half-panicking about the water, though. Sure, I had to do what had become a habit lately—being as subtle as possible about taking slow, deep breaths, clenching my teeth against seasickness that wasn't really seasickness, keeping a clear path between me and the railing at all times in case it stopped mattering whether or not it was seasickness. I'd be thrilled when the summer got here and the nights were hot and muggy; at least then it would be easy to explain why I was sweating.

But tonight I had other things to crowd into my rattled psyche. Those confrontations from earlier were bad news. Real bad. A sign that even though the command was deftly pushing the investigation off to the sides like a kid pushing vegetables around their plate and hoping no one noticed, tensions were still running hot. Something was going to give sooner or later.

It was only a matter of time before someone else snapped. Everything relating to the incident and its bullshit investigation was wearing me down. It was wearing Rhodes down. I'd known all along it was wearing on Chris too, but seeing him explode at Anderson tonight was unsettling as fuck. Thing was, Chris was about as level-headed as they came, especially for an MA. Our rate was known for its hotheads and even bullies, but that wasn't Chris. He'd always been even-keeled and calm. Hell, being around him was a big part of why I'd made a point of learning to get a handle on my temper.

So for him to lose it at Anderson . . . shit. How long before one of us really lost it? I didn't imagine anyone would get violent, but what if Chris had gone on longer tonight? What if I hadn't stepped in? What if Lasby had caught them instead of me?

Pushing out a slow breath, I stared down at my hands on the railing, ignoring the sliver flecks of light on rolling waves in my peripheral vision. I swallowed the nausea and concentrated on the situation back onshore. Chris was pissed about what Anderson had done, and he was pissed about the effect it had on me. He'd been angry already when he'd gone into the locker room. Angry because he'd just seen how messed up I'd been after coming in off watch.

I didn't blame him for being angry, but I was worried he'd finally lose it and say something he couldn't come back from. Something that could be the end of his career. I didn't want that on my shoulders.

I closed my eyes and exhaled, pretending not to notice the nausea burning in the back of my throat. Maybe he was right. Maybe I wasn't as okay as I needed to be. And maybe what I needed was to stop pretending I was before I really did have a full-on flashback or hurt myself or someone else. For my own sake and also for Chris's, something needed to change.

The Navy wasn't going to change anything. As it was, they should have been keeping me landside until I'd had a full psych eval. Any chief worth his anchors would've pulled me off the boat the first time I'd showed so much as a hint of PTSD. He'd have called bullshit on my "all clear."

The powers that be at Big Navy had no way of knowing how messed up I really was, and as long as I was out on the boat, as long as my physical and psychological recovery looked good *on paper*, the incident didn't look as serious. Chief Lasby could sweep it under the rug even though it was a goddamned Bravo class incident that was so, so not being handled the way it should've been.

There was nothing, however, that said I couldn't request a psych eval on my own. The results might pull me off the water and shove me behind a desk, and I didn't like that prospect, but it was better than continuing to sit on this powder keg. Maybe it would kill my career, or maybe it would convince someone on high to transfer me out of HPU. I didn't want to leave HPU, and I didn't want to be anything but a coxswain, but the fact was, I had to start thinking about my health. And about not giving Chris a reason to flatten MA1 Anderson. My career was probably toast no matter what. No point in killing his while I was at it.

I opened my eyes and gazed out at the terrifying dark water.

Tomorrow, I'd make a call.

And we'd see where the chips landed.

NAS Adams had a tiny on-base clinic with a few MDs and two psychologists. Usually that meant a hell of a waiting period to see one of the shrinks, but I got lucky—there'd been a cancellation.

Captain Hayley, a tired-looking white lady with a tight brown bun, perused my file while I sat in a chair in her office. She wasn't wearing blue cammies like I was, so apparently the base was finally getting around to switching to the green uniforms. That, or she'd just transferred in from a base that had made the change. The new uniforms were digicam like the ones we already wore, but with a mix of green and light brown. Ugly as fuck if they asked me, which they hadn't. Maybe these would stick around for the next five years, and I could retire before someone on high decided we needed a whole new wardrobe again. Assuming I lasted that long.

I squirmed in my chair, trying not to think about how my career was hanging by a thread.

Hayley put the folder down and looked at me across her desk. "After everything you've told me, and looking over the reports from the incident, I would highly recommend you visit a military medical facility for a complete psych eval and a more thorough evaluation of the traumatic brain injury. This needs to go in your Navy medical file. Not only so you can file for disability if the damage turns out to be permanent, but so the Navy is aware of any limitations you might have now."

"Thank you, ma'am." I released a breath. It shouldn't have been so vindicating for the doctor to tell me I needed all that, but damn, it was. "So, how do I do that? The nearest military hospital is . . . hell, I don't even know where it is."

"The closest would be either Lewis-McChord or Bremerton in Washington. If you can get yourself up there, I can make some calls and get you in sooner than later." She paused. "Do you have someone who can drive with you? You're okay to drive, but a long trip like that . . ."

"I can ask around."

She nodded. "Let me know if you can't find anyone. I'm sure the base can arrange some kind of transport."

"Thank you, ma'am."

"Do you have any questions?"

"No, ma'am. Thank you again."

She gave me some forms and dismissed me, sending me to the front desk to have them schedule me in at one of the medical centers in Washington. Once that was done, and my appointment was scheduled for two weeks from tomorrow, I headed out to the parking lot.

I was both relieved and anxious. Of course my command—and the Navy, really—wouldn't *want* me to go. If it went in my record that I had any lasting—possibly permanent—effects from the incident, that would mean a disability claim after I was discharged. The bean counters were bitter enough about paying out for vets who'd been hurt in combat. Coughing up even five or ten percent disability for something like this would probably make the assholes break out in hives.

I wasn't concerned about the money or disability claims. I wanted this on my record. I wanted to make sure the Navy had it in writing that what happened out on the water had caused real, quantifiable damage. I wanted someone to see that they had to take me off the water, at least until I had my head back together. If it killed my career, there wasn't much I could do, but maybe I could avoid someone else becoming collateral damage.

In my car, I took out my phone and looked up the Bremerton Naval Hospital. About two hundred miles from here. Sweet. My appointment wasn't on a work night, and the base was well within three hundred miles, so I didn't need to get an out-of-bounds chit signed off. All I had to do was go.

I would need to give Lasby a heads up, though, so I headed over to the security building to get that over with.

As I was walking in, Senior Chief Curtis was on his way out. He paused and looked me up and down. "Glad to see you steadier on your feet these days, MA2. How are you feeling?"

It was tempting to tell him the truth, but I just forced a smile and told him, "Much better. Thank you, Senior."

"Good to hear." He smiled back, then kept walking.

I watched him go, heart thumping and stomach roiling. I could tell him. I could go into his office, unload everything, and let him know why I had to make my own arrangements for my own psych eval when the command should have been all over this.

But those gold anchors on his uniform meant I couldn't trust him. My shoulders sagged. I really wanted to like the guy, and I really wanted to believe he was as cool as he seemed, but those anchors . . . nope. Couldn't do it. Chiefs looked out for chiefs.

I continued down the hall to Chief Lasby's office. With my heart in my throat, I tapped on the door.

"It's open," he grumbled.

I stepped into his office and automatically went to attention. "Chief."

"MA2." The "at ease" was unspoken, but his tone implied it, so I relaxed slightly. He put his pen down and sat back, eyeing me. "What can I do for you?"

I swallowed. "I, um, just came from medical."

"Oh? And what's the latest?"

"She'd like me to go to Bremerton for some tests."

"What kind of tests?"

Technically, I didn't have to tell him, but part of me wanted him to understand how much the incident had fucked me up. How it wasn't just something I could sweep under the rug and forget about. "Psych eval. Probably an MRI or a CT scan to see if there's any long term effects from the TBI."

His lips pursed as he nodded. "I see. You have a lift, or you driving yourself?"

"I've—" I hesitated. He didn't need to know I was going to ask Chris to drive me. "I'll work it out."

He made a quiet grunt of acknowledgment. "And you're going when?"

"Two weeks from tomorrow. Since I have the days off. The appointments are on Thursday morning, so I should be back that night."

He nodded. "All right. Why don't you go ahead and fill in a leave chit? Put it on my desk before you leave tonight. That way if you get hung up or they need you there longer, I've got you covered."

I blinked, surprised he was being this charitable. "Oh. Okay. Thanks, Chief."

"Don't mention it. Have that chit on my desk before the end of your shift."

"Will do."

On the way out of his office, I didn't know how to feel. I'd expected pushback, or at least some annoyance, but . . . nothing. He was completely okay with me doing this. What the hell?

Slowly, cold water spread through my veins. The more I thought about it, the more it made sense that Chief Lasby was okay with me going for the eval. He probably didn't want the incident to look serious on paper, but now that I thought about it, I could see where this might work to his advantage. If I had to guess, he liked the idea of the Navy documenting my TBI so it could be used to question the validity of any statements I made against MA1 Anderson. *Fuck.*

But the wheels were turning, and even if MA1 Anderson managed to get off with that inevitable slap on the wrist, at least someone could validate my problems. Maybe then someone could help me so I could eventually get back to doing my job.

For now, I needed to arrange a ride. I glanced at my watch. Chris would be out on patrol. I could text him, but he was most likely the coxswain today. No point in distracting him—we could talk when he was back on land.

I had my appointment. Things were in motion. Even if the

outcome wasn't the best thing for my career, or helped Lasby keep Anderson's career afloat . . . fuck it. I'd be on my way to getting some real useful *help*.

And I was already starting to feel like I could breathe again.

CHAPTER 16
CHRIS

"**MA2** Ingram, can I speak to you?"

Those were not words I wanted to hear from Chief Lasby. Not today. Not any day. Not when I hadn't even finished pouring myself some goddamned coffee. Especially not when I was still heated over how everything had gone down with Anderson the other night.

Unfortunately, Lasby outranked the shit out of me, so it wasn't like I could say, *No, Chief, as a matter of fact you* can't *speak to me. Please fuck off and eat a bag of dicks.*

So I set down the coffeepot, picked up the cup I'd just poured myself, put on a face that was as close to professional as I could muster, and turned around. "Sure, Chief."

He strolled across the main office. "Listen, I need you to do a duty swap. Two weeks from now, I'm sending MA2 Zachary to CMEO training, and I'm going to be a down a coxswain for a few days. If you can fill in for her, that'll give you a five-day weekend."

Oh. Well. Okay. That wasn't the worst thing he'd ever asked me to do.

In my head, I ran through my schedule, and I didn't have anything going on during the days he was asking me to work, so I shrugged. "Yeah, sure. I can swing that."

"Great." He smiled. "Thanks, MA2."

"No problem, Chief."

He gave a curt nod and headed back down the hall, probably to "his" office. I glared at his back, then rolled my eyes and started mixing sugar into my coffee. The request wasn't unreasonable. Duty swaps were completely normal. I just hated interacting with that asshole.

I'd help any of my fellow Sailors out, especially if they needed a duty swap, but only rank and military bearing kept me from telling Chief I wouldn't piss on him if he was on fire.

My coffee tasted bitter. Or maybe that was just me. The man was going to drive me insane before he finally transferred to . . . wherever he ended up going. Maybe they'd send him to Diego Garcia or something. That tiny island in the middle of nowhere was where careers were sent to die, and I sure as shit wouldn't cry if he went there.

A door opened downstairs. My hackles went up, and I listened as boots came up the stairs. *Now what?*

But as soon as I saw who it was, I smiled. "Hey."

"Hey." Dalton smiled back as he headed straight for the coffeepot, travel mug in hand.

"Junkie," I said.

He eyed me as he unscrewed the lid. "You want to see me without it?"

"No, thank you."

"That's what I thought." He paused to top off the mug. As he put the lid back on, he said, "By the way—are you busy on the sixteenth and seventeenth?"

I sighed. "Actually, yeah." I gestured over my shoulder with my thumb. "Chief asked me for a duty swap while MA2 Zachary is at CMEO training."

Dalton scowled. His narrowed eyes cut toward the hallway that led to the locker room and Lasby's office. "That son of a bitch."

"What? Why?"

"When did he ask?"

"Maybe five minutes before you got here?"

"Fucker." Dalton exhaled. "I told him like an hour ago that I'm going up to Bremerton for a psych and TBI eval. He probably figured out I was going to ask you to come with me."

I clenched my jaw so hard my teeth hurt. "That fucker."

"Right?" Dalton rolled his eyes. "I'll figure something out. I—"

"No, I'll tell him I can't do the duty swap. I can—"

"Chris." He put a hand on my chest and shook his head. "It's okay. I'm probably fine to drive myself, to be honest."

"Are you sure?"

"Yeah." He shrugged. "It's not that far, and I'll just stay overnight at the Navy Lodge. No big deal."

I didn't like the idea. Not at all. He was competent to drive, but how would the eval go? Would something set him off? Fuck with his PTSD? It wasn't the drive *to* Bremerton that worried me—it was the drive *back*.

As if he could read my thoughts—and hell, they were probably written all over my face—Dalton put a hand on my side. "I'll be fine. I promise."

I studied him, then sighed and nodded. "Okay. Just be careful, all right?"

A smirk played at his lips. "Yes, Dad."

"Shut up." I chuckled and pressed a quick kiss to his lips. "Don't make me put you over my knee."

"Ooh. Kinky." He winked, flashing a playful smile.

"You're a dork."

"Yeah, and you—"

Someone cleared his throat.

We jumped apart and turned, and fuck my life but Chief Lasby was standing in the doorway, arms folded across his blue digicams.

My heart hit the floor. Lasby's eyes flicked back and forth between us.

Then, without saying a word, he headed downstairs.

We were both silent for a long moment. Neither of us breathed. Even after the door opened and closed downstairs, we stayed still.

Dalton released his breath first. "Shit." He wiped a hand over his face. "So much for keeping this quiet at work."

I exhaled too and rested my hip against a desk. "Yeah. Damn. Why do I get the feeling he's going to find a way to fuck us over?"

"Because you've been working for him long enough to know that's exactly the kind of asshole he is."

And wasn't that the truth.

We had the next couple of days off, and not a moment too soon. From the second we woke up after sleeping off our shift, we agreed to shut out work until we had to go back. Just us. Relaxing. Catching our breath. Getting out from under the black cloud of Lasby and the investigation.

First things first—well, after a very long shared shower—was breakfast. It may have been three in the afternoon, but for two guys who worked nights, it counted as breakfast. Fortunately, there were quite a few restaurants in town that served breakfast all day, and after maybe ten minutes of searching, we picked one a few blocks from the downtown pier. It was kind of like that one we'd gone to for lunch a while back—family run, no-name, smelled amazing, and probably had recipes handed down from Grandma.

As we chugged coffee and looked over the menus, I kept stealing glances at Dalton. We'd promised to leave work under the radar until our next shift, but it was hard to make all that stress magically go away. Especially after Lasby's underhanded way of keeping me from going with Dalton to Bremerton. And the fact that Dalton needed to go to Bremerton in the first place. Not to mention Lasby busting us together.

Mostly, I was worried about Dalton. I didn't like that he had to wait two weeks for a psych eval he should have had ages ago. It worried me, and it pissed me off. Wasn't the Navy supposed to take care of its own?

I forgot about the menu and just stared at him. It had been several weeks now since the night he'd almost been killed, and it was still hard not to look at him and think about how close I'd come to losing him. It made me want to grab onto him and not let him go, like I could protect him from anything. Or like if he got out of my sight or out of my reach, something would snatch him up. Probably didn't help that I was still having those stupid dreams. I wondered if he noticed how often I woke up during the night and wrapped him up in a bear hug before I went back to sleep. He never seemed to be bothered by it. Hell, he slept right through it almost every time.

No wonder I was so worked up over Lasby screwing me out of going with Dalton. I needed to be with Dalton to make sure he was okay, and Lasby had pulled that stunt. Fucker.

The waiter appeared by our table, and I shook myself out of my thoughts.

"What can I get you gentlemen?" he asked.

Dalton ordered while I quickly skimmed over the menu and pretended I hadn't been zoning out. I settled on the southern style skillet because anything with country gravy on it was always a winner.

While the waiter was taking my order, Dalton took out his phone and frowned at the screen. When we were alone again, he was still eyeing it.

"Work?" I asked, hoping it wasn't.

"No, no." He typed something quickly, then pocket his phone. "Sorry. That was my dad asking me about some stuff. I'll call him later."

"Ah, okay. Long as it isn't work." I paused. "You don't talk about your family much."

He shrugged. "Neither do you."

"Okay. Fair. There isn't really much to tell, though. You know I was a Navy brat."

"And you *still* enlisted," he teased. "Slow learner?"

"Yeah, kinda." I chuckled. "My mom retired the year I enlisted, and my dad retired the year after. They tried to talk me into going to college, but . . . eh, I didn't know what I wanted to do. Figured four years would be enough time to figure it out. Plus I'd have the GI Bill."

"Four years, huh?" Dalton chuckled as he picked up his coffee. "Famous last words, am I right?"

I laughed and clinked my coffee cup against his. "So right. That why you went in? College?" Beat. "Oh right, you said you were a fuck-up as a kid."

"Yep." He sipped his coffee. "I also needed to get the fuck out of Nebraska, and I figured the Navy would get me as far away as anything."

"You do know there's a base there with a detachment of MAs, right?"

Grimacing, he nodded. "Every time I've been up for orders, I've been scared shitless I'll wind up at Offutt." He shuddered. "No thanks."

"Nebraska's really that bad?"

"It's flat and boring and I spent my whole damn civilian life there. I didn't join the Navy to go home."

"Fair enough." I watched him for a moment, and it was kind of funny to realize I knew Dalton so well, and I was so intimate with him, but I didn't know all that much about his pre-Navy life. "So, you're from there?" It was a dumb question, but hopefully enough to keep the conversation moving.

"Well, I grew up there," he said. "I was born in Indiana, but we left when I was two. My dad was having such a hard time after my mom died, he moved us to Omaha so my grandpa and my uncle could help him with me and my brothers." I laughed quietly, gazing out at the surf. "To this day, the whole family is convinced that's why I'm gay."

"What?"

"Because I was around nothing but men my whole life. My grandpa and my dad were both widowers, and my uncle never got married. I had three brothers and no sisters." Dalton laughed, rolling his eyes. "I guess being surrounded by men made me gay or something."

I snorted. "They really believe that?"

"Hey, they have to have *some* sort of explanation besides me being born like this."

"Isn't it usually that there isn't *enough* male influence or something?"

"Well yeah." He smirked. "Unless the guy from an all-male household turns out gay, and then it's *too much* male influence."

"Of course it is." I chuckled. We sipped our coffee in silence for a minute or so before I spoke again. "Can I ask you something?"

"Sure."

I held his gaze. "Why do you still live in the barracks?"

He shrugged. "I don't know. I moved in when I transferred, and I totally planned on getting a place out in town, but I kind of like it, you know? My roommate's a good guy, I don't have a lot of stuff, and I don't have to deal with gate traffic on the way to work."

"It's not . . ." I wrinkled my nose. "Crowded? And loud?"

"Eh. Thing is, I grew up in a house with a lot of people. We lived with my grandpa, and my uncle and his kids were there for a few years too. After that, it was boot camp, MA school, and a ship, which meant a lot of people coming and going at all hours. So it's weird to live completely on my own. The barracks are never totally empty or totally quiet, and I guess I like that."

"To each their own, right?"

"Pretty much." He took another sip of coffee. "So you didn't like the barracks?"

"Nope. It wasn't too bad in boot camp because I was always too tired to care, and I didn't mind the berthings when I was on a ship, but living in the barracks when I could get an apartment?" I shook my head. "No way."

"I can understand that. And I've thought about renting a place, but . . ." He shrugged again. "Maybe I'm just too lazy to go look."

I laughed. "Hey, you've got a place to sleep and shower. Nothing wrong with keeping it."

"Even if I spend more of my sleeping and showering time at your apartment these days." His cheeks colored. "Kind of feel like I should start helping with the rent."

"Don't worry about it. My housing allowance covers all but about fifty bucks of it anyway. I wouldn't ask you to contribute unless we added your name to the lease."

His eyebrows flicked up slightly, and I realized what I'd been implying.

I cleared my throat. "I mean, if we get there, you know?"

He smiled, a little bit of shyness in his gorgeous blue eyes. "Well, if we do, I'm happy to pull my weight."

"I know you are." Even though we were in public, I reached across the table and put my hand on top of his. "Maybe we *will* get there."

He turned his hand over, clasping his fingers gently around my wrist. "It's not something we need to rush into. We did just start dating a little while ago."

I had to stop and think about it, and damn, he was right. "Kind of feels like it's been longer, right?"

Dalton's smile grew. "It really does." His thumb ran alongside my wrist. "It's weird, isn't it?"

I nodded.

Before I could say anything, the waiter arrived with our food, and the moment was broken. Not that my mind strayed from it even as we dug into our breakfast.

Dalton was right that it felt like we'd been doing this a lot longer than a few weeks. It almost seemed like the only thing that had changed was the sex. Like we'd been dating all this time and had only just started sleeping together.

And it took almost losing you for us to take this to the next level.

I tried not to visibly shudder. It scared me to imagine how long we might've gone without ever tipping our hands to each other if the accident hadn't sped things along.

If certain things had happened differently, I might've lost you.

If certain things hadn't happened at all, I might not have had you like this.

Of course I wanted Dalton to be safe and sound above all else. If that meant the accident had never happened and we'd never hooked up, fine. Better than the alternative.

But the accident *had* happened, and we *had* hooked up, and I was sure as shit not complaining about how things were now.

I just hoped that even with all the bullshit going on at work, things between us stayed just like this.

CHAPTER 17

DALTON

After we'd eaten, we wandered downtown for a while. The pier was pretty quiet, and would be until spring, so there wasn't much to do there. There were some decent movies playing at the dilapidated old theater up the street from the pier, and we spent a couple of hours enjoying the hell out of the latest superhero comic book adaptation.

By the time we came out of the theater, it was starting to get dark, but the night was still comfortable. Definitely comfortable enough for my favorite thing to do with Chris (with clothes on)—walking on the beach.

As we walked along the tideline, my mind kept straying back to everything we'd talked about over breakfast. We'd only just touched on the subject of moving in together, but we *had* touched on it.

And . . . I liked the idea.

A lot.

It was way too soon to take that step, but it didn't *feel* like too soon. The thought of being with him all the time made my whole body warm. We were together almost all the time anyway. I hadn't slept in my barracks room in a while—long enough my roommate had started using my bed to fold laundry—and we'd even started doing all the domestic stuff together. Grocery shopping. Cooking. Washing the dishes. I'd never lived with a boyfriend before, but it felt like I lived with Chris. Like the only thing that would change was my name on the lease and my contribution to the rent. Everything else would just keep going the way it already was.

I stole a glance at him in the fading daylight. God, he was beautiful. His clothes hid his gorgeous body, but I'd memorized every inch of him. Smooth, dark skin over perfectly sculpted muscles. A thick cock that I loved to suck until neither of us could take anymore, especially when he got so turned on he threw me down and fucked me into the mattress. Chris was easily the sexiest man I'd ever encountered, and it still blew my mind that I kept winding up in his bed.

It was so much more than that, though. More than any man I'd ever dated, I *needed* him. Not just his mouth or his dick or his powerful arms around me. He was my best friend in the world, and he had my back now when I needed him the most, and that was heady stuff.

How the hell are you mine?

"Hey." He nudged my arm. "You still with me?"

Probably more than you realize.

I laughed and shook myself. "Yeah. Zoning out a bit, I guess."

He looked at me, alarm creasing his brow.

"I'm fine," I said. "It's not the concussion. Just me." *And you. Very much you.*

"Okay. Long as you're all right."

"I'm fine."

He didn't press, and we kept walking. After a little while, he took in a deep breath and let it out. "Today's been nice. Being out like a real couple."

"We *are* a real couple."

Chris didn't respond, and my stomach twisted.

I swallowed. "Aren't we?"

"We definitely are," he said. "Guess it just still kind of blows my mind."

"Yeah. Me too. It's . . ." I stopped. The daylight was fading fast, but when he turned to me, I could still see him well enough. "I fantasized about being with you for a long time, but I had no idea how amazing it would be when it actually happened."

"Me too." He combed his fingers through my short hair. "I thought it might get weird, us fooling around, but . . ." He shook his head. "Weird isn't the word I'd use."

"Neither would I." Heart pounding, I looked into his eyes. "I love you, Chris."

His breath hitched, but he didn't pull away. In fact, after a couple of nerve-racking seconds, a smile started to slowly form on his beautiful lips. "Really?"

I nodded, pretending my face wasn't so hot it was about to ignite. "Yeah. I . . . hell, I think I already did even before I knew I had a shot with you."

The smile came completely to life. Caressing my cheek, he whispered, "I love you too." Then he kissed me.

The relief was almost enough to knock me flat, but Chris's strong arms kept me upright. It was weird, realizing how easy it had been to say all those things. I'd never been sappy or romantic. My lack of romance had driven my last boyfriend up a wall. I'd tried, but it had just never been me.

Not until Chris. Before him, I'd felt silly and corny when I'd tried to say things like that. Now, it was almost like I couldn't get the words out fast enough. Like I might miss the opportunity and Chris would slip through my fingers before I could tell him how I felt.

Maybe that was a side effect of falling in love after a near-death experience. I was way too intimate with my own sense of mortality, and by extension, the mortality of everyone around me. The concept of "losing Chris" didn't necessarily mean someone else winning him over before I had the chance.

He drew back a bit and met my gaze. "I definitely should've come out to you sooner."

I laughed, touching my nose to his. "Just because you're gay didn't mean you were into me."

"No, but I was. And maybe one of us would've said something sooner. We could've been doing this months ago."

I considered it, then shrugged as I cradled the back of his head. "Maybe that would've been too soon. I don't know." I lifted my chin and brushed our lips together. "I think the timing worked out perfectly."

"Me too." He touched his forehead to mine. "It was a fucked up way to start, but I like where it's going."

I smiled and moved in for another kiss. One that kept right on going. Arms around each other, lips moving gently and tongues teasing each other while my heart thumped against my ribs—it was perfect. It was always perfect when Chris kissed me, and now it just seemed like . . . like perfect didn't even describe it anymore. The massive shitstorm still existed at work, and there was still that ball of stress that had taken root in my stomach, but right now, those didn't matter. They barely even registered over the sweet man and his warm embrace and this long, indulgent kiss.

I don't think "I love you" even describes how I feel about you.

Eventually, Chris broke the kiss, but only enough to murmur, "It's a really nice night out. Would be a shame to miss any of it."

"I don't think I'll be missing anything if I'm in bed with you."

Chris laughed, the warm rush of breath tickling my chin. "No pressure, right?"

"Nope." I cupped his face in both hands. "No pressure at all."

"My place?"

"Your place."

CHAPTER 18
CHRIS

Somehow, we made it back to the car, across town, and into my apartment without just giving up and fucking right there in the backseat. Neither of us said anything. I kept a hand on his leg in the car, and the tension in his thigh muscles had me fidgeting the whole way home. I could not wait to have this man in bed.

Finally, he was dragging me down onto the mattress by my shirt, and he stripped that off as soon as he didn't need to hold onto it anymore. Kissing and groping, we yanked off clothes until we were both naked, and then we kept right on kissing and groping.

I loved how needy he was in bed. I loved the idea of Dalton fucking Taylor needing *me* this badly. Couldn't think of anything that had ever turned me on more than knowing I turned him on like this. And that was all before he'd told me he loved me—now it was like being so giddy I was about to burst out laughing and so horny I couldn't contain myself.

I pushed him onto his back again and leaned down to kiss his neck.

Dalton arched into me. "Oh fuck . . ."

"Like that?"

"I love everything you do to me," he purred.

I grunted softly, then nibbled his earlobe. When I finally found some breath, I whispered. "Tell me what you want me to do."

"Fuck me," he pleaded without hesitation, pressing his dick against mine. "Before I go crazy."

"Hmm, I don't know. Kind of like watching you go crazy."

Dalton growled in frustration and dug his nails into my sides. "Ass."

I laughed and bit his neck. "You really want to rush?"

"Who's rushing?" he panted. "If we go too fast, we can just do it again in twenty minutes. C'mon—I want you. Bad."

Far be it from me to argue with that kind of hunger. I sat up and reached for the lube bottle. On my knees between his legs, I paused to slick myself up. Then I pushed his thighs apart and guided myself in.

Dalton closed his eyes, breathing slowly and evenly, and when the head of my dick slid into him, he gave the most amazing little moan. He always did. He loved that moment of penetration.

So I pulled out and gave it to him again. Then again. And again.

"Fucking tease," he growled. "Give me all of it."

I could've kept teasing him, but I wanted him too much, so this time I slid deeper, and it was my turn to moan as my cock sank all the way into him. Dalton exhaled. I rocked my hips again, and now I was moving easily, sliding in and out of his tight hole.

Dalton licked his lips. "Oh Jesus. You feel *perfect*."

"So do you. You always do. *Fuck*, Dalton . . ." I withdrew and pushed in again. I could go so much deeper in other positions, but like this, I could kiss him, and that was what mattered tonight. I wanted to be able to see him and taste him while I was in him.

"Faster," he whispered.

I pushed myself up a little and moved faster, finding that rhythm we both loved. Not quite slamming into him, not pounding him into the mattress, but bottoming out hard enough to make his breath hitch. I hooked my elbows under his knees, and the moan he released made me break out in goose bumps. His back arched, and he tilted his head back as he screwed his eyes shut and swore. Even as I slowed down— slowed way down—he didn't protest. He just writhed and murmured, "Yeah . . . yeah . . . oh yeah . . ."

I couldn't get enough of the view. Every inch of him—of us together—was so mind-blowingly sexy, I didn't think porn would get so much as a twitch out of my dick ever again. Not when I had a mind full of Dalton laid out and open to me. Fingers clawing at sheets and shoulders and whatever he could get his hands on. Every stroke registering in his expression—lips parting, eyes widening, breath hitching. My cock sliding in and out while he just about sobbed for me not to stop.

Everything was happening in super slow motion but still felt like it was going to be over too fast. Every stroke I took inside him seemed like it lasted half the night—long enough to savor every slow, languid slide, and long enough for me to pray I could hold on for one more. A condom would've dulled the sensation enough to hold back my orgasm, but I wasn't giving up this tight, slick heat for anything.

He reached up and pulled me down to him. I let go of his knees, and he wrapped his legs around my waist as I sank onto him, and then we were kissing while we moved together. If this wasn't my favorite thing in the world, I couldn't imagine what was—riding him, kissing him, getting completely tangled up and lost in him.

Dalton broke the kiss with a gasp and shuddered under me. He lifted his head like he was going back in for another kiss, but then let it fall back with a long moan.

"You are so gorgeous like this," I slurred. "You know that?"

"You're one to talk, baby." He slid his hands up my chest, gazing up at me with heavy-lidded eyes. "God, I love you." His whispered words were thick, like he was on the verge of choking on them.

"I love you too." I kissed him, and the soft contact of his lips sent a shiver right through me. My back arched, driving me deeper inside his hot body, and we both moaned, breaking the kiss for a moment before we found each other's mouths again.

Dalton whimpered. I knew that sound, and I loved it—he was close. Coming unraveled. Ready to paint both of our stomachs with cum and make sure my neighbors knew how good he felt.

Gritting my teeth against my own release, I thrust a little harder, just the way he loved it, and he rewarded me with a strangled half sob. A second later, cum shot across his tense, trembling abs, and then I was shooting inside him, coming without making a sound because I couldn't even *breathe* anymore.

I slumped over him, head spinning and lungs screaming for more air than I could find. I tried to say something like "that was amazing" or "holy fuck," but all that came out was a breathless whimper as I touched my forehead to his collarbone.

He held me close, arms and legs wrapped around me, my cock still buried inside him, and we just stayed like that until I started going soft. Then I pulled out and . . . we stayed like that anyway. We were sticky with sweat and cum, but I didn't care.

"Want to grab a shower?" he asked after ages had gone by.

"We probably should." I lifted myself up, looking down at the mess we'd made. "You know we're just going to wind up like this again, right?"

He flashed a Cheshire cat grin. "I'm counting on it, actually."

"Perv." I laughed and kissed the tip of his nose.

We got up long enough for a shower, then tumbled back into bed. Neither of us was getting frisky quite yet, and for all I knew we'd end up going to sleep before one of us woke the other with an under-the-covers blowjob. Either way worked for me.

Long as I'm in bed with you, I'm happy.

That was an understatement. Even the nights when we were too tired or his head was bothering him and we didn't fool around? Perfect. Nights like this where it we'd probably be lazily fucking and napping until we finally crashed? *Heaven.*

"Mmm." He squirmed a little. "I'm gonna fall asleep like this."

"Then fall asleep." I ran my fingers up and down his arm. "I'm not going anywhere."

"I know." He smiled sleepily and met my eyes. "But I want to fuck again."

"We will. Even if we go to sleep."

He made a happy noise and cuddled closer. He was so cute when he was fighting between tired and horny. Like he wasn't adorable the rest of the time. And hadn't been since the day I'd met him. I'd drooled like an idiot the day he'd walked into coxswain training. One look at him, and I'd wanted him. Then we'd become friends, and that want had turned into something a hell of a lot deeper. Back then, I'd have sold my soul just to think I had a *shot* at holding him in my bed. He was the first man I'd ever fantasized about where the fantasy didn't end with the money shot. I'd jerk off to thoughts of having sex with him, and then lie there, blissed out and satisfied, imagining . . . well, this.

And now here we were.

I swallowed. "Can I confess something?"

"Sure."

"All that time I had a crush on you?" I smoothed his wet hair.

"I wanted this—what we're doing now—even more than the sex." It sounded corny as soon as it came out, but Dalton just smiled.

His palm drifted up the middle of my chest. "I'm not going to say no to this any more than I'd say no to the sex."

"Same here. And I mean it—I love you."

"I love you too." He kissed me softly, then rested his head on my shoulder. I loved how we fit together. His body molded easily to mine, and I could spend the whole night with my arms wrapped around him like this.

Smiling to myself, I closed my eyes. I couldn't imagine I'd ever get tired of his warm, solid presence cuddled up against me. It had been ages since I'd had a boyfriend, even longer since I'd had one as affectionate as Dalton. Who was I kidding—no one compared to Dalton on any level. The affection. The sex. The way just looking at him made my heart hurt because I loved him so fucking much.

Please, God. I kissed the top of Dalton's head. *Don't let me fuck this up.*

CHAPTER 19

DALTON

I had a pleasant ache through most of my body as I headed to the HPU building from the parking lot the next morning. Next to me, Chris was walking kind of stiffly too, and I had to suppress a smile. I wondered how many people noticed whenever that happened. Or hell, maybe they thought we were getting old. Damn kids.

My smiled faded as we started up the stairs to the main room. There was a vibe coming from up there, a buzz of conversation I recognized from a mile away. Half excitement, half gossip. Half depressed, half relieved.

I swore under my breath as I trudged up the rest of the stairs to where the activity was coming from. I didn't have to ask—advancement results had posted.

Chris put a reassuring hand on the small of my back. "Moment of truth, right?"

"Yep."

At the landing, I paused for a deep breath. Then we stepped into the room.

As soon as we did, MA3 Powers shot me a sympathetic grimace, and my stomach dropped into my boots so hard, I was amazed no one heard it.

I didn't think it could get worse, but it did—Powers looked past me, and that grimace turned into a grin. "Congrats, Ingram!" Powers came over to give Chris's shoulder a hearty pat. "Now we'll finally have an MA1 who isn't a complete dick."

Oh.

Fuck.

My.

Life.

My lunch threatened to come up my throat, and I focused on tamping it back down. It wasn't like this was a shock. I'd known since the day of the exam that I wasn't getting promoted this time around. The confirmation hurt like hell, though. And it was terrifying. I had one more shot at making MA1. One more, or I was getting booted.

But I wanted—*needed*—to be happy for Chris. His career was secure now. He never had to get promoted again, and he could retire at twenty years.

He deserved it. He'd worked his ass off and should've been promoted ages ago.

So, I forced a smile and joined everyone in congratulating him, but as soon as he met my gaze, I knew he saw right through me. The way his forehead creased and his eyebrows lifted—yeah, he knew. But he didn't say anything. Not yet, anyway.

He waited until the excitement had died down and everyone had dispersed. Day shift was heading home. Night shift was doing boat checks and getting ready to go out on watch. Half an hour after we'd walked in, Chris and I were alone in the main office.

He put an arm around my shoulders and kissed my cheek. "Hey. I'm sorry. I know it's—"

"It's okay. I knew after the exam . . ." That thought didn't need to be finished. I shook my head, then looked up at him, and when I smiled, I meant it. "Congrats. You deserved it."

"So did you."

I shook my head. "Not after I bombed that exam."

"Look, you've got tons of time to study for the next one. And your head's getting better." He lifted his eyebrows as if to ask, *right?*

I nodded.

"And nobody's going to get in your head like Lasby did. If I have to send an armed escort in with you, I will. *Nobody* fucks with you."

I couldn't help a quiet, sad laugh. "You already sound like an MA1."

Chris smiled, but it was halfhearted.

"I'm serious. You'll be good at this." I brought his hand up and pressed a kiss to his fingers. "And I mean it—I'm happy for you."

"I know you are. I'm just . . . I'm worried. About how things are going to play out for you."

"I'll be fine." I swallowed. "You know he's gonna make you LPO, though, right? Anderson hasn't been anywhere near HPU since this whole thing started, and now you're the only MA1 in our section."

Scowling, Chris nodded. "I know." He squeezed my arm. "We'll find a way to make this work, okay? I'll talk to Lasby, and we'll see if we can get switched to opposite sections. Means we won't be working the same shifts anymore, so our sleep schedules will be off, but—"

"I don't care about that. I just don't want to have to split up."

"That is *not* going to happen." He said it so sharply I jumped. "Jesus, Dalton. Don't even talk like that." He paused, and his voice softened. "We'll be okay. I'll work something out with the chain of command. You focus on studying like hell for the next advancement exam."

I managed to smile. "Yes, MA1."

Chris rolled his eyes. "Shut up." He sighed. "Listen, I need to go down and do boat checks before turnover. We'll catch up later, okay?"

I nodded. "Okay."

He glanced around, then stole a quick kiss and a long look before he headed out.

While Chris headed down to the pier, I went into the locker room to collect my thoughts. I tried not to think about what had happened in here that day after Lasby had threatened me and Chris. I loved that memory—not the part with Lasby, but when Chris and I had kissed for the first time—but it was too painful right now. It felt too much like something that was going to get yanked away from me because I had once again failed to make rank.

I leaned against a locker and closed my eyes. My shoulders were heavy. My head was throbbing. I didn't even know if that had anything to do with the nagging after effects of the concussion or if this stress was giving me a headache. I just knew my head hurt. I felt miserable and pathetic and like it didn't matter what I did now. I had one chance left to get promoted, and who was to say I wouldn't blow that one too? I'd had my shit together this time around right up until a boat had smacked me upside the head and a chief had threatened me for good measure. With the way things were going, I could study ten hours a day between now and the next exam, and I'd be abducted by aliens on the way in to take the test.

That thought couldn't even make me laugh. I didn't imagine there was much that could.

The humor didn't last, though. Fact was, I had one shot left to stay in the Navy. Considering the last few weeks hadn't exactly been glowing eval material, I didn't have a lot of faith that I really *had* that shot. My physical recovery seemed to be going okay, but how would I do when I tried to run a Physical Readiness Test? My brain felt more or less like my own again, but what would happen when I sat my next—and last—advancement exam? Even if I didn't have my chief there to sabotage my concentration at the last minute?

I closed my eyes, letting my head fall back against the locker. It was time to do some serious thinking about my post-Navy career. I had the GI Bill. I could always go back to Nebraska. Live at home with my dad and grandpa while I went to school. Grandpa was getting a little fragile anyway—he was in his late eighties now—so maybe they could use the help.

A lump rose in my throat. As much as I would love to be closer to my family, the thought of letting go of this career was even harder to swallow now that I was one step closer to having no choice.

Fuck. I swiped at my eyes. Everything was getting pulled away from me, and I didn't know how to stop it.

I was going to lose the Navy.

I was going to lose being a coxswain.

And deep down, I couldn't help being scared to death that somehow I was going to lose Chris too.

CHAPTER 20
CHRIS

"I need to talk to you, MA1."

I winced. One of the drawbacks of being an MA1—now I was the one the chief would come to when he wanted to pass something on to the section. One rung higher on the ladder meant I was the rung between Chief and everyone else. Fuck.

On the other hand, I needed to talk to him anyway. See about getting me or Dalton transferred out of our section. I hadn't had time to bring it up yesterday, but now was as good a time as any. So, as I always did, I pulled myself together, put on a professional face, and then turned to him. "What's up, Chief?"

He motioned for me to follow him. That wasn't good. This was a private conversation. One for his office.

Inside the office that was basically his, he closed the door. He didn't even hold out for his usual long, awkward silence to unnerve me. The door had barely clicked before he started. "Listen, as you know, MA1 Anderson is out of Harbor Patrol indefinitely." There was an undercurrent in Lasby's voice that I didn't like. Not one bit. "So without him, we don't have an LPO."

My stomach knotted. Oh shit. I knew where this was going.

"So, with you being the only MA1 in the section, looks like you're my new LPO."

Any other time, that would have been great news. Getting a Lead Petty Officer position right after making rank always looked good on an eval, and it was never too early to start looking like someone who should advance to chief. But being LPO muddied some waters even more than getting promoted had already done.

"Uh, Chief." I cleared my throat. "There might be a small problem with me being in charge."

"Oh?" He sipped his coffee, watching me the entire time. As he lowered the mug, he asked, "What problem is that?"

"I'm . . ." I hesitated, not sure how to phrase it. "My relationship with MA2 Taylor. That could—"

"That's not my problem, MA1," he growled.

"No, but . . ." Panic fluttered in my chest. I thought fast, grasping for any solution I could find. "Look, we don't want any fraternization or conflict of interest. Can't we be assigned to separate sections? Different shifts?"

The chief's lips quirked like he was really considering it. Then he shook his head once. "No."

"No?"

"Did I stutter?"

My stomach was doing somersaults and my heart . . . fuck, my heart had stopped. "Chief, I—"

"You're the new LPO of the Harbor Patrol Unit," he said coldly. "Separating the two of you means he's moving, not you, and if he moves, it'll be behind a desk back at the security office."

"That'll kill his chances of getting promoted."

Lasby nodded without even flinching. "Yes, MA1. It will. And if that doesn't, going to Captain's Mast again will."

My stomach roiled. Everything he was saying was wrong, but it was also probably true. Lasby had the power to move us or not. He had the power to keep Dalton working for me just like he had the power to send him to one of those office jobs where careers went to die.

"Your boy's already got a trip to Mast on his record," Lasby went on. "You really want him to go explain to the CO how he's involved with his supervisor when he's already lost rank for insubordination? He doesn't need this. Not if he's going to make MA1 and stay in the Navy long enough to retire."

As the not-so-veiled threat sank in, I stared. I'd believed Dalton when he'd told me about Lasby's threats, and I'd been there for the tirade about the relationship that hadn't existed at the time, but it was still a shock to hear Lasby all but say it out loud. To realize he didn't even *have* to say it—*Do what I tell you, or I will make sure Dalton is fucked.*

"You know the rules, *MA1*." He spat out my rank as if it tasted like bilge water. "Dating a subordinate is fraternization, and the Navy has quite a few regs against that."

"I'm aware of that, Chief." I tried to use an MA1 voice, but damn if the habit of being a lowly MA2 didn't die hard. "But we were already dating when I got promoted. That's why we're asking to work opposite shifts, or—"

"I can't spare a Level II coxswain," he snapped. "I need Taylor in this section."

"Understood, Chief. Then can *I* be transferred to—"

"I'm not rearranging Harbor to accommodate you and MA2 Taylor. You know the regs, and you know your options." He gestured at my lapel. "If you'd like to hang on to that new chevron, I would suggest you unfuck your situation."

"Chief, we're—"

"Dismissed, MA1."

"Chief—"

"*Dismissed.*"

I couldn't move for a few shocked, silent seconds, but eventually I did, and I left the office. As soon as I was out in the hall, I winced—I could hear Dalton's voice coming from nearby. He and MA3 Powers were talking about something I couldn't understand, and every time he spoke, my heart sank a little deeper. He sounded down. His voice was loud enough that he and Powers were probably talking from across the room, but his heart wasn't in it. Hadn't been in much of anything since the results had come out yesterday. Oh, he'd given me an enthusiastic celebratory blowjob when we'd gotten back to my place, but he hadn't wanted anything in return. I didn't think he had the energy, and I was pretty sure he hadn't slept after we'd turned off the light.

I slipped down the hall and into the stairwell without him or Powers seeing me, and I headed outside. I had some time before I went out on watch, so I just walked up and down the pier, trying to think.

We could go to one of the other chiefs, but chiefs protected chiefs. We could request an inquiry into the investigation, but there'd already been enough threats—spoken and unspoken—against Dalton and

Rhodes. Any one of those could come back and bite them in the ass.

No matter how I sliced it, we were out of options. If one of us couldn't go to another duty section or couldn't get a desk job in the security office or . . . *something*—then we didn't have a choice. Every way I sliced it, I was dating a direct subordinate. It didn't matter that we'd been dating already. The Navy just didn't care.

The fact was, I couldn't see any way to end this without ending *us*.

With my heart in my throat, I wrote Dalton a text.

We need to talk.

I stared at it. My throat was tight and my eyes were burning. No, I wasn't ready for that conversation. Not now.

Fuck. I needed to think some more. Then I'd . . . I didn't know what I'd do.

CHAPTER 21
DALTON

I was on my way out of the HPU building lot when I saw Chris. He was down by the pier, leaning on a pylon and looking out at the water. My heart gave its usual happy flutter at the sight of him, and I followed the gravel path down to where he was standing. When I was close enough, I said, "Hey."

As soon as the word came out, he tensed. If I wasn't mistaken, his hackles went up.

The fluttery feeling vanished and ice water filled my veins. "You okay?" I approached cautiously.

He glanced back at me. Oh, no, he was definitely not okay. I couldn't read his mind, but the tightness of his features and the way he flinched when we made eye contact? Oh, fuck.

I stopped beside him. "What's going on?"

Chris pressed his lips together. He returned to staring intently at the harbor, brow furrowed and jaw clenched. I wished like hell I could put a reassuring hand on his shoulder, but that extra chevron on his collar warned me against it.

Then my stomach turned to lead. I glanced at his three chevrons. Then at his face. "Chris, what's going on?"

He dropped his gaze and sighed. "We, um . . ." He chewed his lip, and I gave him time to finish the thought, but he didn't speak, and the silence was about to drive me insane.

"Just tell me what's wrong." The panic didn't seem like it was making it into my voice, but hell if I knew how long that would last. "Talk to me."

He chewed his lip, avoiding my eyes.

The panic was clawing its way deeper. I'd seen Chris nervous before, seen him struggle to say something, but not like this. I didn't know what he was about to say, but I knew—all the way to the core—that it would be bad.

"Whatever it is," I said. "Just say it."

Get it out so I don't have to anticipate it anymore.

Finally, he swallowed and looked me in the eye. "I'm sorry, D. We, uh . . . we gotta stop what we're doing." He gestured at each of us. "This, I mean."

My chest suddenly felt like it was about to implode. Or was already in the process of imploding. And I'd thought the anticipation had been bad. "What?"

He met my gaze, his features taut and his eyes full of regret. "We can't keep seeing each other."

"Chris . . ." The sound of his name slipping off my own lips almost broke me. I swallowed, trying to keep myself together. "We can do this. We—"

"We can't." He shook his head slowly. He wasn't looking at me anymore.

"You . . . want to split up?"

"I don't *want* to, no. I love you, Dalton." He winced like his own words had smacked him as hard as they'd smacked me. He sighed, rubbing the back of his neck. "I don't know what else to do. The regs are what they are. Lasby's making me LPO, and he refuses to move either of us to another section. He's got us by the balls."

I stared at him, struggling to comprehend what was happening. Trying to make sense of what he was saying and what he was doing, and how Chief Lasby could get away with forcing us apart. "Don't do this. We can make—"

"No we can't." He shook his head sadly. "Anyone catches wind we're dating now, we're fucked."

"We just have to keep it on the DL. We—"

"And what happens when someone figures it out anyway?" Chris sighed. "Lasby was sniffing around for it even before we really were dating. If we get caught now, what happens if we go to Mast, huh? You've said yourself your first time at Mast has been following you around for—"

"That was different. I fucked up that time. I deserved it."

"And we'd deserve it now."

My lips parted, but no sound came out. Horror and panic and anger were vying for dominance, but I couldn't sort any of it into words. I was too stunned. Too fucking devastated by what Chris was saying. By what he was *doing*.

Chris sighed. "Don't think for a second that I want this. But Lasby's right. As long as you're working for me, we can't date. Shit, we can't even hang out as friends."

That last part hit me harder than anything. It was true, and it was also . . . *fuck*. Losing my boyfriend was one thing. Not being able to spend time with my best friend? Losing Chris on all fronts? No. Fuck, no. But the regs were clear. Now that he outranked me, now that he was my boss, we couldn't hang out. At all. Even if we weren't dating.

"Chris . . ."

"I'm sorry," he whispered. "I fucking hate this too. But I don't know how to get around it."

I stared at him, unable to speak. This couldn't be real. No way. No, no, no, no, no. Not happening.

But it was. I could feel it in the distance that seemed to be growing between us even though we were both standing still. He'd made up his mind, and to him, it was done. It was over. I was still reeling, but he was already gone.

As if to emphasize that, he finally took a step back. Rubbing his neck and looking anywhere but at me, he said, "I'm gonna go. I'll, uh, see you after I come in off the water."

My mouth had gone dry. My lungs weren't working. So I still didn't say anything.

I just stood there.

And watched Chris walk away.

Working with Chris after that was hell. We both kept our military bearing, and we were civil to each other, but God . . . it hurt. Every time I looked at him, my chest felt like it was going to split open. It was even worse whenever I caught him glancing at me. Halfway through our second shift together as exes, I decided this would have been a hell of a lot easier to swallow if we couldn't stand each other. If one of us had cheated or said something that couldn't be taken back or done *something* to nuke this thing and turn our friendship and relationship sour.

Except we hadn't. We wanted to be together. Being apart—especially when we couldn't *be* apart—was killing me, and if I was reading him right, it was killing him too.

But our shifts weren't the worst. Neither were the nights spent alone in my own bed.

It was our days off.

I didn't know what to do with myself. My best friend and my boyfriend were gone. I didn't want to talk to anyone or go anywhere, but the walls of my barracks room were closing in and the sympathetic glances from my roommate were driving me insane.

Thank God for Diego. Hanging out with him meant getting the hell away from the base, and if there was anyone on the planet who didn't want to talk about the Navy's bullshit, it was him. In fact, with pretty much anything, Diego tended to leave well enough alone. He could read me as well as Chris always had, and he usually knew when I didn't want to talk about something.

Today, he probably knew it, but he didn't leave it alone this time. We'd barely settled onto his sofa, drinks in hand, before he said, "Hey, man." His forehead creased. "What's wrong?"

I flinched, and it took all I had to keep my shit together. I stared down at my soda, and when I was sure my voice wouldn't break—or at least I wouldn't break—I told him everything that had happened recently. After it was all out, I ran a shaky hand through my hair. "It's like the night I went off the boat, everything started coming apart. I'm a wreck as a coxswain. I blew one of my last shots at getting promoted. And now . . . Chris."

Diego shook his head. "That's some bullshit. You need to go above your chief."

I eyed Diego. "What?"

"Everything that's going on? It's seriously bullshit. Plain and simple. That chief is covering for someone who almost killed you, and his homophobic crap is keeping you from the man you love."

"The Navy's doing that," I muttered, thumbing the label on my

Coke bottle. "Fucking fraternization."

Diego huffed, pulling his knee onto the sofa between us and facing me. "The chief doesn't have to keep you in the same section. The only reason your relationship is a problem is because Chief put Chris in charge of you."

"Because Chris outranks me," I said bitterly.

Diego sighed, rolling his eyes. "How many duty sections are there?"

"Four."

"Just in harbor, or all of security?"

"Just harbor."

"See? So there's no reason they can't put your ass in another section so you're not working for Chris anymore." Inclining his head, he looked right in my eyes. "It isn't like you started dating your supervisor. You were dating him, and then he *became* your supervisor. You shouldn't have to break up just because your fucking chief won't shuffle some shifts around. They did it all the time when I was in."

I didn't respond.

"Man, you gotta do something. Especially if they haven't even sent you for the psych eval yet." Diego frowned hard. "What the fuck kind of chief keeps you in Harbor without waiting to see if the shrinks say you *need* to be off the water?"

I flinched. The thought of being taken out of the harbor unit still made my chest hurt. Not as much as losing Chris, but enough. "The guy's an asshole."

"No shit. All they gotta do is move you landside," Diego went on. "Or just put you in a different section and under another supervisor. Then there's no reason to fuck with you and Chris."

"And that's exactly why they aren't moving either of us," I growled.

He knocked his knuckle on the back of the couch. "That's *bullshit.*"

"Yeah, it is," I snapped. "But what the fuck am I supposed to do?"

"Grow some fucking balls and *use* your chain of command, Dalton," he threw back.

I blinked, startled.

Expression softening, Diego took my hand and squeezed it. "I know it's hard, and I know you're scared of reprisal, but don't fucking let this chief kill your relationship."

"He already has." The defeat in my own voice made me cringe.

Diego shook his head. "No, he hasn't. Chris didn't cut you loose because he wanted to. He did it because he was backed into a corner."

"So what do I do?"

"Get rid of the corner."

"*How?*" I exhaled, shaking my head. "Chief Lasby's got all the cards here. Everything he's told us is fucked-up, but he's not *wrong*. And what good will it do to go to a chief or a senior chief?"

Diego watched me silently for a long moment, still gripping my hand. Then he released a breath and sat back. "I don't know. Wish I could tell you. But man, there's gotta be a way. When the Navy fucked me over, it was my word against a damn computer's. You've got a chief who isn't even trying to be subtle about screwing you. So I guess what you gotta figure out is how to show that to someone who can do something about it."

I chewed the inside of my cheek. "Except even if I have bulletproof evidence, it doesn't change the fact that the only people I *think* I *might* be able to trust are chiefs too. How do I know they won't bury this to protect him?"

"You don't," Diego said simply. "Question is—is your career and what you've got with Chris worth the risk? And I think we both know the answer is yes. Well, when Chris isn't jerking you around."

I arched an eyebrow. "He's not jerking me around. He's backed into a corner as much as I am."

"And he's failing you as a friend, a boyfriend, and a shipmate. He's got the rank to do something about what's going on, and he's taking the easy way out by dumping you. That ain't cool."

"It's not that simple. You know it's not."

"No, but neither is cutting you loose. He's a fucking idiot for that."

I blinked, not sure how to take that from a man who'd *also* cut me loose. Even if it had been more of a mutual thing with us, Diego had been the one to initiate it.

Diego closed his eyes and let out a long, resigned breath. Neither of us said anything for a while. When he finally did, he looked at me, his expression full of seriousness and sincerity. "Listen, I got nothing against Chris. But I care about you, and I hate seeing you hurt because he won't step up and be the man you deserve. Especially since it's so fucking obvious he's got you wrapped around his finger."

I straightened. "What? No he doesn't."

"Please." Diego laughed, but there wasn't much humor behind it. "I don't mean you're his doormat or something. I just . . ." He paused. "Let's put it this way—if things could've been different between us, I'd have done just about anything so you'd look at me the way you've always looked at him."

My heart dropped. "Really?"

Diego laughed and gave my arm a gentle squeeze.

I rubbed my eyes. "I'm sorry. I . . . shit, now I feel like kind of a dick for—"

"Dude, no." He shook his head. "What kind of asshole would I be if I got pissy over you being into another guy? I'm the one who called things off with us. I *want* you to be happy. I want us both to be happy—that's why we broke up. So we could be happy with other people instead of making each other miserable."

"True. But still . . ."

"Don't. I'm not bitter, okay? We couldn't have made it work. No way in hell am I doing the Navy wife thing, you know? And I've got you as a friend, so I can't complain." He smiled sadly. "There's a Chris out there for me too. I just gotta find him."

I put a hand on his forearm. "He'll be a lucky man when you do."

Diego's smile turned a bit more genuine. "Ask him how he feels about that after he's put up with me for a few months."

I just laughed. Diego was a pistol, no two ways about it, but whoever finally won this man's heart really would be lucky. If my circumstances were different, maybe it could've been me.

Maybe it still could if the Navy ends up kicking me out.

My heart sank at the thought. As much as I adored Diego, I didn't want him as consolation prize when I lost my career and my . . .

And Chris.

My best friend. My boyfriend. The only man I've ever felt like this for.

I still had my career for now, but Chris had never felt farther out of my reach. The thought hit me hard, and my throat tightened around my breath. If I hadn't had Diego to lean on right then, God knew how I'd have held onto any of my sanity. Maybe we couldn't make it work as a couple, but damn if I wasn't grateful to have him as a friend.

Diego wrapped an arm around me and pulled me in close. He pressed a kiss to my temple and whispered, "I'm serious about Chris. Don't fucking give up on him."

Closing my eyes, I sighed but said nothing.

I didn't want to give up on Chris. Just thinking about it hurt like hell.

But what could I do? Chief Lasby had us by the balls. The Navy had us cornered by a whole stack of regulations. How I felt about Chris didn't matter when there was shit in black and white that said we couldn't have each other.

I don't know how to fix this.

I don't know if it can *be fixed.*

On my next duty day, I headed to work, but I didn't go see Chief Jackson or Senior Chief Curtis. A million times over, I'd talked myself into approaching the chain of command, and a million and one times, I'd talked myself out of it. I could still hear Diego's voice in my head, but my own voice kept shooting him down.

Chiefs look out for chiefs.

So I chickened out. Feeling guilty and ashamed and pissed off that I was letting Lasby win, I walked right past the hall that would lead to Jackson or Curtis's offices and went to admin to take care of some paperwork. When that was done, I passed the hall again. Still didn't stop. Still didn't talk to them. Still didn't have a fucking spine.

No, that wasn't it. I had a spine. I just knew all too well how easily and how badly this could blow up in my face. In *Chris's* face.

Lasby had won. We were fucked. Now I didn't have Chris, and I had one shot at keeping my career. Might as well not torpedo that shot and—

"MA2." Lasby's voice stopped me dead. When I turned, he nodded sharply to the left. "My office."

Ice formed along the length of my spine. Without a word, I followed Lasby into his office. The click of the door behind us echoed through my bones.

As he always did, he let the silence linger until the air in the room was thrumming uncomfortably.

Finally, he spoke. "Things are going to change in Harbor, MA2. I'm down two coxswains right now. Not only is MA1 Anderson still stuck in Admin, but MA1 Ingram is going to be working as the LPO from here on out, so he won't be driving as often. I can't spare him to come out there and fill in for you as a coxswain." He stepped closer, lifting his chin as if that might make him an inch or two taller than me. "You want a shot at making MA1 before you hit high-year tenure, I would suggest you pull it together, get back out on that boat, and be the coxswain the Navy invested in."

I gritted my teeth. "What if the shrinks say I'm—"

"We'll cross that bridge when we get to it, MA2." He closed some more of the space between us, and I swore cold air radiated off him. "But if it turns out your head's too fucked up to do your job? Well, you better start making room in your schedule for TAPS."

My heart sped up. The implication wasn't even subtle—TAPS was a class for Sailors getting ready to transition to the civilian world.

"So," he growled, "are you going to be driving the boat today or not, MA2?"

Teeth clenched against rising bile, I nodded. "Yes, Chief."

"Good. And another thing to keep in mind . . ." His eyes narrowed. "Thanks to the investigation into your incident, the Navy is watching our Harbor unit like a hawk, and if they don't think we're running a tight ship here, people are going to get fired. Not just me, but the LPO. So I would suggest you and your fellow MAs get your shit together. Unless you'd like to see the Navy make an example out of your new LPO."

Acid burned the back of my throat. One MA1 had already fucked up. If another one did, he would fall even harder. Captain's Mast. Stripped of rank. When the Navy wanted to make an example of someone, they didn't fuck around. Any incident, anyone stepping out of line, and Lasby would make sure the hellfire and brimstone landed right smack on Chris.

I had to give the man credit—he knew exactly how to get my balls into a vise.

"Do make myself clear?" he asked in a low growl.

I nodded. "Yes, Chief."

"Dismissed, MA2," he hissed, practically in my ear.

I didn't wait around. I spun on my heel, swung open the door, and walked out of his office, fighting the urge to run.

When I was around a corner and safely out of sight, I paused to grab a few breaths and pull myself together. Fuck. Fuck, fuck, fuck. I didn't know which burn was stronger—the threat of vomit or the threat of tears. Did it really matter? Because I was pretty sure once I gave in to one of them, the other would follow.

I needed air. I needed to be somewhere other than here. I needed to go now before I lost my cool completely.

The door. Just get to the door. Walk fast. Faster. Get to the door.

I strode down the hall, gaze fixed on the exit like a sniper fixated on a target. Nothing else existed or mattered. Get to the door and get out. Everything else could be dealt with afterward.

I made it, and I put my hand on the push bar, ready to step outside, catch my breath, get in my car, and drive down to the harbor building to start my shift.

But one word slammed into my consciousness and stopped me in my tracks:

Enough.

Still gripping the push bar, I clenched my teeth. Fear coursed through my veins like cold water, but the sudden wave of determination was stronger. Chief Lasby had fucked with us enough. He'd threatened us, cornered us, gaslit us, and forced us apart. Now he was using my devotion to Chris to keep me in line. It wouldn't have surprised me if he'd used me to keep Chris in check too. Which would explain why Chris had abruptly cut me loose.

My chest tightened with barely contained rage. I had no proof and no reason to believe anyone above Lasby was an ally, but I wasn't rolling over and taking this quietly anymore. If I torpedoed my own career . . . fine. I was one advancement cycle away from getting booted out anyway. I might never drive a boat again. I had PTSD and TBI. I'd lost my boyfriend and the ability to spend time with my best friend.

I swallowed the acid and stepped back from the door. If there was one thing Chief Lasby had underestimated, it was how little I had left to lose at this point.

Full of determination and scared out of my mind, I turned around and headed back down the hall.

Chief Jackson's door was open, and I wasn't surprised to see Senior Chief Curtis kicked back in one of the guest chairs. They were friends, and everybody knew they sometimes shot the shit in here. And besides, Curtis was leaving for his next command soon, so he wasn't doing a whole lot besides showing up. Curtis just sort of hung around in case he was needed while the new senior chief settled into his old office.

Seeing him there almost made me backtrack again, though. I could face Chief Jackson. Both of them? Shit . . .

Jackson tilted his head. "You need something, MA2?"

"Yeah, I . . ." I cleared my throat. "Can I talk to you, Chief?" I glanced at Curtis. "Actually, both of you?"

They exchanged uneasy glances and both sat up.

"Come in and sit down," Jackson said. "What's going on?"

I came in and shut the door. I started to stand at attention, but he motioned toward the empty seat next to Curtis.

"I said sit down, MA2." It wasn't an order. More like an invitation. A non-negotiable one.

I took it, but I couldn't relax. "I, um . . ." My courage was flagging hard now. I tried to find some comfort in the wedding bands both men wore and the framed photo of a gorgeous redheaded man on Jackson's desk. I knew there was no reason to be scared of any homophobia from either of them.

But there was more to this than Lasby's disgust at my relationship with Chris. There were politics and bullshit involved that, if taken seriously, could do serious, irreversible damage to Chief Lasby's career. I didn't know either of these men well enough to be sure they'd back me up when it meant potentially taking down another member of the chiefs' mess.

Senior Chief Curtis leaned forward, elbows on his knees. He'd always had a pretty mellow tone, but he was so soft-spoken now he almost broke me. "What's going on, MA2?"

I was scared to death. I was about to make everything exponentially worse, I just knew it, and my stomach was sicker than it had been the day after the incident. My mind and stomach roiled with guilt and shame over . . . fuck, I didn't even know.

But with both chiefs watching me intently, I took a deep breath, and everything came tumbling out. The night I went into the water. The pressure and gaslighting. Chief Lasby shutting down the joking about me and Chris together. The threats to MA3 Rhodes.

By the time I was done, I was sweating. If I could've loosened my death grip on the chair's plastic armrests, my hands probably would've been shaking. My voice sure was.

Jackson and Curtis glanced at each other, but they didn't say anything.

I pushed out a ragged breath. "I get that MA1 Ingram and I can't date if he's my supervisor. That's why he requested we be put on different shifts."

"Why was the request denied?" Jackson's tone was neutral, offering no indication of whether he was on my side.

I swallowed. "Because with Chris—with Ingram moving up to the LPO position and MA1 Anderson still working in Admin, I'm the only Level II coxswain in our section who isn't committed to other things."

Both men were silent for a long, uncomfortable moment.

Jackson tilted his chair back as he absently stroked his chin. "Chief Lasby thought you two were dating even before MA1 Ingram was promoted. Is that correct?"

I nodded. "I mean . . . we *were* dating. He didn't like it, and I think he was trying to keep us apart without saying he was trying to keep us apart."

Curtis and Jackson both stared at me.

"Can you give us an example?" Curtis asked.

"The day I made my appointment to go to Bremerton for a psych eval," I said, "I mentioned to Lasby that I'd take care of getting there. I didn't tell him I was going to ask Chris to give me a lift, but Chris and I go pretty much everywhere together. He stayed with me after the accident. It's kind of a no-brainer that he'd be the first person I'd ask. And when I *did* ask, Lasby had *just* talked to him about doing a duty swap to fill in for someone else."

Both men shifted, their chairs creaking.

"Were you able to get a ride?" Curtis asked.

I nodded. "MA3 Rhodes said she'll take me."

"Good," he said with a nod. He turned to Jackson, but neither of them said anything.

Squirming uncomfortably, I blurted out, "You want to know why I did so fucking horribly on the advancement exam?"

Both men looked at me, eyebrows up.

I pushed out a ragged breath and dropped my gaze to the gray linoleum. "Part of it was the concussion. I was . . ." I shook my head as I looked at Jackson. "I was still definitely fucked up from that. But when I was on the way in to take the exam, Lasby stopped me in the hallway. He pulled me aside and told me I needed to be in his office after the exam because the investigator wanted to interview me about the incident. He kept telling me to only tell the investigator what I was absolutely sure I remembered. Leave out anything that was hazy because he didn't want Anderson's career getting fucked over something I *thought* I remembered." I ran a shaky hand through my short hair. "And that was it. I couldn't focus."

"Did he tell you anything else?" Curtis's voice was tight.

I gnawed the inside of my cheek and focused on my boots. "He reminded me that MA1 Anderson was a solid coxswain, that his intent had been to save civilians, and that the boat only foundered because I didn't see the net before we hit it."

Jackson rolled his eyes, breaking military decorum for the first time since I'd known him. "Even if you'd seen the net, there's no way you could have relayed that to the coxswain and had him maneuver in time. Not at that speed."

Something loosened inside my chest. "Yes. Yes, exactly." I gulped. "Plus we were getting thrown around so bad, I could barely stand up. I was looking for shit to hold on to, not nets in the water. And I mean, those nets are almost invisible even in calm seas."

They both nodded with expressions that said *yeah, no shit, everybody knows that.*

"So he's blaming you because you didn't see the nets," Curtis said, tone flat.

"Yeah."

"He also gaslit you and tried to sway your testimony to an independent investigator," Curtis growled. "And he did it right before the advancement exam when he knew it would throw you off your game. Not to mention threatening MA3 Rhodes over that rifle?" He shook his head.

"Downgrading her award too," I said quietly.

Both men stiffened.

"Come again?" Curtis asked.

I moistened my lips. "He told her she might get a NAM, and that's only if she doesn't go to Mast for the gun and breaking protocol. But she was just doing her job, so she doesn't deserve anything higher." My voice wavered a little as I added, "He seriously thinks she didn't go above and beyond? Or that it matters that she broke protocol? I almost *died*. I fucking *would* have if she hasn't done what she did."

Some color was rising in Curtis's face. Jackson's jaw worked. When they locked eyes, something passed between them. Something telepathic. Maybe it was a chief thing, or maybe they'd just been friends long enough to read each other. I couldn't tell.

Then Jackson picked up his phone and dialed an extension. "Hello, MA3. It's Chief Jackson. Would you send MA1 Ingram to my office, please?"

My gut clenched. I turned to Curtis. "What? You guys are—"

"Relax, MA2." He patted the air. "We're on your side."

I didn't relax, though. I couldn't.

Please, don't be lying . . .

CHAPTER 22

CHRIS

I had no idea what to expect on the way into Chief Jackson's office. He was barely even in my chain of command since HPU was separate from the rest of security. On paper, he and Senior Chief Curtis were in our chain, but in practice, HPU mostly did its own thing.

So God only knew why he wanted to talk to me. With everything that had been happening this year, all I could think was, *now what?*

The door was open, so I went in. Senior Chief Curtis was there. And ... *Dalton?* My stomach knotted. What was going on?

Senior Chief Curtis stood and motioned for me to take the chair. While I sat, Curtis leaned against the wall beside the door, arms folded loosely across his chest. Dalton shifted like he was uncomfortable. I could relate.

"You want to tell us what's been going on with Chief Lasby?" Jackson's tone was even. Not baited. Not hostile.

I glanced at Dalton. Then Curtis. Then Jackson. "Which part?"

"How about starting with the night MA2 Taylor got hurt."

I chewed the inside of my cheek, then took a deep breath and told him everything I could remember, all the way up to the part where Lasby threatened me if I continued seeing Dalton. By the time I was done, I thought I was going to be sick.

Jackson looked past me. I could practically feel him and Curtis locking eyes. The tension in the room needled at the back of my neck, and now I was the one shifting uncomfortably.

After a long moment, Jackson picked up the phone on his desk. When he spoke, my blood turned cold: "I need you to come by my office."

He didn't mention any names or ranks, but I knew. Deep down,

I just knew.

The chief and senior chief asked me a few questions about what happened the night Dalton was hurt and about what Lasby and I had talked about recently, but I didn't get the impression I was telling them anything they didn't already know. A few minutes later, there was a knock at the door, and when Curtis opened it, in walked Chief Lasby.

Lasby glanced around the room. His eyes narrowed when he reached Dalton and me. I wondered if Dalton was struggling as hard as I was not to squirm. Lasby glared at Jackson. "Yeah?"

Jackson's eyebrow flicked up, probably at his peer's lack of military bearing. He didn't comment on that, though. Instead, he folded his hands on his belt buckle and looked up at him. "I understand these gentlemen asked to be put on separate shifts. There a reason we can't accommodate them?"

Every muscle in Chief Lasby's body seemed to turn rigid. "I don't have a Level II coxswain to spare, or—"

"What about switching LPOs?"

Lasby glared at him. "I don't think I need to explain my duty sections to you."

"Then you can explain them to me, *Chief.*" Curtis's tone was even, but something in his eyes gave me a chill. Like he was closing in fast on the end of his patience.

Lasby shifted his glare to Curtis. Neither moved. Neither spoke. No one in the room even breathed.

Then, without moving his eyes, Curtis growled, "MA1. MA2. You're dismissed." After a second, his gaze flicked toward us. "No one else comes in here. Understood?"

"Yes, Senior," we both said. We got up and squeezed between him and Lasby. I didn't think I'd ever been so relieved to get out of a room.

To my surprise, Chief Jackson followed, shutting the door behind us.

In silence, the three of us headed down the hall. We weren't twenty feet away when a door-muffled shout stopped us all in our tracks, and we turned back toward Jackson's office. I couldn't understand what was being said, but it was Senior Chief Curtis's voice, and he was *pissed.*

"I didn't think Senior could yell," Dalton marveled.

Jackson chuckled. "Push him far enough or step on the right nerves, and you better believe he can."

We all stared back toward the office for a moment.

Then Jackson turned to us, and he was completely serious. "Curtis and I will look into this. I can't promise we'll resolve everything overnight, but this just became my top priority."

My throat constricted. "Really?"

"Absolutely." He looked at each of us in turn. "You two did the right thing. I'd say you should've come to me or Senior a long time ago, but I know how it is. I get it. But we'll take care of this." He glanced back at his office, then motioned for us to come with him. We followed him to another office, and I realized it was Curtis's. Or, well, it had been. Senior Chief Reyes was sitting behind the desk now, scowling at her computer.

"Hey, Senior?" Jackson said. "You mind if I steal your office for a couple of minutes?"

Reyes glanced at us, then at him, then at her screen. Finally, she shrugged and picked up her cover. "Sure. I could use some coffee anyway."

After she'd gone, Jackson waved us in, but he didn't follow. "You guys take a minute to decompress, all right? Catch your breath, and once Curtis is done with Lasby, we'll come talk to you."

"Thank you, Chief."

He gave us a slight nod and a smile, then shut the door behind us.

As soon as we were alone, Dalton sank into a chair, cradling his head in his hands.

"Headache?" I asked.

"No. Just . . . kind of dizzy." He blew out a long breath. "God, I'm sorry. I just couldn't let—"

"Dalton." I leaned against the desk and put a hand between his shoulders. "Don't apologize."

He didn't speak and he didn't look up. His muscles were so tense under his camouflage blouse, they damn near vibrated. I hadn't realized until now how nervous—downright terrified—he must have been walking into Chief Jackson's office. This could have blown up in his face in so many different ways, but he'd done it. He'd . . . Jesus, he'd fucking *done it*. I was so proud of him I could feel it swelling in my chest even as guilt burned in my gut for putting him in that position. I should have done something. That should've been me, not him. I'd been too much of a coward, but he'd done it, and here we were.

"What you did took some brass balls." I kneaded the back of his neck. "Nobody wants to be the guy who jumps the chain of command and rats out a supervisor, but sometimes you have to. I'm just sorry I didn't do it first."

Dalton lifted his gaze. He searched my eyes, his expression unreadable. Then, slowly, he released his breath. "I just wish there was a different way. But I freaked out. I mean, my career is up in the air right now. If I don't make MA1 next time up, I'm done." Dalton slipped his fingers between mine. "But when Lasby took you away from me, that was too far. Too much."

I nodded. "I know. And I'm sorry I didn't . . ." I sighed, shoulders slumping. "I should've fought harder. I love you, Dalton. I love you, and I want to make this work, whatever we've got to do. Even if we end up on opposite shifts, it's going to suck, but we'll make it work."

He nodded, smiling up at me. "I know we will." As he rose, he added, "And I love you too."

The relief that he was here and we were back on the same page—shit, it was almost enough to break me down. But I didn't want to cry. I just wanted him.

So, without a word, I cupped his face and kissed him, and Dalton sighed as he wrapped his arms around me. God. We were here. We'd made it back to each other. The command was taking us seriously. Lasby was getting his ass handed to him by a pissed-off senior chief. And Dalton. I had Dalton back. Fuck, I thought I might just cry anyway.

Dalton broke the kiss, buried his face against my neck, and we just held onto each other for the longest time. I had no idea if all this shit was really over or if Lasby might find some slimy-ass way to turn this back on us, but I had hope that I hadn't had in a while. I had Dalton in my arms. No way in hell was I letting him go again.

After a while, someone knocked, and we separated.

The door opened, and Senior Chief Curtis stepped in with Jackson on his heels. Curtis's cheeks were flushed, and a hint of sweat gleamed at his hairline. I'd never seen the man so pissed off, and he had obviously come down a few notches before coming in here. It was a wonder he hadn't ruptured a blood vessel or something.

He took a breath as his eyes flicked back and forth between us. "All right, I've got a call in to the team investigating the incident on the water. There's a good chance all of you—including Anderson and Rhodes—are going to be questioned about it again, this time by a new investigator who hasn't had any contact with Chief Lasby."

Dalton exhaled, leaning hard against Jackson's desk like he couldn't even hold himself up anymore.

"I'm sorry you'll have to go through it all again," Curtis said.

"No, it's not that." Dalton ran a hand through his hair like it took all the energy he had left. "Just . . . relieved, I guess."

At that, Curtis smiled. "I can imagine. And I'd oversee it all personally, but I'm PCSing in a couple of weeks." He nodded toward Chief Jackson. "Between him and Senior Chief Reyes, though, you'll be in good hands."

"Anything you guys need," Jackson said, "my office is always open. We will make sure this is a fair and unbiased investigation."

"Thank you, Chief," we both said.

"We're also going to have the awards packages reviewed." Curtis's lips pulled tight, and I thought the angry flush in his cheeks deepened. "There is no justification whatsoever to downgrade MA3 Rhodes's medal."

"Good," Dalton said. "She'll be happy to hear that. Don't know if it'll be enough to get her to re-up, but . . ."

Jackson frowned. "She's not reenlisting?"

Curtis made an unhappy noise. "If I'd jumped into the ocean to save a shipmate, and my command tried to hem me up over losing a fucking rifle, I wouldn't re-up either. They'd have been lucky if I'd finished out my contract."

"Good point," Jackson muttered. "I'll talk to her. She needs to know the command has her back. If she doesn't want to stay in, she doesn't want to stay in, but . . . I'll talk to her."

I relaxed a little. Rhodes definitely deserved better than the raw deal she'd gotten lately, and I was relieved that Jackson and Curtis thought she was justified. Hopefully one of them could talk her into staying in. The Navy was better off for having her.

Dalton and I looked at each other, and we both released long breaths. I didn't think I'd ever felt this relieved. This *vindicated*.

"Anyway," Curtis said. "We'll let you boys get to work. Don't worry about Lasby—he's going to be riding a desk in this building where Jackson and I can keep an eye on him."

I laughed. "Bet he's happy about that."

"Nope." Curtis grinned. Then he shook hands with each of us. "I'll leave you both with my personal email before I fly out. Any time you need help or just some input, don't hesitate to hit me up."

"Thank you, Senior," Dalton said.

"And good luck at your new duty station," I said.

He smiled. "Thanks. I've been dying to go to Okinawa since I first enlisted. Can't wait."

"Oh, you'll love it." I grinned. "My parents were stationed there when I was in junior high. It's amazing."

"Yeah?" His eyes lit up. "Definitely make sure I give you my email, then. You might know some places my husband and I should check out."

I nodded. "I'll do that, Senior."

We shook hands with Jackson, then left the office and headed for the parking lot. On the way down the hall, Dalton laced his fingers between mine. My heart sped up. Technically, we weren't supposed to do this in uniform, but hopefully the powers that be would indulge us this one time.

Outside, we tugged on our covers. Then I took his hand again, and we continued toward our cars. When we reached his car, we stopped, but neither of us let go this time.

I took a breath. "Listen, I'm sorry I ever thought breaking up was a solution. If it helps, I've been miserable as fuck ever since."

Dalton grimaced, shaking his head. "I didn't want you to be miserable. I just wanted you back."

"Me too." I freed my hand and wrapped my arm around his waist, not caring who saw. "And you know I never would have even thought about splitting up if—"

He kissed me, holding onto the back of my head like he thought I might pull away and keep talking. Not a chance. I held him close and let that kiss go on until he was damn good and ready to break it.

When he did, he looked into my eyes and smiled. "We're cool, Chris. You don't have to keep apologizing." He touched my face. "Lasby's getting what he deserves, and I've got you. That's all I care about."

I exhaled and pulled him a little closer. "Yeah. Me too." I kissed him softly. "I love you, D."

"I love you too."

"We should get out of here."

"Yeah, I know." His lips curved into a grin against mine. "We will."

"Will we?"

"Uh-huh. Eventually."

And then he kissed me for real.

And for the first time in what seemed like forever, everything in my world was right again.

CHAPTER 23
DALTON

By the time our shift was over, Chris and I were dead on our feet. Between dealing with the chiefs and our regular long, grueling hours, we were lucky to make it far enough into his apartment to faceplant on his bed. We managed to get rid of our boots and get our phones and keys out of our pockets, and Chris stripped off his blouse, but then we just collapsed, still in uniform, on top of his comforter.

I woke up hours later, feeling more rested than I'd been in a long time. I'd had some pretty shitty anxiety dreams, but those hadn't started until an hour or two ago. For the most part, I'd slept hard. Maybe too long, actually, because my whole body was stiff and sore.

Chris was, as usual, on his stomach with his arm hanging off the bed. I cuddled up against him.

"Hey you," he murmured. "Sleep okay?"

"Better than I have in a while. You?"

"Same."

"I'm gonna grab a shower." I kissed the back of his neck. "Then we can go find some coffee."

"Junkie," he muttered.

I laughed, kissed him again, and got up. Holy fuck, yeah—I was sore. My joints cracked and my muscles argued. Good thing I hadn't decided to take care of that *other* morning stiffness. That could wait until the rest of me could actually move.

I'd been in the shower all of thirty seconds, though, when the curtain moved back.

Chris's broad, warm body pressed against mine. "You didn't really think you'd get to be all wet and naked in here by yourself, did you?"

Whatever comment I might've had vanished off the tip of my

tongue when Chris pulled me back against his thickening erection, and all I managed was "Unnnhhh . . ."

He kissed the side of my neck, lips curling into that grin that always made me crazy. "If I'd been less tired, I'd have fucked you six ways from Sunday last night."

"Stupid work." I rubbed my ass against his cock. "No time like the present, right?"

"Mm-hmm."

My body was still sore, but between the hot water and the hot man, everything was relaxing in a hurry. Too tired for sex? Maybe. Too tired for sex in the shower? Oh hell no.

"God, I want you," he growled in my ear.

I moaned in agreement, rubbing harder against him to egg him on.

Chris picked up the bottle of lube we'd started leaving in the shower, and the click of the top made my knees shake. The slick sound of his hand on his dick sent a shiver of anticipation through me, and when he pushed a couple of slippery fingers into my hole . . .

"Now, baby," I pleaded. "Please."

"I love it when you get all needy," he murmured, still fingering me.

"Always needy when you've got me naked."

He laughed against my skin. "Good. 'Cause I like having you naked too."

"I know you do. Now hurry up and *fuck me*, damn it."

I thought he might tease some more, but he pressed a kiss to my neck as he slid his fingers free. Then he guided himself between us. He slid the lubed head up and down in my crack a few times, just enough to drive me insane, and then he pushed against my hole. I closed my eyes, exhaling through parted lips as I pushed back against him, and when his dick slid into me, my knees almost gave.

It hadn't even been that long since we'd fucked, but it felt like the first time all over again. Or like it had been years since we'd even touched.

God, I missed you.

He worked himself deeper. I rocked with him, swearing and groaning as his thick cock slid in and out. He wrapped an arm around me, keeping us close together, and I braced against the wall and let my head fall back on his shoulder. He kissed up and down my neck as he started to move faster inside me.

"Fuck," he breathed against my skin. "You're so . . ." He trailed off into the most delicious moan. I whimpered softly. My dick desperately needed some attention, so I started pumping it, and we both cursed as I involuntarily clenched around him. He thrust harder. I stroked faster. Between us, we found a perfect rhythm. It was a little clumsy since we were in the shower and trying not to fall on our asses, but damn, it felt good. Not just because he hit every spot just right, not just because he knew exactly how I loved to be fucked, but because he was *here*. It didn't matter that we hadn't split up for very long; it had just seemed like forever because the man I loved—my best friend—had been gone.

And now he wasn't. He was here. Touching me. Holding me. Inside me.

I closed my eyes as Chris pushed me right to the edge.

"Oh God," he murmured against my neck. "God, I love you, baby . . ."

And with that, I was coming. Crying out and shooting my load and trying like hell to keep moving the way I knew he liked it, and then he swore again and pulled my hips back against him, burying his dick as deep as I could take it. Harsh huffs of breath rushed past my neck as his cock pulsed and his hips jerked, and suddenly we were both still.

Panting hard, Chris pressed a kiss to my neck, then pulled out. He carefully turned us around so the warm water was falling over me, and he wrapped his arms around me and kissed me. His mouth tasted like Scope just like mine did; I swore that minty alcohol taste would always remind me of morning sex with Chris.

"I'm so glad you're back," he said after a while.

"Me too." I slid my hands up his sides and brushed my lips across his. "The Navy can take a lot of things from me, but it's not getting you."

Chris hugged me tight. "No, it's not. And I'm sorry for—"

"Don't," I whispered. "I know. It wasn't your fault." Drawing back a little, I said, "The Navy's still going to be a thing, though. This bullshit is done, but . . . I mean, I'll still get kicked out if I don't make

MA1 next time around." I lifted my eyebrows. "What do we do then?"

"Don't know." Chris held me closer to him and kissed my forehead. "We'll deal with that when it gets here. Even if we both stay in, there's gonna come a time when one of us gets orders out of Anchor Point."

My stomach dropped. I hadn't even thought about that. "Shit . . ."

"We'll be okay. If we gotta spend some time apart, we can. And there's . . . I mean, depending on what we want to do when that time comes, there's ways we can get the Navy to keep us together."

I blinked, not sure I was hearing what he meant to say. "You mean . . . like . . . getting married?"

Chris half-shrugged, a lopsided smile tugging at his lips. "Well, if we don't want the Navy separating us . . ."

"Is that the only reason you think we'd ever get married?"

"Of course not." He gave my leg a playful nudge with his knee. "Don't ask dumb questions. You know damn well that's not the only reason."

I laughed, holding him closer. "I would hope not." I kissed him lightly. "So, I guess we'll deal with that when it comes too."

He nodded. "Exactly. No need to make a decision right this second." He ran a hand through my wet hair. "Right now, I just want to enjoy having you back."

"Hear, hear," I said, and I pulled him in for a longer kiss.

Maybe we'd get married someday. Maybe we wouldn't.

Maybe the Navy would keep me. Maybe it wouldn't.

But one way or the other, I knew Chris and I were going to make this thing work.

CHAPTER 24
CHRIS

With Chief Lasby off his back, Dalton pretty much did a one-eighty. He slept better. He talked about going back on the water like it was a foregone conclusion instead of a nightmare. There were still flashbacks and he was still nervous about getting on a boat, but it was like Lasby's bullshit had been pressing on a nerve and making all that worse.

Two months and three psych evals after Jackson and Curtis had stepped in, Dalton and I were drinking coffee in my apartment when he said, "I think I want to get back behind the helm." He took a deep breath. "Like . . . today."

I stared at him. "Really?"

"Yeah." He set his coffee cup on the counter and squared his shoulders. "Even if it's just for one watch. Just to . . . well, test the water, I guess."

I couldn't help smiling. I put my cup next to his and wrapped my arms around him. "You sure?"

Dalton nodded. "The shrink says if I'm ready, there's no reason not to. I can't go back to *being* a coxswain until the next psych eval in February, but I can keep my quals up and get my sea legs back. You know, get my confidence back."

God, that was good to hear.

"Okay." I ran the backs of my fingers down his cheek. "You want to come out on first watch with me, then?"

He smiled, looking like a kid on Christmas. Or, well, a kid who was going skydiving on Christmas—excited as hell but scared shitless. "Yeah." He lifted his chin. "Let's do it."

Because of our relationship and our ranks, not to mention him being on nights while I was on days, we weren't technically supposed to be going out on watch together. Under the circumstances, though, nobody argued. Everyone in Harbor had been rooting for Dalton to get back on a boat, and Chief Jackson was totally on board with Dalton's first watch being with me.

"It's bending the rules a bit," he admitted, "but MA2 Taylor trusts you. Going out there with you is probably the best thing for him."

So, at 1500 the next afternoon, Dalton and I walked down the pier with Simmons on our heels. She had the rifle. On paper, I was coxswain and Dalton was crewman. Back in the office, Powers was ready to come down on a moment's notice if we needed him to take Dalton's place.

At the slip, Dalton paused and gazed at the Metal Shark. It was bobbing almost imperceptibly against the pier; the water was glass smooth in the harbor and gently rolling on the open sea. There was barely any wind either. I couldn't think of a more perfect day to take him out there.

I touched his shoulder. "You ready?"

Dalton gazed up at the boat for another long moment, then turned to me and smiled. "Yeah. I'm ready."

We locked eyes for just a second and then boarded.

I drove for now. Getting in and out of the slip was tricky even for someone whose confidence hadn't been shaken. Better to let him take the wheel once we were out on the water.

In minutes, we were chugging away from the dock. Simmons was behind me in the cabin, the rifle slung across her lap and her attention buried in her phone. Dalton stood halfway in the cabin, holding on to the doorframe for balance. Not that he really needed to, but it never hurt to hang on to something; you never knew when a wave might come out of nowhere and rock the boat.

"How are you holding up?" I asked over the rumble of the engines.

He flashed me another smile. "So far, so good."

"Not gonna get seasick or anything?" I tapped one of the compartments near my knee. "We got barf bags if you need them."

"Shut up." Dalton laughed. Really laughed. And damn if it didn't make me warm all over, seeing him laughing out here, on a boat, with the wind tugging at his uniform. It was like being back at coxswain's school. Back when I'd fallen in love with him.

"Hey MA1," Simmons called from behind me. "You want to keep your eyes on the road?"

I glared over my shoulder at her, and she smirked, eyes flicking toward Dalton. I rolled mine and turned my attention back to the water in front of us. Then I glanced at Dalton again. He wasn't smiling now, but he wasn't scowling either. He looked . . . peaceful. Like he was relaxed and back in his element. If it weren't for the white of his knuckles on the doorframe, I might've bought it.

"Hey," I said. "You still hanging in there?"

Dalton's smile wasn't so easy this time, but it came. "I'm better than I was last time I tried to do this."

I studied him, then tapped the helm. "Think you're ready, coxswain?"

He stared at my hand and took a deep breath. I thought he was going to have second thoughts, but then he stepped into the cabin. "Yeah. I'm ready."

"You sure?"

He shot me a playful glare. "Get out of the way and let me show you how it's done."

I laughed, holding my hands up in surrender. "You got it." I stepped back to make some room for him, and Dalton took my place on the hard metal seat.

Jesus. Yeah. He really was back in his element now. The nerves were still there, and his jaw worked more than it usually did, but he maneuvered the Metal Shark just like he had in coxswain's school. Maybe not at full speed, but it wasn't like we could do that inside the harbor anyway.

I grinned. "You want to take it out to sea?"

Dalton hesitated for a nanosecond before a big old grin spread across his face. "Fuck yeah, I do."

I chuckled. "Hey, Simmons. You might want to buckle up."

"Hey!" Dalton laughed.

"Whatever, MA1," Simmons said. "I buckled up as soon as *you* took the wheel."

"Oh! Oh!" Dalton pointed at me. "She's got jokes, MA1! You

gonna take that?"

I rolled my eyes. "Man, fuck you both."

She smothered a giggle. He elbowed me playfully.

And then he steered the boat toward the mouth of the harbor.

He kept her centered, staying as far from either barrier as he could. We were supposed to do that anyway, but he seemed to be concentrating intently on it, like he wanted to be absolutely sure he was as far from any fish nets as possible. At least the fishermen were pretty good about not plunking them down in the middle of the harbor entrance.

He throttled up, and the Metal Shark passed between the barriers. Now we were in open water, and the boat rocked with a bit more feeling. I kept a hand on the doorframe like Dalton had earlier, but mostly I just kept my feet apart and planted.

Once we were clear of the gate, Dalton looked like he was fighting back another grin. He cut his eyes toward me. "So, as long as we're out here . . . think I should put the old girl through her paces?"

We weren't supposed to screw around on patrol, especially not in the expensive-to-maintain-and-fuel Metal Shark, but if Dalton had the confidence back to do more than just putter around?

"Fuck yeah, you should."

I glanced at Simmons. She'd put her phone away and was watching with a smile.

Dalton took a deep breath. Then he pushed the throttle forward. The engines roared. Water hissed along the hull as the boat sped up.

"Hang on!" he shouted. I was already hanging on, of course, and I still stumbled a bit when he turned hard, kicking up a wall of water as he made a doughnut. He did it again, following it with a figure-eight.

And . . . wow. I'd always loved watching him drive the boats in coxswain's school, but seeing him like this—fearless and enjoying himself—after he'd been afraid to even be near the water? Fuck, I could've cried.

The radio crackled to life. "You boys having fun out there?"

Panic shot through me at first, since we weren't technically supposed to be out here hotdogging, but the smile in Jackson's voice chilled me out. As Dalton slowed down, I picked up the radio. "Just putting the Shark through her paces, Chief."

He chuckled. "Looking good. Nice driving, MA2."

Dalton grinned from ear to ear. "Thanks, Chief."

"When you're ready to be on the watch bill as a coxswain, say the word," Jackson said. "You obviously haven't lost your touch."

Dalton kept beaming as he repeated, "Thanks, Chief." He knew as well as I did—and Chief did—that he wouldn't be allowed to work as a coxswain until the psych eval a year after the incident, but I was pretty sure he got Jackson's message.

You're still a coxswain. You're still a good coxswain. You're not going anywhere.

None of us mentioned that it wouldn't make a difference if Dalton didn't make MA1 on the current advancement cycle. Everyone knew. There was no point in killing the moment for him. After everything he'd been through, he deserved to enjoy this.

"So." Dalton looked at me. "You want your boat back?"

I thought about it, then shook my head. "Nah. I think I'm going to let you drive."

"You sure?" His eyes sparkled. *Please say yes.*

"Yeah, baby." I patted his forearm. "It's all yours."

EPILOGUE
DALTON

The following November.

I usually hated awards quarters. Everyone would shuffle in, usually long before or long after shift so they really just wanted to be in bed. We'd stand in ranks, and somebody in charge—the command master chief, the XO, or the CO, depending on how important the awards were—would talk for a while. Then whoever was in charge would go down the line, give out each award, take a photo shaking hands with the recipient, and if someone got something really cool or someone had reenlisted, there'd be cake. Tasteless, textureless, half-frozen cake, but if there's one thing you learn as a Sailor, it's not to bitch about free food. Especially free cake.

I didn't mind showing up for quarters this morning, though. Not even after a long shift. My pillow was calling to me, and quarters meant I'd be getting to it almost two hours late, but that was okay.

Chris was still on days, so he was as bleary-eyed as I was, shuffling into the security building's largest conference room with coffee in hand.

"Hey." He smiled sleepily. "Shouldn't you be on your way to bed?"

"Yeah, but apparently some assholes are getting awards, so I have to stay awake."

"Damn those bastards," he said into his coffee cup, and he winked.

I just laughed. We didn't touch. In uniform, we had to keep the affection to a minimum. We could date, since he wasn't my supervisor anymore, but he did outrank me, so we had to toe some lines in the name of military bearing and not fraternizing. As if it was any big secret—everyone in the command knew by now.

But it was okay. Tomorrow was a day off for both of us. We'd lounge around in bed until we felt like getting up, and then maybe go out like a normal—if somewhat sleep-deprived—couple. Or we'd just stay home and enjoy being as lazy as humanly possible.

We'd moved in together a couple of months ago after a friend of Diego's had moved out of town, leaving a decent-sized one-bedroom apartment vacant. We'd snatched it up before it had even been listed and locked in a one-year lease at a decent rate. With a couple of ships moving to NAS Adams in the next few months, housing was about to get seriously expensive and tough to find. Whoever moved into our apartment after us would be paying double or triple our current rent.

Our command master chief called everyone to attention. Chris and I put our coffee cups on the tables at the edge of the room, then joined our shipmates in ranks in the middle. We didn't stand together, though. I stood with the other MA2s in my section, and Chris went to the front to join MA3 Rhodes, MA3 Powers, and everyone else who'd been involved in pulling me out of the water last February.

The Coast Guard swimmers and crew were there as well. Rumor had it Chief Lasby had tried to squash their medals too, if only because there was extra paperwork involved when someone from another branch was receiving an award from the Navy. Fortunately, Chief Jackson had personally made sure they were given what they'd earned.

Watching all of them getting their awards and posing for handshake photos with the CO, I couldn't help getting choked up. It was hard to swallow that I would literally be dead if not for them. Rhodes had kept me from drowning, but the fast, precise actions of everyone else had gotten both of us out of the water before the hypothermia or the flailing boat could kill us. One lapse in communication, one inability to make a decision, one person not doing their job, and Rhodes and I could've been dead. But they'd all kept it together in horrendous conditions, put their own lives on the line, and now she and I were here, alive and well.

Everyone was given an award, but it was Rhodes who'd truly gone above and beyond, so there was no Navy Achievement Medal for her. Instead, the CO presented her with the Navy-Marine Corps Medal for Heroism. That was a medal they only gave out for extraordinary acts of bravery outside of combat where a person put their own life in danger. With that on her brag sheet, she was a shoo-in for her next promotion and probably a couple thereafter. Fortunately for the Navy, she'd reconsidered getting out. After Jackson and Curtis had started raining hellfire on Chief Lasby, and the investigation had been properly overseen, she'd felt less disillusioned and less like she was being punished for saving me. I suspected she'd still be guarded with the higher-ups for a long time, but she was giving the Navy another chance. In January, she'd reenlist.

I hoped I'd have the opportunity to reenlist too, but I wouldn't know that until the advancement results came out. They were due out soon, and I felt a lot more confident about my last exam, but there was so much riding on this promotion. From what I'd heard, only a small percentage of MA2s were advancing this cycle. Much fewer than the last couple. That didn't bode well for someone who'd been to Mast and was years behind his peers when it came to making rank.

I shook away that thought. No point in getting upset about it until the results actually came out.

While Captain Rodriguez handed out the awards to the Coast Guard swimmers, I applauded along with everyone else, but I also stole a glance around the room. Noticeably absent in the ranks was MA1 Anderson. Or rather. MA2 Anderson. Senior Chief Curtis's reinvestigation of the incident had left no doubt in anyone's mind that Anderson had acted irresponsibly, putting Sailors' lives at risk despite being warned. He'd gone to Captain's Mast, and Captain Rodriguez had stripped him of one rank, docked him a month's pay, and ordered his coxswain's qual permanently removed. She could have easily sent him to court-martial and potentially ended his career. I wasn't exactly sure why she'd decided to keep it in-house and go relatively easy on him, but I suspected it had to do with his pregnant wife.

I had mixed feelings about that. I wasn't particularly gleeful that a man who was about to be a father had been knocked down a rank and had lost a month's pay, but I was relieved there'd been consequences for what he'd done. Especially since I saw a lot of my younger self in him—the dumb kid who'd been allowed to *be* a dumb kid for too long, only to be abruptly humbled after being slapped upside the head with real-world consequences. It should've happened to him when he was younger and had less to lose, but better late than never. I just hoped he did like I had and straightened his shit out. I suspected he would. After all, he'd been a different man the last few months. Not so full of himself, not so impulsive. There was some humility that hadn't been there before. He may have been a shitty MA1, but he was doing his damnedest to be a solid MA2. I had a feeling that by the time he was promoted again, he'd be MA1 material.

Captain Rodriguez hadn't been nearly as gentle with Chief Lasby. She hadn't even bothered with Mast for him. Once she'd heard about his interference in the investigation—especially his threats—she'd sent his ass straight to court-martial. In the end, they'd knocked him all the way down from E-7 to E-1.

And wasn't it just poetic that, thanks to the high-year tenure rules, he could no longer stay in until his twenty-year mark. At eighteen and a half years, he was stripped of rank and discharged. No retirement. No benefits. The discharge wasn't dishonorable—you pretty much had to commit murder for one of those—but other-than-honorable didn't look so hot on a résumé either. I could only imagine him explaining that in a job interview, along with why he'd been discharged as an E-1 after eighteen years.

Karma's a bitch, ain't it, Chief?

Oh. Sorry. I meant Seaman Recruit.

Maybe that made me kind of a dick, being happy that Lasby's entire career had been reduced to nothing but a shit stain, but I couldn't feel bad for a man who'd threatened me or my Sailors.

Awards quarters finally wound down, and everyone dispersed for handshakes and the most important part—cake.

While the cake was cut and people lined up, I found Rhodes in the crowd and hugged her tight. "Congrats. You totally deserved this."

She smirked as she let me go. "Is it wrong to want to brag that I got a medal for losing a rifle?"

I laughed. "Hey, if I were you, I totally would. Makes a great story."

"Yeah, but I like the other version," Chris said. "The one where you save my man's life." He gathered Rhodes in a bear hug, and I swore there were tears in his voice when he said, "Thank you so much. He wouldn't be here if it wasn't for you."

She hugged him back just as fiercely. When they released each other, they both had to wipe their eyes.

Then I hugged her again. "I know I've said it a million times, but . . . thank you."

She sniffed against my shoulder. "You know I'd do it again in a heartbeat."

"Of course you would." I chuckled as I let her go. "You've got balls of steel."

She laughed, wiping her eyes again. She was about to say something, but right then, Chief Jackson walked up to us.

He extended his hand to her, and as she shook it, he said, "That medal was well-deserved. Congratulations, MA2."

Her lips quirked, and she gestured at her shoulder. "MA3, Chief."

A huge grin spread across his lips. "Not according to the email I just got."

My heart sank. Oh fuck. The advancement results had dropped, hadn't they? God, I didn't even want to know.

Rhodes's jaw dropped. "Are you . . . the results are out? Are you serious?"

"Yep. Well done." Then he turned to me and extended his hand. "That goes for you too, MA1."

I stared at him. "MA . . . 1?"

"Yes. MA1." Still grasping my hand, he clapped my shoulder with his other. "Nicely done. You're going to make a great first class."

"I . . . thank you, Chief." Holy shit. I'd made it? I'd fucking *made it?*

Chris threw his arms around me, nearly bowling me over. "Yeah! You did it, baby!"

I laughed, struggling to keep my balance and my composure. "Oh my God." I still had a career. I was an MA1. Or would be pretty damn soon, anyway. Whoa.

Rhodes hugged me too. "Congrats, MA1."

"Thanks, MA2." I squeezed her tighter than I had earlier.

As we collected ourselves, Chief Jackson's gaze moved to each of us in turn, and his expression was serious, but not hostile. "Listen, what happened to the three of you during that investigation was utter horseshit, and Chief Lasby deserves exactly what he got from it. But if there's any silver lining to it, it's that it has the potential to make the three of you stronger as Sailors and as leaders. From here, there's two ways you can move forward. You can be the type of leader who doesn't pull this shit on the people below you and doesn't take it from the people above you. Or you can . . ."

"Make everyone suffer because we had to suffer?" Rhodes asked.

"Exactly," he said with a nod. Slowly, his expression softened, and the growing smile was made of pride. "I'm pretty sure I know which side all three of you will land on." Some of the seriousness came back. "I just want you to remember how something like this can affect you. Don't forget this happened to you, and don't forget that you can be the reason it does or doesn't happen to someone else."

As one, we all said, "Yes, Chief."

"Good." He gave us a sharp nod. "Turn this into something positive to pass on to your junior Sailors."

"What doesn't kill us makes us stronger, right, Chief?" Chris asked.

Jackson laughed. "Yeah. Exactly." He clapped Chris's arm. "All right. You guys enjoy your cake. Congratulations on the medals and the promotions. They're all well-deserved."

After Jackson walked away, Chris turned and hugged me again. "You made it!"

"I did." I blinked, still shocked by the news. As reality sank in, the relief would've knocked me off my feet if Chris hadn't been holding me up. My career really was secure. Now that I'd made MA1, I could stay in until twenty years and retire. Or I could make chief and stay in longer. But I'd cross that bridge when I got to it. For now, I was just relieved to know I wasn't going to lose everything I'd worked for since I was eighteen.

"Now we definitely deserve cake." Chris herded me toward the table where a gigantic sheet cake had been reduced to about eight remaining slices. As usual, it wasn't great. The more-butter-than-sugar frosting was half-frozen and someone had used ground up cardboard instead of flour, but it was all right. It was something to celebrate a huge stressful chapter in our lives being over. Justice and medals had been handed to those who deserved them, and promotions had saved our careers without a lot of time to spare. The cake might've tasted a bit weird and required more chewing than it should've, but I didn't care because, for the first time since February, I could *breathe* again.

After he'd eaten about two-thirds of his piece of cake, Chris set his plate down and cleared his throat. "So, I'll be negotiating orders in a few months."

I chewed my lip. "Yeah, I guess I will be too." I hadn't let myself give it that much thought because I'd been convinced my career was over. Of course I'd known Chris would be up for orders, and he'd be transferring out of NAS Adams in the next year. In the back of my mind, I'd just accepted that wherever he went, I would move with him and find a job there. Or if he went overseas . . . well, we'd figure something out. Long distance relationship, most likely.

But now we were both going to be negotiating orders.

I set my own plate down and met his eyes. "We can take our chances and try to negotiate orders for the same base or the same ship. But the odds of two MA1 billets being open in the same place . . ."

He nodded. "I don't think I like those odds." He slipped his hand into mine. "I really do want us to be stationed together, though."

"Me too. And . . . you know there's only one way they'll do that, right?"

We locked eyes.

Chris started to smile.

Then I did.

His fingers tightened around mine. "Think we should go talk to the chaplain?"

"You don't think we should finish our cake first?"

He snorted and drew me in closer. "No. I don't. And I'm putting my foot down right now that we are *not* having the commissary make our wedding cake."

I laughed as I wrapped my arms around him. "Deal."

And then, not caring that we were in uniform . . .

Not caring who saw us or who knew or who gave a damn . . .

I pressed a kiss to my fiancé's lips.

I'd never know for sure if we would have found our way to each other without the accident and our chief's bullshit. I'd never know how things would have played out if things had gone differently that day in February. All I knew was that somewhere in the chaos, I'd fallen in love with my best friend.

And nothing else mattered.

Explore more of the *Anchor Point* series:
www.riptidepublishing.com/titles/series/anchor-point

Dear Reader,

Thank you for reading L.A. Witt's *Going Overboard*!

We know your time is precious and you have many, many entertainment options, so it means a lot that you've chosen to spend your time reading. We really hope you enjoyed it.

We'd be honored if you'd consider posting a review—good or bad—on sites like **Amazon, Barnes & Noble, Kobo, Goodreads, Twitter, Facebook, Tumblr,** and your blog or website. We'd also be honored if you told your friends and family about this book. Word of mouth is a book's lifeblood!

For more information on upcoming releases, author interviews, blog tours, contests, giveaways, and more, please sign up for our weekly, spam-free newsletter and visit us around the web:

Newsletter: tinyurl.com/RiptideSignup
Twitter: twitter.com/RiptideBooks
Facebook: facebook.com/RiptidePublishing
Goodreads: tinyurl.com/RiptideOnGoodreads
Tumblr: riptidepublishing.tumblr.com

Thank you so much for Reading the Rainbow!

RiptidePublishing.com

ALSO BY
L.A. WITT

See L.A. Witt's full booklist at: gallagherwitt.com

ABOUT THE AUTHOR

L.A. Witt is an abnormal M/M romance writer who has finally been released from the purgatorial corn maze of Omaha, Nebraska, and now spends her time on the southwestern coast of Spain. In between wondering how she didn't lose her mind in Omaha, she explores the country with her husband, several clairvoyant hamsters, and an ever-growing herd of rabid plot bunnies. She also has substantially more time on her hands these days, as she has recruited a small army of mercenaries to search South America for her nemesis, romance author Lauren Gallagher, but don't tell Lauren. And definitely don't tell Lori A. Witt or Ann Gallagher. Neither of those twits can keep their mouths shut . . .

Website: www.gallagherwitt.com
E-mail: gallagherwitt@gmail.com
Twitter: @GallagherWitt

Enjoy more stories like
Going Overboard
at RiptidePublishing.com!

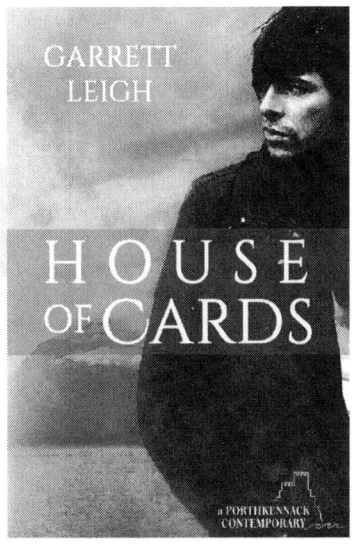

No Small Parts
ISBN: 978-1-62649-502-9

House of Cards
ISBN: 978-1-62649-545-6

78489891R00149

Made in the USA
Columbia, SC
17 October 2017